TROUBLE WITH THE GUY NEXT DOOR

TROUBLE WITH THE GUY NEXT DOOR

USA TODAY BESTSELLING AUTHOR

HOLLY RENEE

For my sisters—

I've always been your crazy little sister.
You've always loved me unconditionally.
I've looked up to you for as long as I can remember, and
neither of you have ever let me down.
Thank you for always supporting me.
Thank you for always making me laugh.
Thank you for being the best big sisters I could have ever
imagined.
I love you, Nickel and K-Dawg.

CONTENT WARNING

This book contains depictions of sexually explicit scenes. It contains mature language, themes, and content that may not be suitable for all readers. Reader discretion is advised.

CHAPTER 1

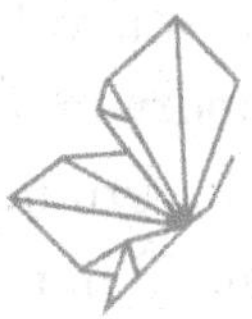

I turned the page and gripped the paperback harder in my hands. It didn't matter how many times those ruffled pages had been turned by my fingers, my heart still thumped against my chest.

I ate the words up one by one, relishing in the story, anxious to get to the part I knew was coming. The page slipped through my fingers as I turned it quickly, not missing a beat as I saw the winged warrior so clearly in my mind. He lifted his sword, ready to fight for his mate, and the loud buzzing rang through the room making me jump.

My paperback clutched to my chest, I looked around the room at all the people busying themselves with their laundry. My dryer still spun beside me, and I cringed I saw a pair of my lace panties slam against the dryer door and gyrate around like they were putting on a show.

The laundromat was packed today, but I had completely forgotten where I was. The smell of laundry detergent filled my nose and blocked the scent of citrus that clung to the skin of the warrior I had so unmistakably smelled a moment before.

A young boy, probably no more than three years old, ran in a circle around my chair. His toy beat against every surface he could find as he smiled wildly. His mother, on the other hand, looked like she was at her wit's end. She chased behind him, balancing laundry in one hand while stretching the other out to grab him. He grinned up at me as he headed my way again, and I imagined him as the mighty warrior in my story. Impossible to tame.

I waved at him as he ran by me, and he came to a sudden stop. He stared up at me, curiosity filling his innocent face, and pointed to the book in my hand.

"Whad are you doing?" His t's sounded like a d, and I smiled at how adorable he was.

"I'm reading." I looked up at his mom who stopped in a huff behind him. "What are you doing?"

"Running from monsters." He grinned before looking over his shoulder at his mom.

"Really?" My voice was in awe. "That's what I'm reading about right now."

He cocked his head and looked down at my book. "You like monsters?"

I shook my head. "No, but I love to read about the warriors who fight them."

His eyes lit up, and he inched closer to me.

"If you want, you can sit beside me, and I'll read to you while your mom finishes her laundry." I glanced at the mom for her permission, but the sudden relief in her eyes was all I needed. She tucked a piece of loose hair behind her ear as her son crawled up in the chair beside me.

"Thank you," she silently mouthed the words to me as she set her laundry basket on the table across from us.

I smiled at her as I opened the book to page one.

The little boy sat attentively as I read the words to him. His eyes got big as saucers as I described the monsters in the book, and he wrinkled his nose when I talked about the girl with golden hair.

We had just finished the first chapter when his mom squats down in front of him.

"Are you ready to go, Jonah?" Her hands reached out and tied his shoelace that had started to come undone.

"We're reading, Mama." He grinned up at me and I returned it.

"I know." She smiled at me as well. "But it's time to go to the park."

"Yay." He pumped his tiny fist in the air and quickly jumped from his seat.

The boy who sat attentively while I read to him was long gone, and he was once again running around full of energy.

"Thank you so much." His mother's eyes tracked his every movement. "You don't know how much I appreciate that."

"It's no big deal." I looked away from her and tucked my paperback into my bag.

"It is." She held my gaze, and I squirmed in my seat. "Just thank you."

"You're welcome."

I went to my dryer as they headed out the door and pulled out my already cold laundry. I should have folded our clothes right then and there, but they were already cold which meant the wrinkles were already setting in. My roommate, Brooke, would be mad, but I was dying to get home to finish the rest of my book.

With my basket against my hip, I awkwardly smiled at the man who sat closest to me before I grabbed my bag and headed out the door. If my roommate and I were responsible adults, we would have gotten our dryer fixed weeks ago. But adulting was hard and buying makeup always seemed more important to Brooke while blowing my paycheck on books would always be more important to me.

The laundromat was a short walk from our apartment building. I stared at the elevator as I stepped through the heavy glass door. It had been broken for the last four days, and I had never hated living on the fifth floor more.

I hiked my laundry basket higher on my hip, and I pulled the door open to the stairwell as I began my long journey home. Each flight had ten stairs in it, and I counted each step as if I was reaching the end of a marathon. Surely someone would be at the top with a congratulatory cookie or something. What I wouldn't give to be living in the book I was currently reading. Then the hero could just lift me in his arms and fly me to the fifth floor.

I snorted out loud at how big of a nerd I was and completely missed the body that came barreling down the stairway toward me. I jumped out of the way with only seconds to spare and several pieces of my freshly laundered clothes fell onto the stairs. They looked like they probably hadn't been cleaned in quite some time, and I quickly squatted down and began grabbing my clothes off the ground. It was as if there was a five-second rule for the amount of time that could lapse before they caught herpes.

I hadn't even looked up at the person who almost caused the near death collision. There was no time to spare. My clothes were collecting bacteria with every second that ticked by, and there was no way I was going back to the laundromat before next week.

"I'm so sorry," a deep southern accent pulled my attention away from my "Don't trust the muggles" shirt that my hand was currently hovering over.

"No worries," I started to say, but I wasn't sure what actually came out of my mouth because when I looked up, I almost fell on my ass.

He was picking up clothes, my clothes, and throwing them in my basket. While I, like a total creeper, stared at him in awe. His jaw was square and had just a touch of scruff covering it. His hair was light brown and styled perfectly in that "I just woke up, ran my hands through my hair, and managed to look like a supermodel" kind of way. My hand was twitching to run my fingers through it to see if it was as soft as it looked. He had on a white T-shirt that stretched across his fit chest and a pair of black running shorts that showed off his muscular calves.

I ran my gaze up his body but stopped dead when I realized there was something dangling from his strong callused fingers. I would have given anything to see my red lacy panties that I was so ashamed of moments before staring back at me. Instead of one of the only sexy panties I owned, the piece of fabric that he held up in front of him with a quizzical look on his face was none other than my loyal, trusty, always hold us together Spanx.

Kill. Me. Now.

"What are these?"

My eyes darted up from the offensive piece of fabric that had the power to suck in my stomach when my will power had all but given up and stared into his laughing, chocolate brown eyes. I reached out and ripped my Spanx from his hand and buried them deep in the basket. I spotted my red lacy panties that probably matched my face at that moment and mentally cussed them for not stepping up when I was in need.

A deep chuckle echoed against the walls in the stairwell and it felt like there were thirty people in there laughing at me.

"Umm..." I trailed off because I didn't know what to say to him. I sure as hell wasn't about to tell him that he was just holding my Spanx.

His phone rang as soon as I opened my mouth to speak again and saved me from making a bigger fool of myself, and he smiled at me and shook his phone in my direction.

"Well, it looks like we'll have to save this conversation for another time."

Over my dead body.

I didn't say that out loud though. I just thought it as I watched his ass jog down the stairs and away from me. I waited patiently for something to jiggle as his feet pounded against each step, but his muscles bunching and releasing didn't count. As he rounded the corner to go down the next set of stairs, he looked back up at me smirking, and I realized I was just standing there with my basket full of shame staring at him.

I quickly spun around holding my hand over my clothes being careful not to drop anything again and headed up my last flight of stairs. I guess it's true what they say about the likelihood of you having a wreck is greater when you're within five minutes from your home because I only had about six stairs before I would have been in the clear.

Instead, I managed to embarrass myself in front one of the hottest men I had ever met.

I busted through my apartment door and Brooke looked up at me from painting her pink toenails like I was crazy.

"Bad week at the laundromat?" she asked before she blew on her freshly painted toes.

"You could say that." I set down the basket on the coffee table and plopped down on the couch across from her.

"What happened?"

"Well to start, the laundromat was packed and it took me a good ten minutes to find an open washer, but then I get home and things only got worse."

"Why?" She finally looked up from her pedicure and gave me her full attention.

"I was walking up the stairs lost in my own world when some guy came crashing into me and knocking our clean clothes all over the floor." My story was very dramatic, and I waved my hands in the air to show all the different directions our clothes landed.

Brooke leaned closer toward me. "Was he hot?"

I wasn't at all surprised by her response.

"I'm not even sure how that is even relevant, but yes, he was incredibly hot."

"What did he look like?" she interrupted me.

"Really, Brooke? I'm trying to tell a story here." I acted exasperated even though I wasn't.

"Sorry. Please continue." She waved her hand like she was the queen finally giving me permission to talk.

"Like I said, he ran straight into me and our clothes were everywhere. He helped me pick them up."

"What a gentleman."

I gave her the evil eye, and she pretended to zip her lips and throw the key over her shoulder.

"When I picked up the last shirt, I looked up at him, and he had my Spanx, my Spanx," I pointed at my chest, "dangling from his fingers."

Brooke's mouth was hanging open at that point, and I was highly surprised that nothing was coming out.

"He asked me what they were." By the sound of my voice, you would have thought he had asked me for a quickie on the stairs.

"What did you say?" Brooke squeaked.

"I did what any sane woman would do. I snatched them out of his hand and didn't reply. His phone rang right after that and saved me from having to talk about it any further."

"Oh my God." Brooke laughed.

"Exactly. I just hope that he doesn't actually live in this building. Maybe he was leaving a one-night stand."

Brooke laughed again and resumed painting her toes.

"What?" I asked.

"I hope you're right because two super-hot guys just moved in next door to us," she pointed to the wall to our left indicating the apartment that we shared a wall with, "and I invited them both for dinner tomorrow night."

CHAPTER 2

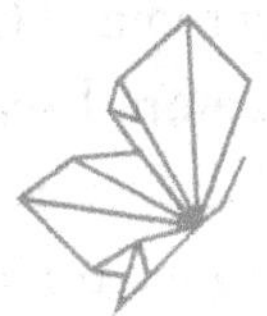

Falling asleep that night was horrible. I tossed and turned and thought about how big of a fool I made of myself in front of my possible new neighbor. I was still praying that he was running out after a one-night stand, but knowing my luck, that wasn't likely. He would probably be sitting across from me at dinner tomorrow night while I did my best to avoid looking at him.

I pulled out my Kindle and relied on my latest book boyfriend to help me get out of my own head and fall asleep. It was a really bad plan because once I got started, I didn't want to put it down. It was around one in the morning when I finally turned it off, and I had to be up early in the morning to meet my client for a shoot.

The sound of my alarm blaring woke me up and I slammed my hand against my phone to shut it up. I felt like I had only been asleep for about ten minutes, and I had every intention to take advantage of the snooze feature. My alarm continued to blare, and after pressing every button on the phone I could find, I finally peeked one of my eyes open to see what the heck was wrong with the torture device.

The light from my phone almost blinded me in my pitch-black room causing me to close my eyes again until I realized that I had just seen two twenty-five on the screen. I sat up in bed and looked around my room. The music was still blaring, and it took me a minute before I realized it was "Take Your Time" by Sam Hunt. While it was a song I loved, it wasn't something I wanted waking me up in the middle of the night unless Sam himself was there to serenade me.

The lyrics were muffled but the beat of the song was clear, vibrating against the wall behind my head. I turned toward the wall and squinted my eyes as if they had enough hate power to get the music to shut off without me having to climb out of bed.

The floor was cold as I walked like a zombie into Brooke's room. I could barely see her through the hall light that was shining into her room, but I knew she was sprawled out in the middle of her queen size bed taking up all of the room. When we first moved in together, we had to share a bed until we could afford another one. It was the hardest few months of my life. I had never been cuddled so hard. We had fallen in love with the apartment, and we decided having the apartment was worth not having everything else in the begin-ning. I didn't realize at that time that Brooke was a complete bed hog and would attempt to smother me to death in my sleep with her cuddles. In the year that we had lived here, we worked hard to furnish it in a style that was both Brooke's and mine. So, it was half girly and half nerdy.

"Shit," I whisper yelled when I felt something stab my foot.

I hopped on one foot and looked down at the eyelash

curler that caused my foot to feel like it needed to be amputated. I had always thought that thing looked like it was used to cause suffering in its victims. Not beauty.

I limped my way to Brooke's bed and plopped down beside her causing her to bounce on the mattress. She didn't even notice. The music was still blaring through the apartment, but it was much quieter on this side of the hall.

"Brooke." I shook her shoulder and her blonde hair swayed with the movement.

"Hello." I shook harder. "Earth to Brooke."

There was no movement whatsoever other than what I was causing. She was completely dead to the world. When I bounced up and down on the mattress and tickled her foot with no results, I chalked her up as a lost cause.

I momentarily considered just forgetting about the music and trying to go back to bed, but when I walked back out into the hall the song changed and cheering broke out.

"Are you kidding me?" I said out loud to myself.

The sound of several voices drunkenly singing the lyrics to a song I didn't recognize had me marching my way out of my apartment and to the apartment next door.

I knocked on the door and waited several moments with no answer. The singing was still going strong, and I wasn't surprised that they didn't hear me. I raised my fist in the air and pounded again, this time louder.

The door swung open and the voices that I thought were loud a moment ago seemed to triple in volume. A tall man who could only be described as a dark Adonis stood in the doorway. His hair was a dark brown that complemented his dark tan perfectly. I couldn't tell what color his eyes were because I was completely distracted by the smooth smile that took over his handsome face.

"Hello, gorgeous. I'm Liam."

He stuck out his large hand and slipped my much smaller, slightly sweaty one in his.

"Are you here for the party?" His gaze roamed down my body and stopped on my chest. I followed his path and tensed when I realized I was still in my pajama shorts that left nothing to the imagination and a white tank top with no bra that literally directed you on which way your imagination should go.

I tucked a strand of my raven black hair behind my ear and crossed my arms.

"No. I'm Kennedy. I live next door." I shuffled on my feet because I hated confrontation. "I was actually coming to ask you to turn the music down."

"Yo, Liam. What's going on?" The deep southern drawl caused me to pull my gaze away from the smile on Liam's face to see none other than the guy from the stairs.

"Well Tucker, our little neighbor here is asking for us to turn down the noise." Liam pointed to me and instantly got a strike against him for referring to me as little. I wasn't a little girl, and I hated being referred to as such just because I was a woman.

"Hello again." He leaned against the doorframe and I watched as his eyes turned to me.

"You've met?" Liam asked as he turned to look at me.

"Yeah. She's the girl I was telling you about earlier."

"So anyway," I interrupted. "I'd love to stay and chat, but some of us have to be up early for work so if you could turn the music down just a bit, I'd appreciate it."

I turned away from them without waiting for a response. I could feel them watching me as I walked and tugged at the hem of my shorts to cover myself.

"Wait," Tucker called out, halting me, and I slowly turned to him. "What's your name?"

I blinked at his question and tucked a loose strand of hair behind my ear.

"Why?"

"Why do I want to know your name?" he asked.

I nodded my head.

"We're neighbors now. I think we should at least know each other's names."

"Well, Tucker." I took a step back toward my door. "As one good neighbor to another," I cocked an eyebrow at him. "Turn down the music and I'll think about telling you my name."

Then I scurried to my door and slammed it shut behind me.

CHAPTER 3

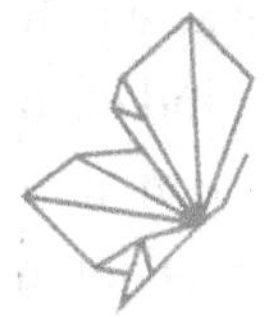

I felt like I had a hangover, and I wasn't even at a party last night. Instead, the party came to me, at least through my wall. The music did get turned down after I went next door, and I couldn't be certain, but I think that most of their party guests left shortly after as well. I had buried my head under my pillow to block out the embarrassment that I felt after my interaction with Tucker and Liam.

Liam was hot, really hot. He had dark brown hair and a tan to match it. As soon as I laid eyes on him, I knew exactly why Brooke had invited them over for dinner.

But he had nothing on Tucker.

When Liam had opened the door, I had breathed a sigh of relief that it wasn't Tucker. After our incident on the stairs, I wasn't sure if I could face him.

I should have known that I wasn't that lucky.

As soon as he made his way to the door, I instantly felt myself become more awkward. More nervous.

And I knew he could tell.

I think I managed to get about four hours of sleep total. I

was sleep-deprived, grumpy, and in desperate need of coffee. Slinging my purse over my shoulder, I grabbed all of my camera equipment and made my way out of the apartment. I glanced at Tucker's quiet door as I passed by.

When I arrived downtown, the couple whose engagement photos I was taking was waiting for me next to an older industrial building. It was kind of my thing. I loved photography. Every single thing about it. I loved taking something that may have looked normal or unimpressive to someone else and showing it to the world through a new perspective. But my true passion was capturing architecture.

I absolutely loved it.

There was something about the sharp lines of an old or new building. The way it stood strong, breaking through the sky in an almost impossible way. The unique curves and details that are so easily looked over. There was something about a structure that was once so grand being forgotten. The delicate rust, the years of wear from the hands that once worked there. I could capture it with my lens and give it life again.

I started photographing weddings, engagements, children, etc... for the money. While it wasn't my true passion, I did love doing it, and it paid the bills. There were a lot more people in the market for wedding photos than there were for architecture. But when I did get a chance to do them, I jumped at the opportunity.

The building that the newly engaged couple was standing by was covered in bright red paint that had chipped and worn off through the years. The brown brick peeked through the bright color and gave the building character that I was sure it lacked when it was freshly painted. It was my favorite building to shoot engagement photos next to. The couple looked to be almost the exact opposite of each other. She was small and delicate somehow with her straight brown hair and bright smile. Her fiancé, on the other hand, sported a massive beard and a man bun on the top of his head. He towered over her, but somehow, they fit together so perfectly.

"Hey, guys." I waved at the couple, Mia and Rob. "It's nice to finally meet you."

Mia walked straight up to me and pulled me into a hug. It wasn't really my thing, but her smile and good spirit were pretty infectious.

"Hi, Kennedy. We are so happy to meet you. We are so excited for today."

I chuckled as I pulled myself out of her grip and stuck my hand out to Rob.

"Hi. I'm Rob."

"Hey, Rob.. Killer man bun." I pointed to the top of his head.

"Thanks." His sweet smile took over his face, and I instantly knew that I was going to like the both of them.

I could usually tell within minutes of meeting the people I was going to photograph if we were going to mesh well or not, and it was important. The people who I felt somehow connected to always ended up with stellar photos. I liked to think that all my photos were good, but there was just something extra special about those. Something magical.

"So," I started pulling my camera out of my bag, "do the two of you have any specific ideas in mind?"

"Honestly," Mia looked over at Rob, "we instantly fell in love with your work as soon as we saw it. We really trust you and what you think will look best."

"Thank you. You two will make some amazing photos." I smiled at her, but on the inside, I was beaming.

It wasn't uncommon for me to get complimented on my work, but every time someone did, it filled me with so much pride that I thought I would burst at the seams. I don't know if it was something I would ever get used to, but I hoped that I didn't.

"Okay. I'd like to start at the front of the building if that's okay with you all. It is the best place to catch the sunlight."

"That sounds great." Mia beamed at me, and I couldn't help being as excited for the shoot as she was.

We went through several poses and moved through downtown taking advantage of all the older buildings as a backdrop. Mia and Rob's love was easy to capture, and their laughter throughout the entire shoot made my job not only easy but fun. By the time we were done, I had a camera full of amazing photos begging for me to edit and a large smile on my face. I hugged the couple goodbye and told them that I couldn't wait to shoot their wedding which was one hundred percent true. Weddings weren't my favorite thing in the world, but when it was for a couple like them, I couldn't wait.

By the time I made it back to our apartment, I was tired but blissfully happy. There was just something about holding my camera in my hand and using the click of my finger to capture something that had nothing to do with me that seemed to make my worries go out the window. It had a way of centering me that I hadn't been able to find with anything else.

I walked through our front door and the smell of marinara sauce hit my nose. It smelled delicious, but it was such a rare thing for Brooke to cook that I was a little concerned about what she was making. But then the sound of male laughter hit my ears and panic filled my chest when I remembered that she had invited our new neighbors over for dinner.

Screw her and her neighborliness.

I tiptoed through the living room to make it to my room before they heard me, but Brooke had some sort of spidey sense and knew I was there without ever seeing me.

"Kennedy, is that you?" she called through the apartment.

"Yeah. I'm just putting my bags down," I yelled back then dragged my butt to my bedroom to give myself a pep talk to come back out and face Tucker.

I took my time and went ahead and plugged my camera into my computer so my images from today would download. I stood in front of the mirror and looked at myself in my black leggings, white blouse, and black flats and decided that nothing else I put on would really make me look any better. I ran a brush through my hair even though it was still stick straight from this morning, then I finally made my way out of my room and headed toward the kitchen.

Tucker was in the living room bent down looking at my book collection with a beer in his hand when I walked in. It took everything inside me not to pull him away from my babies, but I decided that confrontation with our new neighbor for the second time in less than twenty-four hours probably wasn't a good idea.

"Who's got such an eclectic taste in reading materials?" Tucker asked without realizing I was standing behind him.

"That would be me." I walked up beside him when he looked over his shoulder with a large smirk on his face. "Brooke isn't much of a reader."

"I didn't take you for a romance fan." He took a sip of his

beer while looking up and down my body making every inch of my skin tingle.

"What exactly did you take me for then?" I put my hands on my hips. I didn't know what it was about him, but almost every word that came out of his mouth seemed to put me on the defense.

"I don't know. Maybe something less fun or romantic. Zombies maybe?" His grin was even bigger now, and I knew he was trying to get a rise out of me.

"I'm not that into zombies actually. I'm more into fantasy." I shrugged my shoulders.

"Uh huh." He ran his fingers across my favorite books. "A Court of Thorn and Roses. You're one of those girls then." He said it as if he knew everything he would ever need to know about me before taking another sip of his beer, and I fought the urge to pull the bottle away from his lips and smash it over his head.

"Let me guess," I said dramatically. "You're probably really into football, and I bet you're killing it in your fantasy league. But your true champion status probably comes from beer pong."

He laughed deep and long, and I could feel a small smile tugging on my lips even though I didn't want it to be there.

"You're a firecracker, aren't you?" He cocked his head to the side and looked me over again as if he was trying to figure me out.

I was about to come back with some awesome rebuttal that I hadn't even thought of yet when he pointed over my shoulder at the photos on the wall.

"Where did you get these pictures from?" He walked toward one of my shots of an old abandoned barn I had taken a couple years ago. "They are amazing."

"They are just something I collect." I looked away from him before he could read the lie on my face. I wasn't sure why I lied to him. Actually, that's a lie too. I knew exactly why I didn't tell him that I took them. I didn't want him to make a joke out of my work. He was so easygoing. Full of jokes and conniving smirks. My photography was sacred to me, and I couldn't handle him saying something bad about it.

"Dinner's ready," Brooke called out to us.

Tucker waved his hand toward the kitchen and waited for me to walk in front of him. I thought I heard him chuckle when I walked past, but when I looked back at him, he had his beer up against his smiling lips.

Liam was already sitting at our dining room table while Brooke weaved her way around the space and set the last of dinner on the table. I quickly sat down beside Liam in hopes that I wouldn't have to sit next to Tucker. It was childish, I knew that but I hadn't even known him two full days yet, and he was driving me crazy.

I didn't know what made me think my plan would actually work. Tucker pulled out the seat next to me and plopped down with that same irritating smirk on his lips. He knew that I was trying to avoid sitting next to him, I could read it on his face, but I could also tell that getting on my nerves was becoming a game to him.

I wasn't sure what had caused my irritation with him, but I did know that it was overwhelming. He was hot as hell, and he knew it. There was no way that he didn't. He reminded me of every douche bag I had ever dated.

You know the type.

In the beginning, he would treat me as if I was perfect. He would open the door, take me out, and be the guy of my dreams, but as time would roll on, my flaws would come out.

"You're so beautiful for a bigger girl." I couldn't tell you how many times I had heard that non-compliment. It baffled me how anyone ever thought they were giving me kudos for managing to be pretty and thick. My second favorite was, "If you lost a few pounds, you'd be so much prettier."

I always wanted to respond with a, "Yeah? You'd be so much hotter with a few extras inches on your dick," but I never did. I just smiled and pretended like calling me pretty with a disclaimer should make me happy.

I was a confident girl. My photography was amazing, I could beat just about anyone I knew in trivia, and I was pretty, but the one thing that always seemed to bring my confidence down a notch was my weight.

I had struggled with my weight for years. I wasn't obese, but I had enough cushion for me to be in a different category when describing women. My good luck with men was directly related to my insecurities. I was always attracted to the guy who made me feel good about myself in the beginning then dug into my spirit little by little as time went on. I always knew it was happening, and I always said I wouldn't allow it to happen again, until it did.

My last boyfriend, Sam, was the prime example. I thought he was perfect. I wanted him to be perfect, but the only thing he was good at was being a lousy boyfriend. He blatantly told me that he thought I needed to lose weight, and after I cried my eyes out to Brooke, I marched my too big for him ass over to his apartment to break it off. I was pumped. My feminist flag was flying high, and I wasn't going to let anyone make me feel bad about myself. Especially not him. Only it wasn't that simple. I walked in on him sleeping with a stick thin girl who I had seen hanging around his group of friends.

Her name was Ashley, and she was always looking for a man to sink her teeth into. Specifically, a man with money. I had once heard her talking to her friend in the bathroom about how she needed to "lock down" one of Sam's friends who had enough money to take care of her for life. She didn't know that I was in the stall, and I didn't know she was such a whore. But she knew I was dating him.

Sam didn't act remorseful at all when I caught him, and neither did she. She just smiled a smile at me that made me want to smack it off her perfect face, but instead, I walked out and didn't look back. I promised myself I would never date a guy like him again. I hardened my heart to the bull-shit, and I worked out my aggression at the gym. I managed to lose about thirty pounds since he taught me that valuable life lesson, but I didn't attribute my weight loss to the heart-break. All that credit went to me and me alone. It was something I wanted, so I did it.

But I still wasn't comfortable with my weight loss. I got more attention from guys when we went out, and when I looked in the mirror, I loved what I saw. I would never be a thin girl, but I was learning to love my curves. I did still have a habit of pulling down my top when it wasn't perfectly in place. It annoyed the crap out of Brooke.

She saw me as a bombshell, but as my best friend, her opinion was jaded. I knew I would grow more comfortable in my new body, but it would take time. I was still a big girl. I just had a lot more tone than I used to.

I think that was what annoyed me the most about Tucker. The first time I met him, he held one of my most uncomfortable, both literally and figuratively, items of clothing in his hand. While I didn't have the same stomach that I once did, I still wore my Spanx from time to time to make me feel more comfortable, and I didn't need Tucker to be privy to my insecurities.

I didn't even know the guy, but I didn't trust him as far as I could throw him. He was too good looking. His smile was too slick, and his dimples were too deep. Yes. I know how ridiculous I sound, but everything about him was getting on my nerves.

"Where are the two of you from?" Brooke passed the food around to Liam and Tucker, and I thanked God she was there. Otherwise, this dinner would be completely awkward.

"A really small town in Tennessee. You've probably never heard of it." Liam chuckled.

"What brought you all here?" I grabbed a breadstick out of the basket that Liam just handed me.

"Business ventures," Tucker said while looking over at Liam.

"That's vague." I snorted. "Does that mean you're selling drugs or something?"

"No." Liam laughed. "That would probably be more lucrative though. We're actually working on a restaurant downtown."

"So, Brooke." Tucker's voice pulled me out of my own head, and I realized I was wadding up my napkin in my lap. "Are you a professional cook?"

I snorted and every set of eyes turned to me including Brooke's narrowed ones.

"Sorry. There was something in my throat." I avoided looking at Brooke because I knew I would be getting a death glare. The reason why? She was a horrible cook. One of the worst. But she had about three meals in her arsenal that she was damn good at. Steer outside of those three meals, and you would probably be puking for a week. Luckily, tonight she had cooked her top recipe. Lasagna.

"Well, it tastes amazing," Liam said to Brooke and shot her a smile that was causing her to practically swoon before my eyes.

I bit into my own food before I could manage to make any more embarrassing noises, but I groaned when the flavor hit my tongue. How someone could cook something so good then butcher everything else was beyond me.

"Is it as good as it sounds?" Tucker's voice was low but full of humor.

I swallowed the food that was still in my mouth. "What?"

"You were practically moaning over there. I think I know what you sound like when you're about to come." He chuckled at his own joke.

"If that is what it sounds like when you're about to make a woman come then you seriously need some practice."

Liam choked on a sip of his drink and then a coughing fit started that was mixed with laughter. Tucker was laughing too. My insult didn't faze him.

"Like I said, firecracker." He took another sip of beer, and I was suddenly jealous of the bottle that was touching his lips.

"Like I said, practice." I winked at him before cracking my own smile, and internally I shivered a little because I didn't think he would need any practice at all.

CHAPTER 4

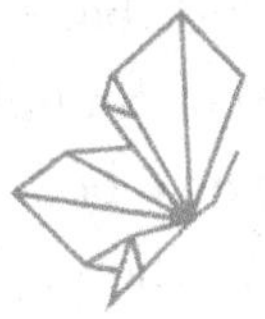

Thump.

Thump, thump.

Thump.

Peeking one eye open, I stared around my pitch-black bedroom.

Thump.

I looked over my head and stared at the wall behind me. I felt like I was having deja vu except this time it was pounding on the wall instead of loud music.

Thump, thump.

My head rattled with the loud hammering behind me, and I could have sworn that I could almost feel vibrations in my bed.

I set up and stared at the wall. Mad wasn't a good enough description of what I was. I needed sleep, and I wanted it uninterrupted.

I wasn't sure which of my new neighbors shared a wall with me, but I knew that I was ready to kill him. They had literally just left our apartment a few hours before. *Did they have a speed dial of tramps just waiting for their call?*

Thump.

I guess that was my answer.

Those man whores.

It ran through my mind that I should have just got up and went to sleep on the couch, but it was my house, damn it. I wanted to sleep in my own bed. In peace.

Light flooded the room when I clicked on my lamp, and I went searching for my headphones and iPod. I pressed the power button and smiled at the image of a cat wearing sunglasses pointing its paw at me saying "You're Purrfect."

I entered my passcode and scrolled through my music to find something that I could manage to sleep through.

Thump, thump, thump.

It would definitely need a beat.

My hand hesitated over the song choices and with a simple title of a song, I got a new idea. I quickly grabbed my speakers and set them on my nightstand, but instead of pointing them where I could hear them, I faced them directly against the wall. I clicked on the song before turning my volume to full blast. I knew it wouldn't bother Brooke. The speakers could be next to her ear, and it wouldn't wake her up.

The lyrics to "Scrub" by TLC blared through the speakers, and I flew back on my bed in a fit of giggles. I could no longer hear the pounding against my wall, but I wasn't sure if it was because they had stopped or because my music was too loud.

Then it happened.

There was a series of rapid knocks against my wall. I paused my music and waited to see what would happen next as my heart raced in my chest. I stared at the wall as if I was expecting someone to jump through it at any moment.

My heart beat louder than the thumping moments before.

A deep laughter echoed through the wall then I heard his gruff voice yell, "Well played, Firecracker."

...

The next day I didn't have a shoot scheduled, and I was thankful that I didn't have to wake up early for work because I had an appointment, *yes, appointment,* scheduled with my mother. Sleep was desperately needed for an appointment with my mother, and I couldn't miss it either. If you missed an appointment with my mother, you would never hear the end of it.

You're so irresponsible.

Maybe if you had a real career, you would understand the importance of keeping appointments.

That one was my favorite.

Neither of my parents approved of my "little hobby" as they so nicely put it. They had expected me to become a doctor like my brother or possibly a lawyer like my dad. I think my mother's biggest dream was for me to marry a doctor or a lawyer like she did, but I disappointed them both and followed my dream. They refused to acknowledge my photography as an actual career.

It didn't matter how much money I made or how many times I got recognized, it would always be a hobby to them. It didn't matter that I was booked out for a few months.

I liked to lie to myself and say that their opinion didn't matter, but deep down, it mattered way too much. But every time someone raved about my work, it seemed to chip away a small amount of the weight of their disapproval. I always avoided them long enough that I almost felt weightless by the time I saw them again, but they never failed to lay it on me again.

We were meeting at a trendy restaurant downtown close to my favorite buildings. I would have settled for a burger joint, but my mom didn't do greasy food or hole in the wall restaurants. She couldn't have it affecting her body or her image. She would drop dead before one of her "friends" saw her in a place like that.

I walked into the restaurant, but I didn't have to approach the hostess because I could see my mother sitting in the middle of the restaurant where she could see everyone and everyone could clearly see her. She smiled up at me but I could see the fakeness in her cheery expression as I always had. She looked down my body, and I almost saw her physically jolt back when she saw the jeans that covered my legs.

Her overly sweet perfume hit my nose as soon as I plopped down in the seat across from her. It was a familiar smell and one that always made my stomach turn.

"Could you not dress appropriately just once?" She acted exasperated but her voice was low so no one around us could hear that she was anything but perfectly happy.

I looked across the table at her flawlessly pressed pink button-down top that I was sure was either tucked into trousers or a pencil skirt. There wasn't much variety where that was concerned. Her perfect brown hair was pulled back in a tight bun that made her face look even more severe than the Botox injections alone could provide. As if she needed the help.

"It's nice to see you too." I pulled my napkin off the table in front of me and laid it in my lap.

The waiter arrived at the table before she could get out another snarky comment, and I ordered a Coke while she ordered a mimosa.

"Drinking at lunch. You must have had a hard day."

"Don't sass your mother in public." She straightened her already perfectly straight top while smiling at the table next to us.

"So what did you want the appointment for?" I cut to the chase.

She looked me over again, and I could feel her judgment with every inch of skin her eyes passed over. I could feel it as if it was a living breathing thing.

"Why don't you let me make you an appointment at my salon so they can do something with your hair? You're not a teenager anymore."

I fingered a strand on my straight hair then looked back up at hers. I didn't know what she expected of me. Why I had to fit some perfect mold.

Her stern eyes were boring into mine when I didn't answer her. "Did you see the new restaurant that they are putting in down the block? They should have just torn down that building and started over."

"I'm not really into new buildings. I like things that are old and decrepit. What's it called?"

She rolled her eyes. "Rock Bottom. How tacky."

Before I could tell her that I really liked it, the waiter returned to our table and set our drinks in front of us.

"Are you ready to order?"

"Yes." She didn't ask me if I was ready. "I would like a house salad with the vinaigrette dressing on the side. Do you know if the dressing is made fresh?" She didn't give him a chance to answer. "If not, I would like it freshly made."

"Yes, ma'am." He turned to me.

"I'll take the cheeseburger with fries, please."

He smiled at me kindly then took our menus and walked away to probably spit in our food.

"Should you really be eating a burger? You've finally lost some weight, and you know how easy you put it back on."

I took a deep breath in through my nose and out through my mouth. If my mother wasn't complaining about my job, then she was complaining about my weight. As you could imagine, having a fat daughter didn't really fit into her perfect storybook life, and I couldn't count the number of diets or work out plans she had forced me to do over the years. She wanted a daughter who was her mini-me. Someone who she could go to the salon with regularly and dress up like a Barbie doll, but a plus size Barbie wasn't in her repertoire. I was never into sweater vests or pastel pink, and it drove her insane.

"So are you going to tell me the real reason why you wanted to meet today?" I ignored her question about the burger.

"Your father and I have been talking, and we think it's time that you stop playing and decide on a career."

And there it is.

"Your father said that he will allow you to come work at his firm as a receptionist while you get into school, and if you choose an approved major, we'll pay for it."

Now I know what you might be thinking. A free education? Score! But nothing with my parents was free. Everything they gave came with strings attached. Except those strings tended to be more like chains.

Did you hear the "approved" portion of that grand gesture? I knew exactly what that meant. I could choose from being a lawyer, doctor, pharmacist, or a similar career. As if there wasn't anything else that could suck my soul out for cheaper.

I was a creative person. I loved to create, capture, invent, get my hands dirty, and not with a bunch of criminals that I got paid several hundreds of dollars an hour to defend. My dad would defend anyone. As long as you could pay, he'd be on your side.

"That's not going to happen." I shook my head at her. "I have a career, in case I haven't mentioned it before, and I have no interest in going back to school."

"When are you going to stop wasting your life? You have no stability in photography. No guaranteed income."

"It is stable. I'm booked out months at a time."

She waved her hand to cut me off. "What about ten years from now, Kennedy? Do you really think you'll be out there taking pictures?"

I swallowed the words that I wanted to spew at her. I wanted to tell her how happy my photography made me. I wanted her to know how well I was doing, but I knew it wouldn't matter.

I had said it all before and she didn't care.

"Have you talked to Jessica lately?" She stabbed her fork into her salad. "She's almost finished with her MBA."

Internally, I rolled my eyes, but I just dipped a French fry into ketchup.

"She will have so many opportunities when she gets finished. She has so many opportunities in front of her now."

I nodded my head and shoved the fry in my mouth.

It wasn't the first time I had heard about how amazing Jessica was, and it wouldn't be the last.

Jessica's mother and mine had been friends for as long as I could remember, and Jessica had always been around. She was always there, and she had always been better than me. At least to my mother.

She would always be better than me to my mother.

Jessica was the perfect version of the daughter my mother always wanted. She was beautiful, she was smart, she did exactly as her parents wanted, but she was also cruel.

I had spent too many years of my life ridiculed by the cruelty that Jessica spewed.

"That's awesome for her, Mom, but I don't want to get my MBA."

I could see the frustration in her eyes without her even saying a word. I could feel her disappointment.

I'd be lying if I said I hadn't considered it, that I hadn't spent too many nights lying awake in bed thinking about it. About doing whatever it took for them to be proud of me. I thought about it all the time.

"It doesn't have to be your MBA. You have several other options." She smiled a large smile and waved at someone making their way over to us.

And just like that my mother dropped everything else to make small talk with her friend who I didn't recognize. She was dressed almost identically to my mother, and I just smiled and finished my meal while they gossiped.

With every passing second, I let my doubts fester. Doubts about what I was doing. Doubts about whether or not I was making the right decisions.

Doubts about me.

CHAPTER 5

I took my time walking home and took in the scenery around me. Each building, every tree. I imagined how it would look through my camera lens. It calmed me. Centered me. I needed it before I made my way back home. If I had gone home directly from the restaurant, Brooke would have known exactly what was wrong with me, and Brooke despised my parents.

She begged me frequently to quit wasting my time on them at all, but for some reason, I apparently liked to torture myself. I knew the likelihood was practically impossible, but somewhere deep inside of me, I hoped that one day my parents would actually love me for who I was. It was a dream that would never come true, and I needed to stop wasting my time on it. I knew that. But it was easier said than done.

By the time I made it to our building, I was emotional, irritated, and exhausted. A long bubble bath, a large glass of wine, and a good book were exactly what I needed. What I wasn't in the mood for was the loud music that filled the hallway as soon as I made it to our floor.

The sound of me knocking on their door could barely be heard over the music, so I continued to knock until I heard movement from the other side. I never thought I was such a picky neighbor, but the constant noise coming from their apartment was about to drive me insane.

The door jerked open and my jaw hit the floor. In front of me stood a very shirtless and very muscular Tucker. His hands were covered with yellow rubber gloves, and one hand held a bottle of cleaner while the other was latched around a rag.

"What have I done now, Firecracker?"

"Do you need hearing aids?" I dropped my gaze down his tan body tracing the ridges of his abs and practically drooled when I got to the deep V of his hips.

"I don't think so." He chuckled, deep and masculine.

I traced my way back up each ripple of muscle before I noticed he was watching me. My blush was creeping up my chest.

"Well, you're going to if you don't turn down your music. Are you always so loud?"

"I haven't really noticed, but it's good to know that you are noticing me." He smirked, and I simultaneously wanted to suck his bottom lip into my mouth and smack the smirk off his lips.

"I wouldn't take that as a compliment when you're in everyone's face."

"I guess you're right, but Brooke doesn't seem to mind my 'loudness,'" he actually did air quotes, "as much as you do."

He was right, but Brooke rarely complained about anything. It was just who she was.

"I'm really not in the mood for this today, Tucker. Please just turn down the music."

His smirk instantly dropped from his face, and he stood taller.

"Are you okay?" He actually looked concerned.

"Yes. I just need some peace and quiet."

"Done." He looked me in the eyes. "I'll be here for a few more hours before I have to run some errands if you want to talk about it."

"No, thanks." I tucked some loose hair behind my ear. "I'd rather go listen to the characters in my book." I hitched my thumb over my shoulder.

"Well let me know if Fabio has any tips for me." He laughed softly and started to run his gloved hand through his hair but thought better of it.

"Will do." I chuckled, and he smiled at me.

By the time I made it to my door, I could no longer hear the music, and I could kiss Tucker. I liked to think it was only about the music and that it had nothing to do with his pouty lips or scruff on his face. I just needed alone time with a good book to get my head back in line. It would do the trick like nothing else could.

I set my bag down next to the door and Brooke looked up at me from her place on the couch.

"You're home early." I hadn't expected her to be home from work yet. She managed a trendy salon that was just down the road from us, and she absolutely adored her job. It was both great and torturous for me. I got to get my hair done for free by one of the stylists, but Brooke also liked to use me as her dummy for any new products that came in. Sometimes I smelled like a flower bomb blew up in my face. But I couldn't refuse her. I never would.

"I'm actually not. You were gone a really long time." She looked at me concerned.

I looked down at my phone, and I realized that she was right. It had been about two hours since I walked out of the restaurant where my mother sat with her head held high.

"Yeah. I lost track of time."

"How did lunch go?" She watched me like a hawk, and I knew she was looking for any tells on how it really went in case I lied to her about it.

"Same old, same old." I plopped down on the couch beside her, and she pulled me into her side.

"Want to talk about it?"

"Nope."

"Okay. I know I've said this a million times, but you don't need them." Her voice was soft.

I nodded my head at her even though I couldn't really bring myself to believe that deep down.

"We've got each other, and we're all each other will ever need." She pulled me in tighter.

Did I mention that Brooke was the best friend ever? Despite our difference in opinions on clothing, books, style, and who the hottest Hemsworth brother was, I couldn't imagine anyone else being here with me. She was my person in this world.

"I know, babe." I snuggled in tighter against her.

"Now go get one of your books, take a bath, and then we're going out tonight. No arguments."

I swallowed the one that was on the tip of my tongue.

"You don't have a shoot until tomorrow evening, and we need a night out."

"Yes, ma'am." I got up and walked past her to head to the bathroom. She was right. A night out wouldn't hurt us.

"Now that's the attitude I like to see." She slapped my ass and pressed play on her TV show.

She was completely right. We were all each other would ever need.

CHAPTER 6

I was ashamed of myself. Not so ashamed that I probably wouldn't do it again, but the kind of ashamed where I would make the unbreakable vow to never speak about it to anyone.

Everything was going fine. My body was submerged in the hot water, my paperback was perfectly balanced on the side of the tub, and the story I was reading was good. But the sex scenes, they were hot. I could feel a tingle in my stomach when the hero lifted the heroine off the ground and slammed her into the wall, and I decided that was exactly what I needed. To be slammed. But of course, as slightly anti-social and completely single, my chances of that happening at the moment were pretty slim.

So I took the problem into my own hands.

Literally.

I closed my eyes as my hand slid down my body, and I imagined the hero's light blond hair as he threw me on the bed and had his dirty way with me. It was perfect. My stomach tightened as I imagined my hand as his. I sped up as my imagination did.

Then it all went downhill.

The hero's hair changed from the perfect sun-kissed blond to a light brown. His bright blue eyes morphed into a dark brown shade, and somehow it managed to get so much hotter.

If I had any sense whatsoever, I would have stopped what I was doing and cleared my head. But I was too far gone, and apparently, Tucker was going to be the guy to take me to the end.

My body lost control as I imagined his hands running down my body, his scruffy facial hair dragging against my skin. I could see his satisfied smirk in my head when he successfully got me off, and once again I had mixed emotions. I wanted to kill him, slap myself, and then beg him to do it again.

I sank my head under the water, the warmth covering my already overheated body, and I screamed out my frustration. Clearly, self-care wasn't the best option for relieving my stress today. It seemed to make me crazier.

When I got out of the bath, Brooke was waiting for me in my bedroom. She was sitting on my bed acting innocent, but I knew the look on her face.

"Hell no." I pointed straight at her while holding my towel up with my other hand.

"Why not?" She pouted.

"Because I'm not a Barbie."

"I know you're not a Barbie, but it's not a sin to let me do your makeup, you wench."

I smiled at her insult.

"What do I get out of it?"

"To look extra gorgeous tonight." She smiled.

"Try again."

"You can choose what we watch next movie night." She knew she had me with that one and you could see the victory all over her face.

"Deal." I huffed before plopping down at my vanity like a brat. "But don't make me look like a slut."

She put her hand over her heart like that would somehow make her innocent. "Me?"

"Yes. You." I looked at her through the mirror. "I know your makeup bag is filled with slut dust. You sprinkle that crap around like you're a fairy and poof! Sluts everywhere."

"Glitter is not slut dust."

"Whatever you say, slut dust master."

...

By the time everything was said and done, my hair and makeup looked awesome. She lined my green eyes with a sharp, black liner that winged out at the edges and created a sultry effect on my eyes. The rest of my makeup was light except for the bright red lip that, despite my doubts, looked awesome with my hair and light skin tone. She piled my hair on top of my head in a large bun that made me happy because I wouldn't have to deal with it all night.

I put on a Brooke approved pair of black skinny jeans, a white V-neck T-shirt, and a pair of Brooke's black sparkly sandals. I drew the line at heels. Especially if I wanted to make it through the night.

The bar that we chose was pretty packed, but we still managed to get a seat at the bar. The place was ordinary. Nothing special. Just a hole in the wall place where people came to drown their sorrows or drown themselves between each other's legs.

Brooke ordered a martini, and I ordered a whiskey sour. Somehow our drink choices seemed to fit our personalities perfectly. I looked around the bar and watched the people around me. It was an ordinary night with ordinary people.

The guy to my right was leaned into the pretty blonde sitting on the stool who was clearly giving him the "Fuck off" vibes. He either didn't have a clue or didn't care. I wasn't sure which was worse.

The hottest guy in the bar had already saddled up next to Brooke, and she was giggling and throwing him her flirty eyes. And yes. Flirty eyes are a real thing. Not all women are accomplished in the art, take me for example, but Brooke was the master. She could bat her eyelashes a few times and men were eating out of the palm of her hand. I was in awe of her skill.

Just watching her made me smile.

"Hey there, hot stuff." I heard a voice call from behind me.

Please don't be talking to me. Please don't be talking to me. Please don't be talking to me.

The man leaned against the bar and stared at me expectantly.

"I'm sorry?" I asked before taking a sip of my drink.

"What's your name?" He moved in closer to me and beer sloshed out the side of his glass.

"My name is Kennedy."

"Kennedy." He rolled my name over his tongue. "That's a good name. I could see myself calling it out."

"Did you seriously just say that?" I looked around me as if I was being punked.

A snort came from my side, and I turned to see Brooke trying to hide her laughter.

"What? You're not interested in knowing my name? Don't you want to know what it would feel like to scream it out?"

His stale breath blew in my face and I fought the urge to retch. I didn't know if it was from the smell or from his words.

"What's your name?"

He was drunk, and I could see the fuzziness in his vision.

"Brad." He took another sip of his beer. "Do you want to get out of here?"

"Sorry. That's not going to happen." I shook my head softly.

"You don't have to be a bitch." He snarled up his nose. "You're not that good looking anyway."

I pretended like his words didn't hurt me.

He brushed against my side, and I clearly heard the "slut" he tried to say under his breath.

It was the exact reason I wasn't the bar scene kind of girl. I wasn't into empty compliments, if that's what you want to call it, or the empty hookups.

It was the lack of expectation and romance. I wanted sweet words, passionate touches, and grand gestures. I needed to be swept off my feet, not expected to drop to them and open my mouth as soon as I met a guy.

Instead of letting the jerk get to me, I ordered another drink and turned toward my best friend.

"Why are guys so sleazy?" She wrinkled up her nose.

"It's not all guys. At least I don't think so. It just seems to be the men in this bar."

"What's your idea of a perfect guy?" She practically sighed as she said it.

"Well he has to be hot, preferably a six pack, sweeps me off my feet, is alpha enough to piss me off just a little bit, and then he will fuck me like a champion and make it all better again."

"You just described one of your book boyfriends," she said blankly.

"I know and wouldn't it be wonderful if one of them were real." I fanned myself dramatically.

"I think you need to quit reading and get out more. You might actually find a guy that interests you." Her eyes were searching the bar looking for a victim.

"Or maybe you should read more and then you wouldn't have such low standards."

She stuck her tongue out at me, and I laughed.

"You know I'm not a reader. If I was though, I would start with Pride and Prejudice. Mr. Darcy is dreamy."

"You got that right, babe. He is the king of angst."

"Well, I say since there are obviously no Mr. Darcy's in this place, we should drink our fill then go back home and watch him be amazing."

"That sounds like the best plan you've had all day." I raised my glass to hers and we toasted to Mr. Darcy and the unrealistic expectations he gave us.

Brooke and I managed to consume way too many alcoholic beverages, and by the time we made it back to our apartment and started Pride and Prejudice, we were a giggling hot mess. Wine was consumed and our worries went out the window.

When I finally climbed into bed in the early hours of the morning, all concerns regarding my mother were gone, and all that was left were thoughts of Tucker. I had been trying to clear him out of my head as well, but there was something about knowing that he was lying in a bed just behind the thin wall behind me that just wouldn't budge. I was still reeling from my earlier lapse of judgment in the bathtub, but something deep inside my gut was telling me how much I loved the thoughts of him. I completely blamed it on the alcohol and his abs.

I mean did he really have to have abs like that. And that V cut. That was just ridiculous. Nobody really needed that. The only thing it was really good for was tracing it with your tongue. It was really just a cocky display to even have it, but God, I loved it. The urge to run my tongue over his entire body was fierce, and I needed to snap myself out of it.

My body was on fire, but I refused to give into it. One Tucker masturbation a day was all I was allowing myself. I was drawing the line there because clearly, my libido was needing some ground rules.

CHAPTER 7

The blaring music coming out of my phone caused me to shoot up in bed and almost fall off the side. I slapped at the screen without even looking at it. The noise was killing my damn headache. Clearly, I had a few too many drinks the night before.

When my music didn't stop, I finally peeked an eye open toward the wall I shared with Tucker. But this time, it wasn't him. I looked over at my phone and saw that I was actually getting a call. I probably should have let it go to voicemail since my mouth felt like I had been chewing on cotton for about seven hours straight.

"Hello." Oh dear God. I sounded like a man.

"Hello. May I speak with Ms. Hayes?" A woman's voice came through the line.

I held my hand over the speaker of the phone and cleared my throat. "This is her."

"Hi, Ms. Hayes. This is Chloe Rule. I am the Manager of Rock Bottom. We are a new restaurant in the area."

"Yes. I've heard of it," I said almost confused.

"Well we are looking for a photographer to do some promotional shots and our owners are asking for you by name."

"Me?" I almost squeaked out.

"Yes." She laughed softly. "Apparently they saw some of your images through a friend and were highly impressed. Can you come in to meet with me about the vision we have to see if you feel like you would be a good fit?"

"Absolutely. I would love to."

"I know it's short notice, but could you come in this afternoon? I'd like to get things squared away."

"Yes. I have a scheduled shoot at six this evening, but I could come in around two if that works for you." I was practically bouncing on my bed.

"That sounds great. Do you know where we are located?"

"Yes, ma'am."

"Oh, God. Don't call me ma'am. I'm young and rocking. You just made me feel old."

"Okay." I laughed. "I'll see you at two."

"Sounds good! See you then." Chloe ended the call, and I jumped on top of my mattress and screamed at the top of my lungs.

This was a huge opportunity for me. Doing a campaign shoot for a highly anticipated restaurant could completely change my career. It could give me the boost I'd been needing to take my photography in the direction I'd always envisioned.

After doing my happy dance for a few more minutes, I leaped off my bed and ran straight out my bedroom door and into Brooke's. The apartment was still dark and I momentarily looked at the clock to see that it was nine in the morning, and Brooke was probably going to kill me.

I jumped up on her bed without any warning, and she almost head-butted me in the crotch when she shot up in her bed like a ninja.

My hands protected my lady bits then I jumped onto her lap and pinned her shoulders to the bed.

"What the fuck are you doing, you crack head?"

"Wake up. Wake up. Wake up." I shook her shoulders.

She slapped at my hand, and I couldn't help laughing at the scowl on her face.

"What is wrong with you? Get off me."

"I can't. I'm too excited."

"Why? Did a new book release today?" she asked sarcastically.

"Don't be a snob. I'm excited because I just got a phone call from the manager at that new restaurant Rock Bottom, and they want to meet me about taking photos for their advertisements."

"Seriously?" she shouted.

"Yes," I squealed before I was thrown off of her, and she jumped up on her bed.

"Oh my God! This is amazing!"

I stood up with her, and we jumped on her mattress giggling and hollering like a couple of pre-teens who just got asked out on their first date.

A pounding on the front door stopped our celebration, and we looked at each other in confusion as we tried to catch our breath.

I jumped off the bed and Brooke followed on my heels. I

had no clue who could be here at nine in the morning, but there was no one and nothing that could ruin my good mood.

I pulled the door open and standing on the other side was none other than our new neighbors. They were both dressed in gym shorts, tennis shoes, and cut off shirts that were covered in sweat.

"Are you all okay?" Tucker asked in a rushed tone.

"We're great. Why?" I asked.

"Well, we just got back from our run, and it sounded like the two of you were being murdered in there." Liam pointed into our apartment as his eyes scanned the area for a threat.

"Kennedy just got the best news ever. We were celebrating."

"Did she win the Nobel Prize?" Tucker asked, now amused.

"Not quite," I said, but Brooke was already spilling out my news.

"Have you all heard of Rock Bottom?"

Tucker and Liam exchanged a look, but I couldn't decipher what it meant.

"Yeah. We've heard of it." Tucker was almost hesitant as he said it, and now I was worried that it was actually an undercover sex dungeon or something.

"Well, she has a meeting with their manager to possibly become their photographer."

"Really?" Tucker said almost smug, and it pissed me off.

"Yes, really. Apparently, the owners saw my work and asked for me by name."

Liam chuckled at my attitude I assumed, but the two of them were really starting to get on my nerves.

"Well good luck," Tucker said as he turned away from the door and started walking toward his apartment.

"Thanks," I said back almost suspiciously. I didn't know what it was, but something felt up with the lot of them, but I decided that I was sticking to my original plan and no one was going to ruin my day.

CHAPTER 8

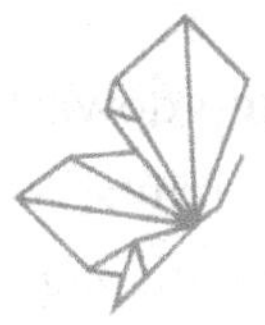

My closet had never been so empty before. I had almost every piece of clothing that I owned strewn out in my room, and I still hadn't found one thing that would be suitable to wear for my meeting.

"Dear God. What happened in here?" Brooke looked around my room at the disaster I had made.

"What the hell am I supposed to wear?" I sounded like a maniac, and it didn't slip my notice that I was kind of acting like one.

"Okay. First off, calm down."

I threw myself back onto my bed and landed on a pile of clothes. I pulled a deep breath in through my nose, and instantly, I started to feel a little bit better.

"Second, I have the perfect outfit for you to wear."

"You do?" I turned my head to the side and looked at her.

"Yes. You go get your butt in the shower, and I'll get the clothes."

I didn't move at first so she kicked my foot that was

dangling off the edge of the bed. "Get a move on." She shooed me with her hands.

"So much for calming down." I teased then ran into the bathroom before she managed to get a hold of me.

She was right though. She did have the perfect outfit for me to wear.

I was currently walking down the sidewalk in a pair of black skinny legged dress pants, a white blouse, and a hot pink blazer that I somehow managed to love instead of hate. It was trendy, professional, but still managed to show personality.

The building that currently held Rock Bottom was one of the oldest buildings in the downtown area, and it was a building that I had photographed many times. The outside of it at least. The last time I peeked in one of the broken windows, the inside was covered in dirt, trash, and broken glass. I couldn't wait to see what had been done with the space.

The front door was large and ornate, and it felt heavy in my hand as I took a deep breath and pulled it open. There was no way that I could have been prepared for what waited for me inside.

If I hadn't snooped in the windows months ago, I wouldn't have believed that this place had ever been anything but beautiful. The name Rock Bottom made so much more sense as I walked into the room.

There was a large light fixture hanging in the center of the room that was made out of agate slices that looked like a large crystal formation.

The light reflected off each piece and bounced around the room creating a display of light that was out of this world. My right finger was twitching to grab my camera and capture the amount of beauty that was in front of me. I was imagining the angles and exposures I would need to capture the perfect image.

There were several people bustling around the space. Some were stocking the expansive bar that resembled a massive rock, but with a smooth top, some were cleaning the pretty immaculate space, and some I had no idea what they were doing. But they all seemed to work like a well-oiled machine. Everyone was doing something individually, but they were all working toward one goal.

The walls were painted a grey that was so dark that it was almost black, and it seemed to set a mood that I had never seen created in another bar or restaurant. It was seductive and dark. Dangerously sexy. The tables against the wall had large booths the color of deep magenta that looked like you could lie on them and be lost for hours. The color was feminine and sensual. I was in love with it.

A small girl came out of a door behind the bar, and she smiled as soon as she saw me. She made her way toward me. She was short. Probably only five foot three inches, but it was easy to tell that she had enough spunk for a six-foot man. Her hair was cut short in an effortlessly stylish pixie cut, and it was black like mine except hers had streaks of pink in it that made her somehow look like a badass and a fairy at the same time. She was dressed head to toe in black and the only source of color other than her hair was the sleeve of bright tattoos that covered her left arm.

"Hi. I'm Chloe." She stuck her untattooed hand out to me.

I gripped her hand in mine. "Hi. I'm Kennedy."

"I was hoping that was you." She crossed her petite arms across her chest. "I don't trust the guys too much so I was a little leery about them choosing our photographer, but I already like you."

I smiled at her, and I felt my shoulders relax a little. "Well, I hope they made a good decision. I brought in my portfolio," I patted my bag on my side, "so you can take a look at the work I've done so far."

"That sounds great. Let's go take a seat over here."

We walked to the edge of the restaurant and took a seat across from each other in one of the booths that I was eye fucking earlier.

"This place looks amazing." I looked up at the artwork that was on the wall, and I couldn't believe the amount of style one place could hold.

"Thank you. The guys and I have worked really hard on this place. You'll meet them later in the process. They know enough to trust me with the creative decisions."

I smiled at her, but she didn't look like she was joking at all. "Well here is my portfolio." I slid my crisp black portfolio in front of her. "My favorite thing to photograph is architecture and since that is the majority of what I would be shooting in here; I put those in the front."

Chloe opened my portfolio, and I held my breath. There was always something about the first few seconds that someone took in your work. It wasn't exactly an expression they made or a specific comment, but there was a feeling that you got as to whether your work resonated with them or not. It was one of my favorite moments in the world. It was also one of the most nerve wracking.

Chloe's eyes skirted across the image in front of her, but I couldn't get the feeling. I wasn't sure what she thought about it just yet. I purposely chose the first image in my portfolio as a photograph I had taken of the outside of the building we were in. It was a stormy day, and the deep grey clouds made the perfect backdrop against the building.

"Can we buy this image?" Chloe's eyes darted up to me.

"What?" I was completely caught off guard.

She pointed down at the photograph in front of her. "Can we buy this image to hang inside the restaurant?"

"Yes, you can," I said almost as if it was a question. "Are you still interested in me photographing the inside?"

"Um. Hell yes. You're hired if you will do it."

"You haven't even looked at any other images," I pointed out stupidly.

"I don't need to."

CHAPTER 9

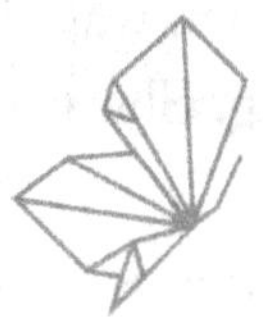

There was a spring in my step on the way home that hadn't been there before. After Chloe and I discussed all the details about their vision for my work, we signed a contract and agreed that I would start the following week once everything was in its designated place within the restaurant.

It was by far the biggest contract of my career. A part of me wanted to run to my parents' house and shove the contract in their face, but another part, a much bigger part, wanted to impress the pants off of the owners of Rock Bottom in a way that I didn't need any validation from my parents. Not that they would give it to me anyway. I could probably be photographing covers for Vogue, and they would still snarl their nose at me.

I couldn't wait to tell Brooke about it though. I knew she would be just as excited and proud as I was. More than likely, she would also want to go out and celebrate as well.

As I rounded the corner to our apartment building, I saw Tucker standing out front in similar attire to what I always saw him in, gym shorts and a T-shirt. Not that there was anything wrong with what he was wearing, even I could admit that he looked hot as hell. He was leaned back against our building, and there was a tall, leggy blonde standing in front of him. Her hair was curled in perfect spirals down her back, which was almost completely bare in the dress she was wearing. She was gorgeous. She was my exact opposite.

I pulled out my cell phone and tried to keep my head down as I passed by them. The last thing I needed was for him to think that I was eavesdropping in on his conversation with tonight's one-night stand.

"Hey, Firecracker."

I rolled my eyes at his nickname for me that apparently was going to stick around and looked up at the giant smirk on his face. There was just something about his damn smirk that looked like trouble. It made me want to get into trouble.

"Hi." I waved awkwardly at him and the blonde who was now staring at me like I was her enemy and continued to walk toward our door.

"Hey. Wait up," he called behind me, and I took a deep breath to calm myself enough to deal with him. I was in a good mood, damn it, and I wasn't about to let him bring me down.

I reached out for the door handle, but his large hand bumped mine out of the way as he grabbed the handle and pulled the door open for me. I looked over my shoulder at him and his friend, and I was surprised to see that she was no longer with him.

"Finished already?" I asked sarcastically.

"What?" His smirk widened and a dimple showed on his right cheek.

"Are you finished already?" I waved my hand in the direction that the woman was just standing in.

"Somebody sounds jealous." He walked in behind me and the door slammed at his back.

"Because there is something to be jealous of? I just feel sorry for her is all." I grabbed the handle to the stairwell before he could get to it, and I saw his eyes narrow on me slightly.

"And why would you feel sorry for her?" He looked more curious than irritated.

"Because you just love them and leave them. Do you even let them know the score before you pound them into my wall and then send them packing?"

"Well aren't we Miss Judgmental." He jogged ahead of me on the stairs then stopped on the landing to look down at me.

"I'm not judgmental. I'm just observant."

I was so being judgmental.

He placed a hand on each side of the stair railing and leaned down into my space when I made it to the top. The smell of his cologne mixed with something more, something delicious, hit my nose, and I momentarily forgot everything but him.

"Don't you ever want to just forget about all the rules and let a man fuck you with no expectations other than a mind-blowing orgasm?" His voice was as smooth as molasses, and when I looked up into his eyes I knew he was not only toying with me but that he knew he was also getting to me.

I pulled the lapels of my blazer tighter around my chest and prayed that he couldn't see that one damn sentence out of his mouth was already turning me into a pile of mush.

"No. I don't," I said with as much authority as I could

muster when all I really wanted to do was throw my clothes off and let him take me against the stairs.

"Then you've never been fucked correctly." He tucked a piece of hair behind my ear before his conniving smirk took over his face once again. He straightened himself back up and opened the door to our floor. "After you, Firecracker."

I picked my jaw up from the floor before I walked through the door and prayed that I could keep it together long enough to make it to my apartment. "I wish you would quit calling me Firecracker."

Tucker chuckled but ignored what I said.

"How was your consultation you had today?" He changed the subject like he wasn't just talking about orgasms. Mind-blowing orgasms that he could give me.

"It was great, thank you. I signed a contract with them."

"That's awesome." He walked past me and pulled keys out of his pocket as I started putting mine in my door.

"If you want to celebrate, you should come over later. I have a wall that can take a good pounding, as you said, and it seems to really just hit the spot."

I momentarily looked over at him and that damn dimple of his before I walked into my apartment and shut the door with a groan. It amazed me how a cocky, playboy could get me so worked up, but when his laughter carried through my door, I knew that Tucker was doing nothing more than playing a game. But he didn't need to forget who he was playing with because he was right. I was a firecracker.

CHAPTER 10

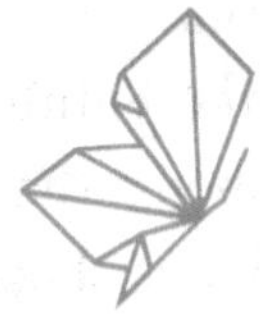

I hadn't laid eyes on Tucker in three days, and it was a good thing. Obsession with my new neighbor wasn't something I needed on my plate right now. I had too many other things to worry about instead of being concerned with what every noise was that I heard in the apartment next door.

Especially at night.

It was driving me mad hearing the noises coming from his apartment when I was lying in my own bed fantasizing about him. I was pathetic.

My job shooting Rock Bottom started in just a few days, and I was excited and anxious. I needed this job to boost my career to the place I wanted it to go, but I was so damn worried about screwing it up. My parents would just love that. It would seal the deal that I wasn't meant to be a photographer. That I was making mistakes.

I had just finished an engagement shoot, and let me tell you, it wasn't one of my favorite jobs of all time. The bride-to-be must have had some major pre-wedding jitters because she was a bitch. I had never been ordered around like that on one of my jobs. I felt like I was taking photos of my mom or one of her socialite girlfriends, and I made an effort to avoid anyone who even resembled them.

Their pictures would be gorgeous. She didn't have a single hair out of place, and she also made sure that her fiancé stayed in line for the entire shoot, but there was a disconnect. I hated my photos that I didn't feel somehow connected to the people I was shooting. It literally drained every bit of my creativity out of me.

By the time I was walking into my apartment, I was tired, irritable, and ready for a nap.

What I wasn't prepared for was walking into my apartment and seeing Tucker sitting on my couch with his feet on the coffee table and a beer in his hand.

He looked up from the TV when I closed the door and smiled at me like he was genuinely happy that I was there. I searched the apartment for traces of Brooke or anything else that would give me a sign as to why Tucker was in my place.

With no luck, I gave up and finally just asked him. "Why are you here?"

"Welcome home, honey. It's nice to see you too. How was your day?"

I stood in place and stared at him like he was insane because I was ninety-nine percent sure that he was.

He started laughing and rubbed his hand against the white T-shirt covering his stomach. I watched his hand and thought about the taut abs that I knew lay underneath that obstructive fabric.

"The cable company is working on our TV today so Brooke said that I could hang out here and use yours." He leaned back against the couch and tucked his arm behind his head.

For a moment, I thought about why the hell Brooke would tell him that was okay without telling me, but that thought was overtaken by the overwhelming thoughts of straddling him and kissing that damn smirk off his face.

"You okay?" He turned his head to the side and smiled harder.

I shook my head and tried to clear the crazy thoughts that seemed to be clouding my head throughout the day and attempted to act like I wasn't a psycho.

"Yeah. I was just surprised that you were here is all."

I hung my bag by the door and suddenly had no clue what to do with myself. It was my house, damn it.

"You want to watch a movie with me?" he asked as he watched every move I made.

"Umm..." Watching a movie was actually my plan when I finally made it home, but I wasn't exactly sure that I wanted to do it with him.

"You don't have to." He sat up and dropped his feet to the floor. "I can head home and get out of your hair."

"No. It's fine. Let's watch a movie." I walked to the kitchen and pulled out a couple beers. "I get to pick the movie, though."

I handed him one of the beers as I sat down on the opposite end of the couch.

"Deal, but please don't pick anything too girly."

I huffed and held my hand over my heart.

"You clearly don't know me very well at all."

"And whose fault is that?" He took a sip of his beer, and I sat shocked by his question.

"What do you mean?"

"You basically avoid me any chance you get. Did you know that Liam and I have had dinner with Brooke three times since we moved in? Three." He held up his fingers as if he was driving the point home. "You've only been present for one of those."

"I'm a busy girl." My voice showed my irritation.

I had been busy because I had been booked up with shoots, but I had also been avoiding him. When Brooke called me one night to let me know they were coming over for dinner again, I took my time finishing up my shoot.

He nodded his head in agreement, but I could tell he had more to say on the subject.

"Are you sure you're not avoiding me?"

"Why would I be avoiding you?" How did he know I was avoiding him?

"I don't know. It just seems like it."

"Ego much?" I moved my feet up on the couch.

"Okay." He grinned. "If you aren't avoiding me, then tell me something about yourself."

"What do you want to know?"

"Anything."

He was staring straight into my eyes and it was unnerving as hell.

"Okay." I looked away from him and searched for something to tell him. My eyes focused in on one of my photos. "I took those photos." I pointed to the photos on my wall that he asked me about the first time he was in my apartment.

He chuckled, and I turned my head back to scowl at him. "You finally going to be honest about that, huh? You lied to me about it the first time I asked you about them."

"I didn't lie. I was evasive."

"Same thing."

"Okay. Tell me something about you." I pointed my beer toward him while digging my toes into the couch cushion.

"Let's see here." He tapped his fingers against his thigh. "I'm originally from Tennessee."

"You already told me that. What made you move here?"

"Work." He shrugged his shoulders like it was no big deal.

"And what exactly do you do for work?"

"What do you think I do?" He angled his body toward me and his perfect lips formed a grin.

"Well, my first thought would be a male escort from all the sounds I hear coming from your apartment, but I think I'm going to go with a personal trainer."

He lifted up his shirt and ran his hand over his abs. "I can see why you would think that, but you would be wrong on both accounts. You do know that I have a roommate right? How do you know it's only me making all that noise?"

Because I listen to your moans and fantasize that I'm the woman you're pounding into the wall.

That statement would never come out of my mouth so I came up with the next best thing. "Liam seems a lot more wholesome than you."

He busted out laughing and bent over clutching his stomach.

"You're fucking with me, right?" he asked through his laughter.

"No. He seems like a sweet guy."

"The next time you go on a date you should let me meet them first. You are a bad judge of character." He was still laughing, but he didn't realize how accurate his statement was.

"Don't worry. I have no plans to start dating anytime

soon." I downed a quarter of my beer and leaned my head against the couch.

"Why not?" He arched one of his eyebrows at me and draped his arm over the back of the couch. It wasn't until that moment that I realized how close we were sitting. His leg was only a few inches away from my toes.

"I'm just not interested in dating any douchebags right now, and you were right, it's what I seem to attract."

He laughed and stared down at me. His eyes trailed from mine and paused on my lips. I took a deep breath to stop me from throwing myself at him, and that one breath seemed to snap him back to his senses.

He looked back up at me and smiled that damn dimpled smile of his. "So what movie are we watching?"

I shrugged my shoulders. "It's up to you." I didn't have it in me to try to choose a movie I knew he would like. I was too tired after today.

"Are you sure you trust me?" he asked with laughter in his eyes.

Not one damn bit.

...

WARMTH WAS WRAPPED around my body as I bounced slightly. I had no clue what the hell was going on, but I didn't want to open my eyes either. They were so heavy.

I felt a hand adjust under my knees and my tired eyes popped open.

"What..."

"Shhh," his deep voice whispered right next to my ear.

I turned my head to look up at him, but I could barely make him out in the dark.

"You fell asleep on the couch. I'm taking you to bed."

"I can walk," I argued.

"I got you."

"Put me down. I'm too heavy," I whined.

"Are you kidding me? You are not too heavy. Don't ever say that again." He sounded like he was actually mad about my comment. His hand tightened around me as if I was about to jump. I wasn't going to though. It felt too damn good to be in his arms.

The night had been great. We binge watched Game of Thrones instead of watching a movie, and we talked about which characters we loved and which ones we wished would get killed off. We ordered pizza, drank beer, and laughed. A lot. It was kind of scary that it was one of the best days I had in a very long time.

Even after it started out as shit. Tucker managed to turn the whole day around, and as he laid me down in my bed and whispered good night into my ear, I couldn't stop the smile that seemed to be permanently on my face since I walked in my apartment and saw him.

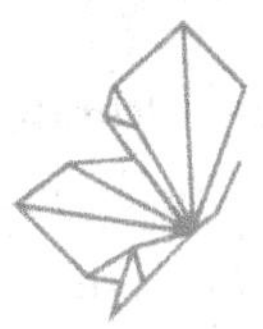

"Leave me alone, Brooke." I pulled my blanket higher above my head and buried myself in the fluffy heaven.

"Get up, sleepy head," a voice that was way too deep and far too sexy said above me right before the blanket was jerked from my body.

"What are you doing?" I screeched as I grabbed for the blanket to cover myself back up, but Tucker held it in his hand far enough away from me that there was no way I was going to reach it.

I crossed my arms to hide my breasts that bounced freely since I was only wearing a black tank top and a pair of pajama shorts.

"You promised last night that you would go out on my morning jog with me." He smiled.

"I did no such thing." I don't think I did at least, but I also drank four beers last night and lightweight wasn't a strong enough term to describe what I was.

"Yes. You did. You told me that I wouldn't be able to

keep up with you because and I quote," he made little quotation marks with his fingers, "you are the bomb dot com."

I groaned and threw my arm up over my face to hide my embarrassment.

"Let's go." He tugged on the bottom of my foot. "I'm ready to be blown away."

He was teasing me, and although, I was about to embarrass myself, there was absolutely no way that I was going to back out now. I was too damn competitive.

"Well, get out of my room so I can get dressed."

"Why?" he asked. "After the bonding we did last night, we're practically besties. We should be able to dress in front of each other by now."

He sat down on the edge of my bed and raised his eyebrow in challenge. I knew he was just trying to get a reaction out of me, but something about him thinking that I wouldn't rise to the challenge pissed me off.

I stood up from my bed and stretched my arms above my head. His eyes immediately dropped to my breasts, and I smiled to myself.

There was a little extra sway in my step as I made my way to my dresser. With my back turned to him, I took a deep breath to force down my nerves and whipped my tank top off. A deep hiss sounded from behind me, and I almost did a little happy dance. I pulled my bra from the top drawer of my dresser and put it on with my back still turned to him.

"So where exactly are we going jogging?" I asked as I clasped the back of my bra.

No response.

"Tucker," I called out his name to get his attention and looked over my shoulder when he still didn't answer.

He was still sitting on my bed looking like a god in his

cut off T-shirt and a pair of black sweats. His eyes though, they were on me. He was taking in the back of my body as if he was hungry to get a taste.

"Tucker?" I called out again.

"Yeah." His eyes were on my ass and didn't move when he answered.

"Where are we going?" I giggled softly.

He looked up to my face at this point, right as I pulled a T-shirt over my head.

"I usually go to the trail at the park."

"Okay," I replied before pulling my pajama shorts down my legs and trading them for a pair of yoga pants.

I bent down and grabbed a pair of socks out of my drawer before sitting on the bed beside him and putting on my socks and shoes. Tucker was still staring at me, and he looked like he may have seen a ghost.

"What?"

"I can't believe you just changed in front of me."

"You said we were besties now," I pointed out. I tried to calm the pounding of my heart. There was something about the way he was watching me that I couldn't shake. There was something about it that made me feel alive.

"Yeah, but I didn't think you would actually fall for that."

I didn't think I would either.

I stood from the bed and stretched my arms once more.

"Well let's go, bestie. It's time for me to smoke your ass."

He stood from my bed and smiled at me. "After you."

...

"I think my legs are going to fall off," I huffed.

"What's wrong? Can't keep up?"

He was in front of me running backward like a show-off.

"I really didn't want to show you up on our first jog. I know how sensitive a man's ego can be." My words were choppy as I tried to breathe.

"Does that mean you're going to go on more jogs with me?" He brushed his hair off his sweaty forehead.

"Maybe."

"What if I sweeten the deal a little?" He had such a playful look on his face, and it was impossible not to smile with him.

"And how are you going to do that?" I asked.

"There is an awesome little waffle place right over there." He hiked his thumb over his shoulder. "I'll take you there for breakfast. My treat."

"Doesn't that kind of cancel out the workout we just did?"

"Nope. It's the reason for the workout we just did." He winked before turning around and leading me to breakfast.

"What do you get here?" I asked as we sat down in a booth right beside the window. My thighs were shaking from trying to keep up with him through the jog. I knew he had taken it easy for me, and I appreciated it. I would have probably been laying somewhere on the side of the trail by now if he hadn't.

"Chocolate chip waffles," he said as if there was no other option in the world.

I laughed. "Of course, you do."

"You don't like chocolate chip waffles?" he asked, dumbfounded.

"Not really. I think I'm going to get this one with fresh strawberries." I pointed down to the menu.

"Well, when my waffles come, don't even think about asking for a bite."

"What if I want one?" I tightened my ponytail on top of my head.

"Do you want one?"

I wasn't sure if he was talking about him or the waffle. Either way, my answer was the same.

"Maybe."

CHAPTER 12

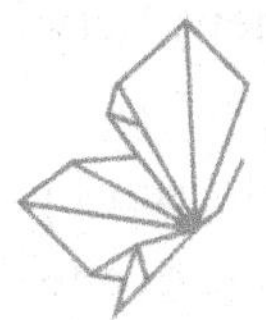

I knew the moment I walked into the country club that I shouldn't have come.

My mother was sitting with Jessica and her mother, Mrs. Russell, and they all fit together so perfectly. They fit in with everyone else in the room. Everyone except me.

I adjusted my glasses on my face as I made my way to their table.

"Hey, Kennedy." Jessica grinned at me before pressing her wine glass to her lips.

Our mothers turned toward me at the sound of my name. Both of their eyes calculating. Judging.

"Hey." I pulled out the chair next to my mother and took a seat.

"It's about time you got here. I was about to give up your seat," my mother said it quietly, but I knew Jessica and her mother could hear her.

"I'm ten minutes early." I looked around the room that was practically still empty.

My mother rolled her eyes as if my answer was ridiculous, but then planted her fake smile back on her face.

It was the annual mother daughter luncheon, and I had been forced to come for as long as I could remember. There were very few faces in the room that I didn't recognize, but very few that I actually knew. Very few that I would consider my friend.

"So, Kennedy." Mrs. Russell's pale pink lips pulled into a tight smile. "Are you seeing anyone?"

"No." I shook my head. "I'm not really looking for a relationship right now."

"That's good. That gives you plenty of time to think about your career."

My mother grinned at her friend, and I rolled my eyes.

"I have a career, Mrs. Russell." I took a sip of the water that sat in front of me in a crystal glass.

"I know, dear," she said sarcastically. "But you have time to consider your options and think about what you really want to do."

I nodded my head because there was no use arguing.

"Jessica just graduated, and she's so excited." She smiled over at her daughter with pride in her eyes. "Tell her, Jessica."

"It's the best decision I've ever made." Jessica tucked her perfectly curled hair behind her ear. "I can always talk to the Dean for you if you're interested."

"That's sweet, Jessica." There wasn't an ounce of that girl that had ever been sweet. "I'll let you know if I change my mind."

A woman stepped up to the podium at that moment saving me from further conversation about my future, and I sighed in relief. She started talking about how much money they had all raised for charity, about the events they had planned for the rest of the year, and how excited they were to see all the daughters.

After about fifteen minutes of her droning on and on, I excused myself to the bathroom.

I searched my eyes before I removed my glasses and splashed water on my face. My lungs filled with air as I took a deep breath for the first time since walking through the front door. I let the silence surround me, and I reminded myself that I would be home soon. I would be away from these people.

The bathroom door opened and I glanced up in the mirror just as Jessica walked through it. I patted my face with a paper towel before pushing my glasses back onto my face.

Jessica leaned against the counter next to me and watched me closely. She stared at me the way she had since the moment I met her.

"You know they aren't going to stop, right?" She crossed one heeled foot over the other.

"I'm aware." I looked in the mirror and straightened out my already straight hair.

"Why don't you just drop this whole photography gig and go to school? You'll have everything handed to you on a silver platter if you do."

"I don't need everything handed to me on a silver platter, Jessica. I'm doing fine on my own."

"Really?" She laughed and my spine straightened. "Look at you. You're a mess."

I recoiled as if she had hit me. Every cruel thing she had ever said to me came rushing back.

"No wonder you don't have a boyfriend, Kennedy." She

turned toward the mirror and pulled her lipstick out of her purse.

I watched her as she rimmed her lips as if she had done it a million times.

"You've lost some weight, but that isn't everything." She glanced at me through the mirror with a saccharine smile on her face. "You're going to have to try harder if you want to end up with someone who's worth a damn. Someone who your parents will approve of."

Tucker flashed in to my mind at that moment, but I wouldn't let him stay there. I wouldn't let myself consider what my parents would ever think of him.

"I don't care if my parents approve of me and my choices." At least that was what I told myself.

"Don't you?" She cocked her head. "If you didn't care, you wouldn't be here right now."

I narrowed my eyes at her.

"You've just never managed to measure up. Not in high school. Not now. Maybe you have the right idea. Just stop trying."

My stomach flipped with the anger that ran through me, the anger that was always there when I was around her.

"You're right." I smiled as her as she faced me again. "I will never be you, Jessica. I will never be the woman my mother approves of."

She looked so smug and I wanted nothing more than to wipe that look straight from her face.

"And I couldn't be prouder."

She stared at me as I walked past her, but I didn't spare her a glance.

CHAPTER 13

Tucker and I fell into a routine over the next week. The first couple days, he came, pulled my ass out of bed, then we went jogging. After that, I managed to pull myself out of my comfy cloud of blankets and get ready by the time he showed up at my door.

The jogging was getting easier with each day that passed and so was spending time with Tucker. I seemed to crave it. Every morning when I woke up, I had a smile on my face knowing that he would be there shortly. It was pathetic, but I couldn't help it.

We were on our last lap and somehow I didn't feel like I was going to die.

"Look at you," Tucker said beside me. "You're doing so much better already."

"I know," I said dramatically. "I was checking out my ass in the mirror last night, and I think I need to go out for a night on the town."

I laughed. He didn't.

"Your ass looked amazing even before you started

jogging with me. If a guy didn't realize that then he doesn't deserve you."

"Awww. Thanks, Tuck." I played off his comment as if his words weren't affecting me.

"You're not going to quit calling me Tuck are you?"

"Nope. You're my bestie, and besties need nicknames for each other. You call me Firecracker."

"That's true, but that name is awesome. Couldn't you call me something like Thor or Beast?"

I stopped mid stride because I couldn't help bending over in laughter.

"Beast?" I snorted.

"Did you just snort?" He looked offended.

"Did you just call yourself beast?" I was still laughing, and my words were muddled.

"Yes. I am a beast." His arms were flexed in a super hero pose, and I almost fell to the ground in laughter.

"Is that funny?"

"Yes." I wiped at my eyes.

"If you saw other parts of my body, you would call me beast too."

"Only men with small penises brag about their penis being a beast." I pointed down at his crotch.

The laughter was knocked out of me in the next moment when Tucker threw his shoulder into my stomach and lifted me from the ground.

"What the hell are you doing?" I squealed.

People who were walking by us were all staring. I was laughing like a maniac, and Tucker was strolling through the park like I wasn't hanging over his shoulder like a rag doll.

He smacked my ass. "That's what you get for offending my best friend."

I snorted again. "I thought I was your bestie?" I teased.

"You are the newest addition. He is my oldest. Tried and true."

A pang went through my chest thinking about how tried his penis was, but I pushed it away.

"I hope you've had your tried and true tested."

He bounced me on his shoulder, and I screamed when I felt like I was going to fall head first onto the sidewalk.

"Don't be mean. I'm not a whore."

"No. I think the correct term is man whore."

He swatted my ass again, and I giggled.

"The beast is just fine. Thank you very much."

He pulled me off his shoulder and slid me down to the ground against his body. Goosebumps broke out on my skin, and I prayed that my sports bra was strong enough to hide my arousal. He pushed some stray hairs that were stuck to my sweat off my forehead. I was looking up at him, and he was looking down at me.

I wanted him to kiss me.

I needed him to kiss me.

"Waffle place or smoothies?" His voice broke through the trance I seemed to be in.

"That's a dumb question." I took off toward the waffle shop and tried to clear my head of the insane thoughts I was just having. "I'll race you there," I called behind me.

He caught up to me quickly and passed by me without any effort at all. He didn't even look back.

...

I walked into my apartment and waved goodbye to Tucker. There was a giant smile on my face, but I dropped it as soon as I shut the door and saw Brooke staring at me curiously.

"What?"

"Nothing." She still hadn't stopped staring at me.

"Spit it out. I know you have something to say." I grabbed a bottle of water out of the fridge and plopped down on the couch.

"You and Tucker seem to be getting really chummy."

"Yeah. We're becoming good friends."

"Uh huh." She smiled. I didn't like the smile she was giving me.

"Uh huh, what?"

"Are you sure that you are just becoming friends? Nothing else?"

"Yes, Brooke. I'm sure. Tucker isn't interested in a girl like me." I rolled my eyes at her.

"But you are interested in a guy like him." I couldn't tell if it was a statement or a question.

"It wouldn't matter if I was. We would never be together."

"Okay. If you're not interested then you should let me set you up. I have the perfect guy in mind."

"I'm going to do a hard pass on that one." I chugged some water down.

"Why? If you aren't interested in Tucker than you should be free to date whoever you want." She thought she had me backed into a corner, but she was dead wrong.

"I am. That's why I'm not going to date a guy that I don't want to date."

There was no way in hell I was going on a date that she set me up on. I had been down that road before, and it typically came to a screeching halt before our entrees made it to the table. Not going to happen. Nope.

"Please?"

"Seriously, Brooke. You are the world's worst matchmaker." It was harsh, but it was the truth.

"I am not. I just haven't found the right man for you yet. This guy's name is Jake, and I met him at work yesterday."

"That's just what I need," I interrupted her. "A great guy you met at a salon."

"He was there working, asshole. He's an electrician, and he is hot as hell."

"So why don't you date him?"

"Can't. I'm going to go out with his work buddy, Andrew." She fanned herself.

"So, let me get this straight. You're going to go out with his super-hot friend, and you are leaving me the leftovers?"

"No. They are both equally hot. I was just drawn to Andrew." She sighed, and I rolled my eyes at her again.

"Please don't go falling in love on me. You haven't even gone out on a date with him yet." She always did that. She would go on two dates with a guy, and all of a sudden, she was in love. Then I was the only one there a week later when she realized he was really a douche nozzle.

"I'm not in love. This is called swooning. I'm allowed to swoon over a man's looks. Just because you're being negative doesn't mean I have to be."

"I'm not negative," I said, offended.

"Says the girl who won't even take a chance on a guy."

"I'll think about it. Okay?" I wouldn't really think about it, but she didn't need to know that. I just needed her off my back.

"Fine. Do you want to get dinner tonight?"

"Tucker's going to pick up Chinese food and come over to watch Game of Thrones later. You want me to tell him to pick you up something?"

She groaned and threw her hands in the air like I was supposed to know what that meant.

"You frustrate the hell out of me."

"Is that a no?" I asked cautiously.

She rolled her eyes and I grinned. "I want chicken fried rice."

CHAPTER 14

"Holy shit! I told you this was going to happen." I pointed to the screen where Game of Thrones had just ended.

Tucker pulled his wallet out of his pocket then slapped five dollars into my hand.

"This is shit. Complete shit."

"You should just go ahead and learn now that you should never bet against me," I bragged.

"She's right," Brooke said to the right of me, and I had almost forgotten she was there. "What I am more concerned with is Jon Snow's body. Did you see how hot he looked?"

"Yes." I fanned myself. "He is the ultimate."

"The ultimate sissy. His muscles aren't even that big." Tucker started flexing his muscles, and I couldn't help but laugh.

"Feel it." He held his bicep out toward me, and I squeezed it.

"I don't know. You're feeling a little soft to me."

His face was in pure shock, and I laughed even harder.

"There is nothing soft about me," he pouted.

"Put the lip up buddy. Not everyone can be Jon Snow."

"What time do you have to be at work tomorrow, Kennedy?" Brooke interrupted our banter.

"I told Chloe I would be there around ten."

Tucker stood from the couch we were sharing and started picking up the mess from our Chinese food.

"I need to make sure all my camera equipment is ready before I go to bed."

"I need to head out anyway." Tucker smiled over at me. "Liam is going to get jealous if I don't hang out with him at some point."

"Tell him to back off my bestie." I pointed at Tucker and made a serious face.

"Will do, Firecracker." Tucker walked over to where I was still sitting and cupped my head in his hand. His lips touched my forehead, and I closed my eyes and focused on not sighing out loud.

"Night, ladies."

"Goodnight." Brooke and I called out at the same time.

Tucker walked to the front door and smiled at me before the door shut behind him.

I turned my head toward my best friend, and she was staring at me with her finger pressed against her lip.

"What now?" I asked.

"You are so fucked."

...

Butterflies took off in my stomach as I walked into the door of Rock Bottom. My camera was in my hand and my stomach was in my throat. I wasn't sure why I was so nervous about this job, but I was. The excitement and inspiration that I usually felt when going to a shoot didn't compare to how I was feeling at that moment.

My hands shook as I fiddled with the strap of my camera bag. I took in the space that laid before me just like I had the first time I stepped into it. It was just as impressive. The only difference was that everything seemed to be in perfect order. There were no workers walking around the space. It was empty, quiet, and intimidating.

Chloe walked out of the back of the restaurant as I walked into the space, and I let go of the breath I was holding when a large smile lit up her face.

"Hey, girl! You ready to get started?" She stood beside me, her head barely making it up to my chin.

"Yes. I'm excited."

"Well, the place is yours. There is no staff here today except for me. I'm going to go back to my office and get out of your way. Let you do your thing." She hiked her thumb over her shoulder and pointed to the door that she just walked through. "If you need anything, I'll be in there."

"Okay. Sounds good." I pulled the strap of my bag off my shoulder and started setting out my equipment as she made her way back to her office.

Taking a deep breath and shaking out my hands, I tried to relax myself, and get my head in the zone.

I pulled my equipment from my bag. Deep breath.

My lens clicked into place against the camera. Deep breath.

The tripod legs separated, and I set it exactly where I wanted it. Deep breath.

With my camera in my hand, I began walking around

the space and taking shots to test the lighting. Before I even had a chance to question it, I was in my zone.

I took picture after picture. Light gleamed off the chandelier made of agate slices, and I captured it in every angle I could manage. I walked toward the back office to talk to Chloe, but I found what I was looking for as soon as I walked through the door.

I set the ladder up in the middle of the room, I climbed to the very top and began shooting again. The angle was completely different and completely mesmerizing, and I became wholly lost in what I was doing.

The shades of magenta against the dark grey walls created an amazing contrast, and my finger clicked rapidly against my shutter until it was the only sound I could hear. I climbed on top of the large rock bar and lay on my back to capture angles that I hadn't yet managed.

"This really isn't that kind of bar." Her voice came from somewhere behind me.

I pulled my camera away from my face and turned to look for Chloe. She was standing in the middle of the bar smiling at me, and she looked like she just belonged there. She had meshed her style into Rock Bottom so perfectly, and I couldn't stop myself when I picked my camera back up and started snapping shots of her standing in her kingdom.

"What are you doing?" She laughed.

I caught the laughter on my screen.

"You do know it's already three o'clock, right?" She tucked her hair behind her ear, and it was the first time since I met Chloe that she had ever looked the least bit insecure.

I set my camera on the bar and swung my legs around the bar until I was in a sitting position.

"I had no idea. I guess I was kind of lost in my work." I

stretched my arms above my head to loosen up my muscles that were sore from lying on the hard bar.

"I know. I came in here once to see if you wanted to go get lunch, but you were up on that damn ladder, and there was no way I was interrupting you. But now I am starving so I couldn't help it." She rubbed her stomach over her black T-shirt.

"Well, where are we eating?" I hopped down off the bar and starting packing up my equipment.

"Sushi?"

"I knew that I liked you, Chloe."

She laughed as I carefully put my camera away.

"Do you think you got enough images?"

"I think so. I'll start editing them tonight, but I took a ton. I just couldn't stop myself."

"This place is pretty great, huh?"

"It's incredible. You should be proud."

"I can't take all the credit. The guys have worked damn hard to make this place what it is."

"Why haven't I seen them here before?" I was curious to see the men behind such a seductive, sexy place.

"They work a lot of nights and a lot from home. They'll be here next week though. That's why I wanted to wait to photograph all the staff. We'll have everyone here, and you'll get a chance to meet them."

I nodded my head at her.

I slung my camera bag over my shoulder, and we made our way to the door just as it was opening.

I blinked, completely confused as Tucker walked through it.

"Tucker?" I looked over at Chloe, but she didn't seem confused at all.

"Hey, Kennedy." He pulled me into a small hug, but I stiffened.

"What are you doing here?" I looked around the restaurant.

"I work here." Him and Chloe exchanged a look, but I was too busy trying to wrap my head around what he had just said to read into it.

"Why didn't you tell me you worked here? Is this the place you've been helping open?"

"Yeah." He shrugged his shoulders. "I didn't realize this was the place you were shooting."

I watched Chloe as she watched him, but I didn't know her well enough to know what she was thinking.

"Kennedy and I are going to lunch. Want to join?"

Tucker looked down at me with a smile. "I've got some work to do, but you two go and have fun."

Chloe pulled the door open, and I turned to look at him.

"I'll see you later," he said softly, and I waved.

...

When I arrived home from lunch, there was a large package in my mailbox, and before I even looked at it, I knew what it was. I held it against my chest as I walked into my apartment. I held it against my chest as I set my bag down and sat down on my bed.

I took a deep breath then laid the package in front of me.

The school emblem practically jumped off the page as I stared down at it, and I stared at it for a long time.

It was my father's alma mater and the exact school my brother had attended. Exactly like he was expected to. As I was expected to.

I ripped open the tab on the back and pulled out the stack full of papers that lay inside.

Information on the school, information on their programs, and information on the programs I specifically requested. Business and law.

Just the thought of both made my stomach roll.

But I had let Jessica get to me. I had let me mother get to me.

I would never be good at business or law, never love doing it, but just looking at it wouldn't hurt me.

It would only help me with my family. With my parents.

I read over the papers carefully, page after page, but I couldn't quit thinking about the photos I had taken of Rock Bottom.

I would have to cut down on the number of shoots I booked to go to school. I would be too busy. I would have to put all my focus into school.

Just the thought alone made my chest ache.

"Kennedy, you here?"

I scrambled off the bed at the sound of Brooke's voice and tucked the packet in the drawer of my bedside table.

CHAPTER 15

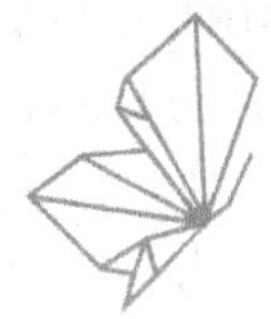

"What's up?" Tucker busted through my door, and I paused with popcorn halfway to my mouth.

"You know..." I cleared my throat. "In some countries, they think knocking before walking into someone's house is appropriate."

He waved his hand in the air and dismissed everything I just said.

"I have good news." He bounced down on the opposite side of the couch and planted his feet on my coffee table.

"And what would that be?"

He stuck his hand in my bowl of popcorn, and I attempted to smack it away, but he was too quick.

"Well." He popped some popcorn in his mouth. "Liam and I are going to head down to Tennessee for a four-day weekend on the lake."

"That sounds awesome."

It did sound awesome, but a pang of anxiety filled my chest at the thought of him being gone. Being around him on a daily basis had become my new normal, and I wasn't sure how I felt about him being gone.

"It would be even better if you would come with us."

I choked on a piece of popcorn.

Not gracefully either.

I felt the kernel get stuck in my throat, and I bent over coughing which also led to me knocking over half the bowl of popcorn.

Tucker laughed before he scooted closer to me on the couch and started patting my back.

"Are you okay?"

He handed me my water when I finally was able to take a breath. I gripped the bottle in my hand and swallowed it down.

"What?" My voice sounded rough.

"Are you okay?" He repeated himself.

"No. Not that." I waved my hand around like a maniac. "What you said before that."

"You should go to Tennessee with us?" he said almost as if it was a question.

"Bingo." I took another drink of water.

"It will be fun. You don't have any shoots this weekend. You told me so yourself the other day."

"I didn't tell you that so you could use it against me."

"I'm not using it against you. It will be fun. I swear."

I eyed him skeptically. "I'll have to talk to Brooke about it."

"Good luck." He smirked. "Brooke already said yes."

...

The trees were lush and green with a spattering of

yellow, orange, and red mixed in. Summer was ending and fall was beginning, but it was still hot as can be in Tennessee. I took a deep breath of the air around me and there wasn't even a hint of smog. It was clean and refreshing, and it made me realize how different this place was from home.

We had just stepped out of the car after the long drive to Tennessee, and I needed a long stretch and a shower. There was just something about being in a car for so long that made me feel like I had been traveling for days. It was probably the fact that I fell asleep as soon as we started the drive and didn't wake up except for pee breaks.

Tucker and Liam were pulling our bags out of the trunk and Brooke was walking around with her phone in the air praying to the phone gods for service. There were two other cars parked in the driveway of the large cabin we had just pulled up to, and Tucker explained that some of their friends would be meeting us here. I wasn't sure if that made me more nervous or less.

On one hand, I was nervous as hell to meet Tucker's friends from Tennessee, but on the other hand, I was scared to spend the weekend with just the four of us.

The cabin sat right on the lake, and although the water was a deep green, it looked perfectly calm and was begging me to run and jump in it.

"Welcome home, ladies," was yelled from the front porch of the cabin, and I turned to see a blond surfer looking guy leaning over the railing and looking straight at Liam and Tucker.

"Fuck you, Ryan," Liam called back to him while shutting the trunk and making his way up the stairs.

Tucker saddled up beside me and lifted my bag over his

head. "I'm glad you packed light. Did you see how much Brooke packed?"

I looked up at Liam at that moment and saw his muscles straining as he carried Brooke's bags (Yes, plural) up the stairs.

"That's Brooke for you. She never packs light."

Tucker and I made our way into the cabin behind the others, and I was blown away by how gorgeous the place was. There was a large open living room that allowed access to a shiny kitchen and a dining room that had an amazing view of the land outside it. A large porch wrapped around the entire cabin, and I couldn't wait to sit out there with my Kindle.

Tucker set our bags down just inside the door then he and Ryan pulled each other in a hug while slapping each other on the back.

"Where's Jase?" Tucker asked his friend.

"He's upstairs getting everything settled. He'll be down in a sec."

Right about the time he finished his sentence, a sound came from the top of the stairs and a guy who I assumed was Jase made his way to where we were. And I couldn't stop staring at him.

He had dark brown hair almost to the point of black, and he was tall. Taller than anyone else there, and his piercing green eyes looked like they were pure trouble. We could almost be twins if he wasn't over a foot taller than me and didn't have a jaw that was chiseled by the gods.

He stuck his hand out to Brooke, and I watched his movements like a hawk.

"Hi. I'm Jase."

Brooke was looking at him with a dumbfounded look on her face, and I was sure that it matched mine.

"Brooke."

He smiled a megawatt smile at her before turning to me.

"Hey, gorgeous. What's your name?"

"I'm..." My voice squeaked, high. I cleared my throat. "I'm Kennedy."

"Cute name." He shook my hand, and I could feel my blush creep up my chest.

"Okay. That's enough. Get off my girl." Tucker stepped up closer to me.

"Your girl?" Ryan acted shocked. "I thought you said they were just your friends."

"We are friends, but Kennedy is my bestie so she is off limits." Tucker was staring right at Jase, and he didn't even look at Ryan as he spoke to him.

"We'll see," Jase said quietly before winking at me and making me blush harder.

"Come on, Kennedy." It was one of the first times I had ever heard Tucker use my real name. "Let's go get settled into our rooms."

Jase chuckled as Brooke and I followed the boys up the stairs and to our rooms. There were three open rooms left so Brooke and I volunteered to share one so Tucker and Liam could each have one to themselves. When we finally shut the door to our room, it was like a dam broke loose.

"Did you see him?" Brooke fanned herself.

"How could I not see him?" I plopped back on the bed and a few pillows fell to the floor.

"He is so hot. He looks like dirty sex."

"What?" I leaned up on my elbows to look at her.

"You know what I mean. He looks like he would just be

straight up dirty sex. He would be the one to tie you up and make you beg for him to spank your ass." She pointed her finger at me. "And I promise you, we would beg."

I couldn't stop laughing at her description of him, but God, she was right. That was the exact vibe he was giving off.

"I wonder if he's single."

"Like it matters," she scuffed. "Your watch dog isn't going to let that man anywhere near you."

"Whatever. He doesn't have a choice."

...

After taking showers and changing clothes, Brooke and I made our way back downstairs. We had put on our bathing suits, but unlike Brooke, I had covered mine with a T-shirt and a pair of shorts. Brooke was rocking a hot pink bikini, and she was strutting her stuff in all her glory. It was something I would never be able to do.

I also had on a bikini (Because it was a battle I couldn't win with Brooke), but I had every intention of wearing my T-shirt into the water. She didn't need to know that though. It was my way of winning an argument without actually arguing.

When we made it downstairs, the guys were already out by the water. I popped my oversized sunglasses on my face to block out the bright sun and followed Brooke out toward the lake bank.

Tucker was in the water when we arrived so I laid out my beach towel and took a seat. I needed to work up the courage before I shimmied my shorts down my legs and made my way into the water.

Brooke set her bag down next to me and didn't hesitate as she headed over to where Liam, Jase, and Ryan were all standing in the water. I envied her confidence. I had never seen her in a situation where she doubted herself or her self-worth. She always knew exactly what she wanted, and she went after it. No worries. No insecurities. She was fearless.

I watched her through my sunglasses as she stood waist deep in the water and charmed the socks off of each of the guys. Liam was looking at her with a small smile on his face, but I wasn't sure if it was out of friendship or something more. The few times I had been around Liam, he was carefree and laidback, and I had a hard time getting a read on him.

A splash of water against my skin pulled my attention away from watching them, and I screamed as Tucker bent down and flung his dripping wet hair in my direction.

"What the hell are you doing?" I screeched.

"Coming to get you. Come swimming."

"By getting my clothes wet?" I shook out my top.

"I'm sorry, firecracker." He smiled his dimpled smile at me. "Do you forgive me?"

"I guess." I smiled back at him. I couldn't help it. He was too infectious.

"Well. Strip down and let's go."

I stood from my towel, and I looked around me to make sure no one's attention was on me before I popped the button on my shorts and worked them down my legs. I began walking to the water, but Tucker gripped the back of my shirt and pulled me to a stop.

I looked over my shoulder at him.

"What's this?" He tugged on my shirt.

"It's a T-shirt." I looked at him as if he was an idiot.

"I know that smart ass. I meant why are you still wearing it?"

"Because I want to." I crossed my arms over my stomach and prayed that he let the subject drop. It was a wasted prayer.

"You are not swimming in a T-shirt. Take it off."

"You can't tell me what to do. I want to wear it." I huffed.

He finally let go of my T-shirt but moved his hand to cup my chin. "Take it off, firecracker." His voice was soft, and I knew that he knew this was an insecurity for me. I could see it in his eyes. He was telling me that I could be comfortable with him, and he didn't even have to say the words.

I gripped the edges of my T-shirt and my hands hesitated. Inhaling a deep breath, I closed my eyes and pulled the shirt over my head. Tucker's eyes roamed down my body, and I had to fight the urge to run and pick up the T-shirt that I just tossed behind me. I fiddled with the tie on my bathing suit bottom to stop myself from covering my stomach with my hands.

Tucker caught the movement and his eyes went there before meeting mine. "You're beautiful."

I looked away from him. "Thanks, Tuck."

He placed his hand on my chin again and pulled my face back in his direction. "You are beautiful." He sounded out each word, and I stared into his eyes and tried to see what he was seeing. All I saw was truth.

It was pure.

It was overwhelming.

I felt lost in him, in his words, in being around him.

Then Brooke's squeal rang out through the air and the moment between us was broken. I looked over my shoulder just in time to see Brooke fly through the air and land in the water like a cannonball. Liam was bent over clutching his stomach in laughter, and I had no doubt that he was the guilty party.

"And you said he was nicer than me." Tucker started walking toward the water and I slowly followed him.

"I'm not sure if that is exactly what I said."

"It was something like that. You basically said that you liked him more than me." He pouted out his bottom lip and he looked so damn adorable.

My toes hit the cool water and I dug them into the soft dirt underneath.

"Now I know you're lying. There is no way I could like Liam more than you."

"Aww, babe."

Babe coming off his lips sent a shiver through me, and I hoped he attributed it to the cool water and not to the fact that he could practically make me swoon with just one word. One little word and my heart was fluttering in my chest.

Tucker reached his hand out for mine, and I gave it to him with no hesitation. His skin was warm and rough against mine. He had a callus on his palm right under his middle finger, and I couldn't stop myself as I ran my finger back and forth over the tough skin.

He was pulling me toward him slowly, and I stared at his dimpled grin and wished that we could be something that we're not. I would never be good enough for someone like Tucker. He was perfect in both looks and personality, and I didn't compare to him. I was his friend. His bestie. Nothing more. No matter how bad I wanted it.

When I was just a few short inches away from his body, he placed his hands on my hips and lifted me into the air. I was so lost in my own thoughts that it took me about two seconds too long to realize what was happening. My ass hit the water right before the rest of me sunk to the bottom of the lake. I barely managed to gasp a breath of air before I went under.

It was a good dose of reality though.

While I was fantasizing about what we could've been, Tucker was throwing his good buddy into the water. We had completely different ideas about each other, and I needed to get myself in check. The bottom line was that Tucker was my friend, and if I wanted to keep him in my life then that was where he needed to stay. I wouldn't go ruining things by making a move on him.

When my face broke the surface of the water, I took a deep breath of air and tried to clear my head.

Tucker was my friend.

Tucker wasn't into me.

I repeated the mantra in my head before opening my eyes and looking over at him. He had a large playful smile on his face. His dimples were in full force, and his wet hair was in disarray, a few pieces falling into his brown eyes. His chest was bare, and water rivets were sliding over his muscled chest and abs as they made their way back to the water. And there I was again. Overwhelmed and completely in danger of making a fool of myself.

I pushed my hair out of my face and took off swimming in the direction of Brooke. I could hear Tucker's laughter behind me, and although it made me want to go right back to him and breathe in his laughter like it was air, I needed separation. I was drowning in everything that was Tucker, and I didn't want him to throw me a floatation device.

I wanted him to drown with me.

CHAPTER 16

Brooke and I were lying out in the sun while the guys still swam and goofed off like teenagers. Brooke was on her back, and I was pretty sure she was asleep because I hadn't seen her move in the last ten minutes. But I did have my Kindle in front of me so I couldn't be held accountable for what happened around me while I was reading. I could easily get lost in the world a book created.

I picked up my Kindle to help get me out of my own head, but the hero reminded me of Tucker, and it was driving me insane. The only difference was the hero was actually interested in the heroine, plus he had a ton of magical powers.

I caught movement out of the side of my eye, and I pulled my attention away from my Kindle long enough to see Jase lying down on the grass beside me.

"What you reading?"

"A book." I didn't mean to be a smart ass. I really didn't, but I hated when someone talked to me when I clearly had my nose buried in my book.

Jase's deep chuckle washed over me as he leaned back on his elbows and stared at me through his aviator sunglasses.

"So what's the deal with you and Tucker?"

"There is no deal. We're just friends." I set my Kindle down and gave him my full attention.

"Is that why he's staring daggers at me right now?" He smirked, and his bright white teeth shined in the sun.

I turned my head and looked over my shoulder as inconspicuously as I could, and Jase was right. Tucker was staring straight at the two of us and he did not look happy.

I tucked my chin back against my chest before he could see me looking at him and looked back at Jase.

"He's a man. He just doesn't like when other boys play with his friends. It's nothing more than that." I wiped a stream of sweat off my forehead.

"So that tells me about him, but what about you?"

"What about me?"

Jase tilted his head and studied me. I felt unnerved under his stare. Exposed. I wanted my T-shirt.

"How do you feel about Tucker?"

"Tucker is my friend." I reiterated it to him again.

"Bullshit someone else."

I narrowed my eyes at him even though he couldn't see it behind my sunglasses.

"You look at him like he makes the sun rise in the morning. So why don't you tell me the truth about how you feel?"

"It doesn't matter how I feel. We will never be anything more than friends."

"I really thought you were so much smarter. I'm a little disappointed."

I scoffed at him. "That was rude. I am smart."

"Then open your eyes, sweetheart."

I stared at him before turning my gaze toward Tucker. He was laughing at something Liam was saying, but he didn't take his attention off of me and Jase. His muscles looked tight, and I smiled at the thought that he could possibly be jealous.

"For the record, we would have made beautiful babies."

I dropped my head to my towel and laughed at Jase's comment. He shot me another megawatt smile before standing up and heading back to the water. I watched him walk away, and I thought about what he said. Not the part about babies, but about Tucker.

Sure, Tucker may have gotten a little territorial when his friend was flirting with me, but he wasn't interested in someone like me. The girls I had seen him with were leggy, glamorous, and the total opposite of me. Tucker was into girls who stayed around for one night, and I wasn't that girl. I felt too much. I felt everything.

Especially with him.

Tucker already had too much of an impact on me. If I allowed him to get too close, he would destroy me. I would be bottoms up before I even realized that he had spun my world around.

...

We were sitting around a large fire pit in the backyard, and I couldn't stop laughing. It was partly due to the fact that Tucker was cracking me up, but I think the alcohol that was pumping through my system was making him so much funnier than he actually was.

"Do you guys remember the time we took those girls skinny dipping over by the dam?" Ryan chuckled.

"Yes, asshole. We remember," Tucker called out.

Ryan and Jase laughed, but Tucker and Liam were giving a look to their friends that screamed shut the hell up.

"What happened?" I giggled while looking over at Tucker sitting next to me.

"Nothing."

"Let me tell the story," Ryan spoke at the same time as Tucker and Liam.

Tucker ran his fingers through his hair.

"Tucker, Liam, and I picked up these chicks. Super-hot. I mean smoking." He moved his hands in the air to motion out an hourglass figure. "We went down to the lake to, you know help set the mood." He raised his eyebrows up and down.

Everyone laughed including me even though a bolt of jealousy shot through me.

"So, we all walked down to the water, and I laid on the charm. I had to work double time to make up for the lack of game these two had." He pointed to the guys.

"Whatever." Liam groaned.

"Well we decided to play a game of truth or dare, and I being as smooth as I am, dared two of the girls to make out."

I rolled my eyes but still smiled. I didn't really expect anything less.

"They agreed to, but they had one stipulation. Two of us had to kiss first."

Brooke laughed and a small amount of beer shot out of her mouth and dropped down her chin. She wiped her face with the back of her hand and the smile on her face was contagious. "You mean to tell me that two of you made out."

"We did not make out," Tucker growled.

"Hush, Tucker. I'm telling this story."

Tucker crossed his arms over his chest, and he looked so damn adorable when he pouted.

"So, I wasn't about to kiss another man because I'm not gay," Ryan continued.

"Oh, fuck you," Liam called out, and I laughed hysterically.

Tucker gave me an evil eye, and I kicked his arm with my foot. He grabbed a hold of it with his hand, and electricity shot across my skin. He pulled my foot into his lap before grabbing the other one and setting it on his lap to join the other. His warm hand ran over my skin as he mindlessly rubbed a trail from my ankle to my knee. I squeezed my thighs together to try to stop the goose bumps that I was sure were about to break out across my skin.

"So, like I was saying, somebody had to kiss the other one so the girls would do it, and these two right here," he pointed to Liam and Tucker, "volunteered. The best and worst part about it was after I watched two of my best friends in the entire world swap spit, the girls backed out."

Brooke and I laughed loudly, and my laughter only increased when I saw the look on Tucker and Liam's face. Tucker tickled the bottom of my foot, and I snorted and tried to squirm out of his reach.

"We did not swap spit. We pop kissed," Liam said, exasperated.

"You two kissed." You could barely understand my words through my laughter. "It puts all the noises coming from your apartment into a new perspective."

"You little shit," Tucker grumbled before he lunged at

me. My feet had barely hit the ground from his lap when I was thrown over his shoulder.

"What the hell are you doing?" I was still laughing, but I couldn't help it. The only thing I could see in front of me was his perfect ass in a pair of sweat pants, and I didn't even hesitate when I swung my arm out and smacked it.

He stopped walking and swirled around as if he could see me behind him.

"Did you just smack my ass?"

"Put me down." I giggled.

"Hell no. Especially not now."

"Please, Tucker. Where are you taking me? You don't even like girls."

I heard a loud booming laugh behind me and I knew it was Jase. His laughter was drowned out though when the sound of Tucker's footsteps became loud, and I realized that he was walking out onto the dock.

"Tucker!" I screamed. "I swear to God. You better not throw me in."

"And what are you going to do about it?"

Instead of answering him, I wrapped my arms around his waist and held on for dear life.

"I'm not letting go. You can't make me."

Tucker came to a stop, and I could hear the soft lapping of water against the dock. The wood creaked under our weight. His hand that was holding my legs moved slowly up my thighs until they reached the edge of my shorts.

"Let go, firecracker."

"Not happening." I squeezed tighter.

He lifted his hand from my legs and then it came down on my ass. Hard.

"You asshole!" I squirmed, but he had still had a strong grip on my legs.

"You hit mine first. It was fair game."

"I didn't hit you that hard."

"I'm sorry. Poor thing." His voice was teasing, but I didn't care one bit about his voice when I felt his hand come down once again on my ass. This time it was soft though. He laid his hand against the same spot he had just smacked and caressed it slowly as if he was taking away the pain that he had just caused.

My breathing became shallow, and I clamped my eyes shut. My heart was pumping against my chest.

His hand moved over my shorts slowly, and I bit my lip to stop a whimper.

"Tucker," I whispered softly.

But he didn't answer.

Instead, he jumped off the dock headfirst with me still attached to his body.

The cool water surrounded me, cooling off my skin that had just become much too hot. I opened my eyes and looked around, but I couldn't make out a thing in the dark water. There could have been a million different things in that water. All within an arm's reach from me, but I couldn't see them. The only thing I managed to find was Tucker who still had his hands on my legs, and it seemed to be a pattern. Regardless of what surrounded me, the only thing I could see was him.

A little drunk, a lot turned on, and completely wet (from the water not the before mentioned lust), I marched out of the water and away from a laughing Tucker. I wasn't really that pissed off about him throwing me in the lake, but I was pissed. I was frustrated. Sexually frustrated, and I didn't need him playing games with me. I wasn't a strong enough woman.

The grass crunched under my wet feet as I made my way into the cabin. Water was dripping off me and my clothes clung to me like a second skin. The guys were all laughing by the fire as I walked by and I gave each of them a sweet smile before flipping them the bird. Their laughter only increased and fueled my anger.

Water slipped down my skin and splashed against the hardwood floor as I stomped up to my room. I wasn't going to clean it up either. Tucker threw me in. He could clean it up.

I had just made it to the top of the stairs when I heard his loud footsteps behind me. He was taking the stairs two at a time, and I knew he was coming for me, I could tell by the evil smirk on his face.

"Don't even think about it, Tucker." I turned and tried to make it into my room before he could get to me.

Suddenly I was jerked to a stop by his hand on mine. "Aww. Don't be mad at me. It was just a joke."

"I'm not mad." I pouted. A full-on pout.

"Really?" He chuckled while squatting down until he was eye level with me.

"You don't know much about women, do you? Laughing at me is only going to make me madder."

"So, you admit that you are mad."

I crossed my arms and stared at him.

"You are so damn beautiful when you're angry." His voice was low. So low that he couldn't miss the small gasp that escaped my lips.

His finger traced a rivet of water that was falling down my neck before moving along my collarbone. He stared down at my lips and I poked out my tongue to trace them, tasting the water that remained there.

He leaned his head into me and rested his forehead against mine. "You should go take a shower. You're freezing."

Then he pushed himself away from me and headed into his own room. He was wrong though. I wasn't freezing. I was on fire.

CHAPTER 17

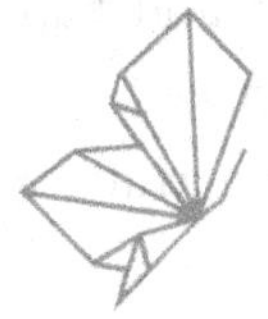

The next day, the guys all wanted to go four wheeling, but I decided to stay back. Space from Tucker was my number one priority. I was falling too deep into a fantasy about him, and I needed to clear my head.

Tucker teased me about being too scared to go riding with them, and I let him. I would much prefer him to think I was scared rather than the truth.

Sorry, Tucker. I really don't want to go because just the thought of having my body pressed against your back all day has me about to combust.

That would have gone well. I can't even imagine what his reaction would have been. Instead of worrying about it, I decided to distract myself. First, I cleaned and tidied up the place. Those four men were messy. It was like living with a bunch of teenagers. After that, I decided to relax on the porch with my Kindle.

I had just gotten to a good part when I heard a voice.

"Hello?" It was definitely a woman, and instantly, I felt my hackles go up. I had no clue who she was here to see, but just the thought of someone stopping by for Tucker was making my jealousy sky rocket.

I walked around the porch to the front of the house and by the front door stood a gorgeous woman. She had chocolate brown hair that fell to her shoulders in soft curls. Her eyes were the same dark color and had small lines surrounding them from years of smiling.

When she spotted me walking around the porch, her warm smile lit up her face.

"Hi," I said awkwardly.

"Hello."

"All the guys have gone out on the four wheelers."

"Oh. That's all right." She was still smiling, and I got the feeling that it was a look she wore a lot. "I'm Josephine, but most people call me JoJo."

"Hi, JoJo. I'm Kennedy." I waved, and when I realized how ridiculous I looked, I put my arm down.

"Kennedy! It's so nice to meet you. Tucker has told me a lot about you."

"Oh." I tucked a stray hair behind my ear.

"I'm Tucker's mom."

"Oh..." Realization hit me along with butterflies. "It's really nice to meet you as well. Do you want to come inside?"

I felt like an idiot. I hadn't even thought about the possibility that I would meet Tucker's parents while we were here, yet there I was all alone at the cabin with Tucker's mom.

"I actually brought some food over for dinner tonight. Do you mind helping me carry it in?"

"Of course not." I set my Kindle down on the porch railing and walked down the stairs with her toward her car.

She pointed up at my Kindle. "You a big reader?"

"Yes. I'm a self-proclaimed book worm."

"Me too. I don't go anywhere without my Kindle."

"Same here." My voice was a little bit higher than a moment ago, but I loved when I could talk about books with someone.

She opened the hatch on the back of her SUV and the back was packed down with food.

"You feeding an army?" I laughed.

"Have you seen the boys eat? They used to eat me out of house and home when they were teens."

"I see your point."

We both filled our arms with the delicious smelling food that I was dying to eat and carried it into the house.

"The cabin is much cleaner than I expected. They must be on their best behavior with you here."

"No," I shook my head. "I just cleaned."

"Figures." She laughed.

"Did you have a friend that came with you as well?" She looked around the space as if she would appear.

"Yes. Brooke came with us. She's my roommate and best friend. She went four wheeling with the guys."

"Why didn't you go?" She didn't seem nosy. Just curious.

"I just wasn't up for it. I wanted to stay home and read."

She smiled knowingly. "Speaking of, how about I make us a couple glasses of sweet tea then we go out on the porch and talk books."

"That sounds amazing."

...

It had probably been around three hours since Tucker's

mom arrived at the cabin. It felt weird to call her JoJo even though the name totally fit her. I was in love with her. She was funny, kind of a smart ass, and so nice. We also had similar taste in books, and we fangirled together as we talked about books and authors that we loved. She also told me stories about Tucker and his friends from their teen years, and I had laughed hysterically. She didn't ask me about Tucker and me though, and for that, I was thankful. It wasn't a subject that I really wanted to dive into right then.

The sound of four wheelers pulling into the driveway pulled my attention away from JoJo who was telling a story about a time when Tucker was trying to sneak out of the house at two in the morning and didn't think her and her husband had a clue. Laughter and heavy footsteps made their way onto the porch, and JoJo smiled when Tucker and the boys came into view.

"Mrs. Moore," Liam called out before pushing Tucker out of the way to get to her.

"Hey, Liam." She stood, and he pulled her into a hug. "I've missed you."

"I've missed you too."

Tucker looked over at me, and I smiled at him before he went to his mother. He was covered in mud. Speckles of it were all over his handsome face, and when he smiled at his mother, he looked like a much younger version of himself.

Watching Tucker interact with his mother did absolutely nothing to help me want to stay away from him. It was obvious that he loved his mom dearly. He wrapped her up in his arms as soon as he made his way over to her, and the way her face lit up showed how much she missed him.

She wiped his sweaty chocolate brown hair off his forehead and spoke to him in a low voice that the rest of us couldn't hear. He put his arm around her shoulders, which only went up to his chest.

"What have you two been up to?" he asked while looking over at me.

"We were talking about books, life, and..." She hesitated so I finished for her.

"Stories about you," I smirked.

"Which story?" His eyes crinkled at the corners.

"Oh. Don't worry yourself about that." JoJo patted him on the chest.

"Great," he muttered under his breath.

My phone rang in my hand, interrupting us. When I looked down at the screen, I clicked ignore as soon as I saw my mom's name. It wasn't quick enough though. Tucker saw it too.

"You can take that."

"No. I'm good." He looked at me with an odd expression, but I started talking to his mom again before he could ask any questions.

I didn't care about telling him about my parents, but I didn't want to do it in front of his mother. She was so nice and it was easy to see that she was an amazing mother. And my mom, well, she wasn't. I was a little bit ashamed to even talk about her in front of JoJo.

I liked to think that I would be a good mother one day. I hoped I would be at least. I would rather not have kids at all than to resemble my mother even a small amount. My children would never be told that they weren't good enough. They will never be ashamed of their own bodies; of the decisions they made in life.

My phone rang again, but this time, it was my brother calling. I knew he was only calling because my mother put him up to it, but I also knew they wouldn't stop until I answered. I never spoke to my brother unless we were forced.

I smiled up at JoJo and Tucker. "Excuse me. I am going to take this."

My flip-flops slapped against the deck as I walked around the house and put the phone to my ear.

"Hello."

"Kennedy. It's Justin."

I rolled my eyes.

"Yeah. I have caller id. What's up?"

"Mom has been trying to reach you. Why didn't you answer your phone?"

"Maybe because I didn't want to talk to her. Is that all you're calling about?"

"No. It's not. I'm calling to invite you to a family dinner on Monday. I've got news to share with the family and I would like for you to attend."

Oh, dear God. I felt like I was being invited to tea with the queen.

"What kind of news?" I asked, but deep down I already knew the answer. He had always been one hundred percent in sync with my parents' plan.

Prom king. *Check.*

Ivy League college directly after high school. *Check.*

Choosing one of the approved professions. *Check.*

And now. Marriage before thirty. *Check.*

I was sure she was a real debutant too. Her hair would probably be perfectly quaffed; her nails were probably in a constant perfect French manicure. I would bet that the majority of her clothes were pastel, and she probably considered it a sin to wear ripped jeans.

My mother's idea of a perfect daughter.

"Can't you just do as you're told for once?"

It took everything inside me not to ask him why, but I knew that would only start an argument. It wasn't exactly something that I wanted Tucker or anyone else at this cabin to see.

"Okay. When and where?"

"Monday at six. At our parents'. Please dress appropriately."

And there it was.

Every time I spoke to Justin, he reminded me more and more of my parents. It made our already strained relationship even more so.

"Noted," I said in a short, clipped tone.

"Okay. We will see you then." He didn't give me time to respond. Instead, he hung up the phone and the line went dead in my ear.

I stared down at my phone in annoyance and took a deep breath.

"Everything okay?"

Tucker's voice made me jump.

I looked over my shoulder as I tucked my phone into the back pocket of my jeans.

"Yeah. It's fine."

"Who was that?"

His eyes were narrowed and anger burned in them.

"It was my brother. Why?"

His eyes narrowed even further. "You look upset."

"I'm not really a fan of my brother. Or of my whole family, actually."

"Did they hurt you?"

"Not in the way you're thinking. They are just different than me. I've never been good enough for them."

"That's bullshit. You're one of the best people I know. They aren't good enough for you."

My heart ached and fluttered at the same time.

"I don't speak to them much. My brother was just calling to ask me to meet them for dinner so he can share news."

"Okay. But if you don't want to go, you don't have to."

"I do."

"No. You don't." He moved closer to me and gripped my chin in his mud-covered hand. Tilting my face up to look at him, he said, "Whether you go or not is your choice, but I don't like you being around anyone who puts this look on your face." His thumb rubbed back and forth against my cheek. "They don't deserve you." His voice was low but it hit me harder than anything that had ever been screamed at me.

"Tucker." My voice was hoarse, and I tried to fight back the tears that clogged my throat. It pissed me off that I was letting my family get to me once again, but every time I spoke to one of them or about one of them, I was left emotionally raw.

"It's okay, Kennedy."

I could feel myself breaking. Falling too deep into him. I dropped my head to his chest and wiped at the tears that had managed to escape.

He held me close to his body, and I felt his lips touch the top of my head. His warmth was surrounding me. I felt safe. I felt something that I shouldn't have been feeling.

I desperately wanted to lift my head and touch my lips to him, but I couldn't handle his rejection. Especially not at that moment.

"Are you okay?" Brooke's voice broke through my Tucker fog, and I took a step back out of his embrace.

I wiped under my eyes and tried to school my features before I turned to her.

"I'm good." I smiled at her, but I knew it was weak and I knew she would see right through me.

She narrowed her eyes at me, but she didn't say anything. I knew she was sparing me in front of Tucker, and I appreciated it, but I also knew that I would get the fifth degree later.

"JoJo is cooking dinner. Do you want to go help her?"

"Absolutely." I walked toward my best friend, but Tucker caught my wrist right before I was out of his reach.

I looked back at him, and he looked like he was struggling with what he wanted to say. His thumb rubbed over my knuckles and a chill followed in its wake.

"You can always talk to me. You know that, right?" Worry was etched across his handsome face, and I wanted to take it away.

"Of course. I'm fine. I swear."

He hesitated, but he finally let my fingers slip out of his hand. I followed my best friend into the house to help cook dinner, and I ran my fingers over the skin he had just touched. As if he had branded me, I could still feel him even though I was walking away.

CHAPTER 18

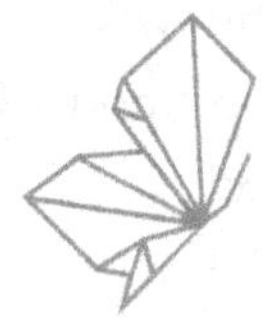

"Are you going to date my son?"

"JoJo!" I looked over at her like she was crazy.

"What? You said that you two were just friends, but then he came home and looked at you like that." She waved her hand around in the air.

"Like what?"

"Like someone who is completely infatuated," Brooke piped up, and I shot her the evil eye.

"Bingo," JoJo replied while stirring the sauce in front of her.

"He wasn't looking at me like someone who is infatuated. He was looking at me like a friend. He was just worried about me." I shrugged my shoulders.

"I'm his friend too." Brooke pointed to her chest. "He doesn't look at me like that."

"Whatever."

"I'm his mother. I have never seen him look at a woman like that." JoJo looked at me with a small smile on her face.

"Trust me. You all are reading into something that isn't there. It will never happen."

"What won't happen?" Tucker's voice caused my back to go stick straight, and I made big eyes at JoJo.

"We were talking about whether or not Ramsay Bolton could ever take down Jon Snow."

"Oh. Kennedy loves Jon Snow. She doesn't think anyone can take down her Jon Snow."

I took a deep relieved breath that he hadn't heard our conversation. "That's because they can't."

"I know, Mrs. Snow." Tucker wrapped his arm around my shoulders and looked down to me. He was smiling and his damn dimple was showing.

"Don't make fun of me." I poked him in the ribs.

He chuckled then wrapped his other arm around me and pulled me into a hug.

"Never, firecracker." He kissed the top of my head before he let me go and headed back outside with the guys.

When I finally got my bearings back, I turned back to JoJo and Brooke to help finish cooking. JoJo had a large smirk on her face and an eyebrow raised at me. Brooke's arms were crossed over her chest, and I could tell that she was dying to say something.

I raised my hands before either one of them could. "We are just friends."

"Keep telling yourself that, sweetheart." JoJo winked at me. I would keep telling myself that because I wouldn't get my hopes up otherwise. If there was one thing that I was one hundred percent certain about Tucker Moore, it was that he had the power to ruin me.

...

"Wake up, sleepy head." My body shook, and I grumbled.

"Go away." I swung my hand out in the air trying to connect with the asshole who was trying to wake me up from my nap.

"Firecracker. Get up," Tucker's deep voice called out but I wasn't sure if it was the real Tucker or dream Tucker. Because the man was invading my every thought. I couldn't get away from him.

"Come on. I want to take you somewhere."

His face was soft and a small smile rested on his lips. I couldn't tell him no.

"Where are we going?"

I sat up in bed and stretched my arms over my head.

"It's a surprise. Just make sure you wear jeans and tennis shoes."

He looked down at my legs, and I followed his gaze. I was wearing a pair of Captain America sleep shorts that barely covered any skin.

"Okay. Give me a few minutes to get ready."

Tucker nodded his head then walked out of the room.

After throwing on the clothes he told me to, I left my room in search of him. Brooke was sitting on the couch with Liam when I made it downstairs, and she was still in her bathing suit.

"Are you not going with us?" I asked.

When Tucker said he wanted to take me somewhere, I assumed he meant with everyone else.

"Nope." She smirked at me. "Tucker said it's just you and him tonight."

My heart rate took off at her words. I pulled the ends of

my long sleeves down over my palms and tried to hide my awkwardness over being alone with Tucker.

"Do you know where we're going?"

"No, and she couldn't tell you if she did." Tucker walked into the living room dressed similar to me in jeans and a T-shirt. Except he looked good enough to eat. "You ready?"

"Yeah." I walked toward him hesitantly because I wasn't sure if I was actually ready for whatever he had planned for us.

Tucker grabbed my hand in his much bigger one and led me outside to where his four-wheeler was parked.

"We're going four wheeling?" My voice squeaked, and Tucker chuckled.

"Yes. Is that okay?"

"We're going alone? What if it breaks down? What if it gets stuck?" What if I don't think I can stand to have my body pressed against yours while we frolic through the woods?

"Don't wound my ego. I can fix a four-wheeler. Plus, we have these things called cell phones." He waved his around before slipping it into his jean pocket. "What happened to my firecracker?"

"Nothing happened. I'm just making sure we are being safe."

Tucker chuckled again before putting his hand on the handle of the ATV and lifting his leg over to straddle the seat. "Come on." He patted the seat right behind him.

I took a deep breath and made my way over. I placed my foot in the same spot he had put his and gripped his shoulders as I climbed on. As soon as I was settled, I dropped my hands to my sides.

Tucker started the machine and the loud rumble met my

ears and the vibrations shook my body. I looked around for something to hold on to. Tucker's large body was seated between my thighs and blocking any chance of holding on to anything in front of me. Behind me, there was some sort of black railing, and I decided that it was my best option. I weaved my fingers below the metal and held on for dear life.

"You ready?" Tucker yelled over the rumble of the ATV.

"I think so."

"You need to hold on."

"I am."

Tucker turned then and looked at me, and I could tell he wanted to laugh. There I was leaning backward holding onto the four-wheeler for dear life, and we hadn't even moved yet.

"No, Firecracker. You need to hold on to me."

"I'm fine like this."

"Yeah. If you want to break a wrist."

I immediately let go of the railing, and he pulled my arms around his waist. My chest rested against his back, and I could feel the heat of his skin through my shirt. He was too big for me to manage to clasp my hands together so I rested them against his stomach, feeling his taut abs that lay beneath his shirt. As soon as he took off, I let out a small scream and clasped his shirt in my fists.

After the initial shock, I finally poked my head out from where it was hiding against his back and watched the scenery as we flew by it. We were riding through a wooded area with lots of bumps as we rode over rocks and fallen branches, but the lake stayed visible in my sight the whole time. The water was perfectly smooth now that the sun was going down, and it looked completely peaceful. The waves caused by boaters and swimmers were long gone and left in their wake was water that looked like it had never been touched. Smooth as glass and reflecting the bright orange of the sinking sun.

The wind whipped the hair that had fallen out of my ponytail around my face. I started to pull my hand away from Tucker to tuck it behind my ear, but as soon as my hand lost contact with him, Tucker's much larger hand grasped mine in his and pulled me closer into his back. He tucked my hand back against his stomach before moving his back to the handlebars.

I rested my face against his back to protect it from the wind, and I inhaled his scent. There was a hint of his cologne mixed with the spicy smell of his body wash. It was intoxicating. It was a smell I had loved since the moment I met him, but this was the first time that I was allowed to really take it in without him thinking I was a lunatic.

Tucker's left hand touched my knee and my legs tightened around him. His hand squeezed my skin before I was bounced in the air as he made some jump that caused us to become airborne. My arms tightened around his waist, and I buried my face deeper into him. We landed with a hard thud, and I smacked him in the arm as soon as I knew we were safe.

"What was that for?" he yelled over his shoulder.

"You know what. A little warning would have been nice."

I could feel his laughter against my body even though I couldn't hear it.

We rode for about five more minutes before he pulled to a stop and turned the four-wheeler off. I lifted my face away from his back to look around. We were parked next to a small creek that was surrounded by rocks, flowers, and trees. The sun peaked through the trees touching the water and flowers that hid below.

Tucker climbed off before reaching his hand out and helping me. He messed with the back of the four-wheeler pulling things out while I took in the view that surrounded us. I don't think I had ever been to a place this beautiful. The water flowed through the creek gliding over rocks and making the most peaceful sound.

Being out in nature wasn't something that I was used to. Sure, I went to parks and things like that, but I had never really ventured to places where I could see nothing but nature. This place looked untouched by human hands. It was refreshing, serene, and beautiful.

"I brought your camera in case you were interested."

I turned my head toward Tucker to see him pulling my camera, a blanket, and a small bag out of a compartment in the ATV that I didn't even realize was there.

"Thank you." I walked toward him and pulled my camera into my hands. I was itching to look around me with my lens and capture everything.

I pulled my camera out of my bag while Tucker laid the blanket on the ground. Holding my camera up against my glasses, I started getting lost in it. I captured the light that was coming down through the trees. I squatted low to get the perfect shot of the water cascading down over the rocks. I took my time, and by the time I came up for air, I felt much calmer. Much more grounded somehow.

I looked back at Tucker, and he was sitting on the blanket watching me. His small smile was genuine and breathtaking. I lifted my camera again and captured it before he could look away.

"How did you find this place?" I pulled the camera away

from my face and looked at the picture I had just taken. It was perfect.

"My sister and I used to come here all the time with our dad. It was one of our favorite places in the world."

"Where is your sister now? Do I get to meet her?"

"I wish. She couldn't miss classes. She is going to come visit in a couple of weeks though. You'll get to meet her then. You'll love her. She's super dorky, but she's awesome."

I knew how much his sister meant to him just by the look on his face.

I sat down beside him on the blanket and put my camera safely back in its bag.

"You love nerdy girls and you know it."

"You're right. I do." The seriousness of his voice made me look up at him. His brown eyes were staring down at me, but I couldn't tell what he was hiding behind them. My eyes dropped to his lips, and I wanted so badly to lean over and press mine to his. But before I got the chance to embarrass myself, I laid down on the blanket and stared up at the sky.

"Why do you do that?"

"Do what?"

He was practically leaning over me, and he was blocking my chance to pretend like I was looking at something else.

"Every time we get close. Every time we talk about something real. You close down on me."

"I do not." My stomach ached in unison with my chest.

"You do." He brushed a piece of hair out of my face. "You were just giving me this look, and then you shoved it down and planted on one of your fake smiles."

"I did not do that. I don't even know what you're talking about." *I so knew what he was talking about.* "What look?"

"The look where you wanted to do this." He leaned his

body down over mine and his hand went to my jaw. His face came down over me and his lips touched mine. The kiss was soft. Just barely there, but I felt it. I felt it so deep that I knew it was something that I would never forget.

A soft, breathy moan slipped from my lips, and Tucker kissed me again. This kiss was very different from the last. His hand thrust into my hair and gripped it at the root to perfectly position me where he wanted me. His other hand tightened on my jaw as his tongue traced my lips and begged for entrance.

My lips opened on a sigh, and he took the opportunity to slide his tongue along mine. When I tasted him, a hunger like I had never known took over me. I met his every move with one of my own. When his teeth sank into my bottom lip, I sucked his tongue into my mouth. His hand in my hair tightened, and the hand on my jaw moved to my thigh, just below my ass.

His body was leaning over me. His weight pressing me into the blanket. My skin was tingling even though he barely touched me. My breathing was erratic, but I didn't need air. I only needed him.

I could feel him pressed against my thigh, and he was just as turned on as I was. My body bowed into him and suddenly he pulled away.

He stared down at me. His hand still wrapped in my hair. Both of us tried to catch our breath as we searched each other's eyes. I wasn't sure what to do with myself. Not that I had many options. I was basically a puddle beneath him who would bend to his every move.

He pressed his forehead to mine, and I could feel his breath against my lips.

"I knew you were a firecracker." His voice was gruff and his words were a whisper.

A smile took over my face, and I buried my face in his neck.

We stayed like that for several moments. Just holding onto each other and that feeling that I had never felt before. My heart hammered in my chest, and I couldn't even form a complete thought. The only thing that ran through my head was the feel of his lips against mine. When Tucker did pull away, he sat back down on the blanket and stared up at the sky for several moments.

"Do you know how long I've wanted to kiss you?" He turned and looked at me.

"I have a pretty good idea."

He smiled at me and fixed my glasses that had gone crooked during our kiss.

"Are you going to tell me any more about your family?"

My stomach ached just at the mention of them, but I knew he wasn't asking to upset me. He genuinely wanted to know more about me.

It made me both excited and scared.

"There isn't a whole lot to say." I shrugged my shoulders. "My family thinks they are better than everyone else. Including me. I've never quite fit in with them."

"You do know that is bullshit, right? You say they are better than you like you actually believe it."

I sat in place and thought about what he had just said. I didn't believe that. Did I? I had always been the black sheep of the family. The one they hid in the back of family pictures. The one my mom always spoke about as if I wasn't in the room. I used to get upset. I would sit in my bedroom surrounded by expensive things and I would cry. I cried myself to sleep.

But I wasn't that sad girl anymore. More than anything, I was pissed. I hated my parents for what they had done to me. I hated them for making me feel like I was less than. Less than them. Less than worthy.

"I don't believe it. It's just hard sometimes. They've made it difficult for me to trust people. To trust their motives. Every time I get a phone call from them, I question what they truly want from me. Why do they still call me when they would prefer that I wasn't a part of their family at all?"

Tucker's eyes were on me, and I could see the sympathy shining in them. I hated that look. I fucking despised it. There was a moment where something else flashed across his face. It looked like guilt, but I knew I was being crazy.

"Listen, Firecracker. I need to tell you something."

As soon as the last word left his mouth, a raindrop hit my cheek and ran down my neck. I looked up to the sky and watched the dark grey clouds roll above us. Then the sky opened up and rain began pouring down on us.

Tucker and I both jumped up off the ground and started packing up our stuff. He pulled my camera bag out of my hand and stuck it back in the compartment on the four-wheeler. When he jumped on, I followed his lead and hopped on behind him.

I was already soaking wet, and I could barely see through my glasses. Tucker patted my hands to make sure I was holding on and then took off back in the direction of the house. The rain pelted against us as we sped through the trees.

It was exhilarating.

By the time we pulled up to the house, there wasn't a

single spot on us that was dry. My jeans clung to my legs and my feet squished in my shoes. It was already dark outside, and for the first time since we left the house, I realized that we had been gone for hours. Being with Tucker was easy. I never checked my phone, the time, or my feelings when I was with him. We just were. No questions asked.

He grabbed our stuff and the two of us took off running toward the cabin. We took a look at each other when we finally made it to the shelter of the porch, and God, he was beautiful. His clothes were stuck to his skin and left absolutely nothing to the imagination. His normally perfect hair was flat against his head with random pieces stuck to his face. His face was scruffier than normal, and the rain drops glistened against his skin that had become much tanner since we arrived in Tennessee.

Tucker chuckled, and I stopped checking him out long enough to look up at him. "Well, that didn't go quite like I was planning."

"And what exactly was your plan?" I wrapped my hands in the bottom of my T-shirt and wrung out the excess water.

"You have no idea how gorgeous you are, do you?"

I looked back up at him and saw his eyes skirt over my bare stomach before moving to my face. I didn't respond to him immediately, and apparently, he wasn't in the mood to wait.

"It's taking everything inside me not to throw you up against the wall and fuck you. I want to trace every fucking inch of your skin with my tongue."

Dear God.

My thighs clenched involuntarily and my chest heaved. I had never heard Tucker speak like that. But damn, I loved it.

I loved everything that he said, and I prayed that he did all that and more.

"Then do it." It was my voice that said the words, but I had never been so bold. I was typically the one who was timid when it came to sex. I rarely expressed my wants and needs.

I didn't have much time to think about it though. My back hit the front door right before his mouth slammed down on mine. He gripped my hands in his and held them above my head. Both of our chests were heaving and my breasts pressed against him. The feeling of the cold fabric and his body against mine was causing goose bumps to break out across my skin.

I had never been so turned on in my entire life.

Tucker's hands ran over my body leaving a trail of heat and lust behind.

His hand reached behind me, and I would have tumbled to the floor if his hands hadn't been holding me when the door opened.

The cabin was dark inside, and I heard no sound of movement. I momentarily moved my mouth away from Tucker's to look around. There was no one to be seen.

My ass hit the back of the couch, and I looked back up at Tucker. His hands toyed with the edge of my shirt, his rough fingertips a barely there caress against my skin. He slowly lifted my shirt over my head and threw it behind him. His eyes took in my breasts momentarily before he moved his mouth to the skin that was pouring out of my bra.

He licked and teased the sensitive skin, and just when I thought I couldn't take anymore, he dipped his tongue below the lace fabric of my bra to taste my nipple.

I kicked my shoes off in a haze and began pulling his

shirt off his body. The wet fabric clung to him and regardless of how hard I pulled, it seemed to get stuck. Tucker chuckled softly then pulled it the rest of the way off while my hands went to the button of his jeans. I had managed to pop the button and lower his zipper before he pulled my hands away.

He made quick work of my jeans, pulling them down my legs and leaving them in a puddle of fabric on the floor. His jeans hung low on his hips, the edge of his boxers resting against the muscles that disappeared below the fabric.

His hands went to my ass and he lifted me in the air. I didn't expect it, but I wrapped my arms around his shoulders and my legs around his waist. It wasn't until that moment that I started feeling self-conscious about my body. Tucker had this way of making me forget anything that was worrying me before, but when he had me practically naked and in his arms, my insecurities started to sneak their way back in.

He took off in the direction of the stairs with me in tote.

"I can walk, Tucker," I murmured.

But he didn't respond. Instead, he pressed his lips to mine again. He caressed my tongue with his. He nipped at my lips before taking the sting away with a trace of his tongue. I was so distracted that I didn't even notice that we had made it upstairs until he dropped me onto the bed and pressed his weight into me.

He leaned back and took a long perusal of my body. I could feel his eyes on me as if they were his hands. Each drag of his eyes burned my skin. When his eyes dilated and he took a deep shuddering breath, it was burned into my memory.

My hands were resting on my stomach, and he pushed them away slowly.

"You are so gorgeous." His words were breathless, but they carried more weight than I could imagine.

He peppered slow, soft kisses against my collarbone before moving down my body. My head was pressed into the mattress and my eyes were clamped shut in pleasure. He was barely touching me, and already, I was coming apart.

I felt my bra snap open behind me moments before the cool air of the room hit my bare skin. It didn't last long though. His warm mouth latched on to my nipple and my back arched off the bed. Tucker took that opportunity to wrap his arm behind my back and hold my body closer to his mouth.

He took turns, showering each of my breasts with attention. By the time he trailed his mouth down to my belly button, I was a whimpering mess.

"Please, Tuck."

"What do you need?"

What did I need? It wasn't a question that I wanted to spend too much time thinking about, but somehow an answer still rolled off my lips.

"You."

He swirled his tongue into my belly button before he dropped to his knees at the end of the bed. His warm breath touched my inner thighs and it set a fire in my veins. I was burning from the inside out. My body begging for more than he was giving me.

I jolted when his nose ran along the edge of my panties. His lips pressed against my center, and I knew that he was aware of how bad I wanted him.

His rough fingers ran over my hips before I felt my panties being slowly pulled down my legs. I held my breath waiting for his first touch, but when it didn't come, I leaned up on my elbows to look down at him.

His brown eyes were staring up at me, and they were hungry. Dark and daring.

"Keep your eyes on me."

Then his mouth disappeared against my flesh, and I barely managed to hold myself up. His eyes stayed on mine as he licked, bit, and sucked on my skin. It was too much, too intimate, and too intense. I was falling apart at an embarrassingly fast pace.

"Please, Tucker." I wasn't sure what I was asking for, but he did. He grabbed my hips in his hands pulling me closer to his mouth, my arms buckled underneath me, and my control snapped as he sucked my clit into his mouth.

His hair was threaded through my fingers and I pulled it hard as I rode out my orgasm against his mouth. There was no shame. No hiding. I laid bare for him completely at his mercy.

I watched him as he wiped his mouth with the back of his hand. My stomach tightening again just at the sight of his smirk outlined by his perfect dimples. He made his way back up my body, kissing every inch of skin that he passed. My toes dug into the sides of his jeans that were still covering his body, and I pushed them down his hips. He helped. Stopping his worshiping of my body long enough to kick both his jeans and boxers off his body.

Tucker's mouth assaulted my neck as I took him in my hand and felt the smooth skin of his penis for the first time. He hissed through his teeth then sank them into the sensitive skin where my shoulder and neck met.

I arched my hips off the bed and silently begged for more.

His cock rubbed against me, coating him in my wetness. Driving me insane with lust.

He leaned past me, reaching into the drawer on the bedside table. With a condom in his hand and determination on his face, he placed the condom between his teeth and ripped it open before rolling it down his length. I watched as his hand ran over himself, and I had to bite my lip to stop the small moan that was about to escape.

Tucker gripped my thighs in his hands, spreading them apart and lifting them near his sides. He stared down at my center before he leaned his body down and placed a kiss on my stomach. My belly fluttered as anticipation coursed through my veins.

He scattered slow, lazy kisses up my body, paying special attention to my breasts and my neck before he made it to my mouth. His tongue teased mine as he teased me in the same rhythm with his length. When he finally pushed into me, I was writhing beneath him and begging him to give me more.

He slid into me slowly. Taking his time making sure that he didn't hurt me. I pushed against him. My body begging for his touch. For more. For him.

I could see it the moment his control snapped. His brown eyes turned darker. His normally cool demeanor gone. His hands on my thighs tightened, digging into my skin. Digging into my resolve.

He bit down on my neck at the same time that he slammed his body into mine. The contrast from moments before was vast. No longer was he careful and calculated. He was a man controlled by lust. Animalistic. Savage.

My thighs were spread as far as they could go by his hands, and my body jolted up higher and higher in the bed with every thrust. His mouth was running over my body. A drag of his lips. A soft kiss. The bite of his teeth. The swipe of his tongue.

My back arched off the bed when his teeth sank into the sensitive skin covering my ribs. He took advantage of my position and flipped us over so I was straddling his hips. My hands were on his chest helping balance myself as I began to move, and his hands were on my ass, digging into my skin as he set the pace.

I couldn't get enough. I needed to get closer to him. I needed more.

He knew exactly what I needed too. He sat up against the headboard, and one of the hands on my ass slowly crept up my body.

"Your body is fucking unreal," he whispered close to my ear.

His words and the feel of the sweat on his chest made me breathe harder. My body had taken over, and any logical thoughts that I had were long gone.

His tongue traced the moisture of my own skin, driving me insane. Pushing me closer. My hands were on his shoulders using him as leverage as I worked myself up and down on him. Faster and faster. His hand wrapped in my hair, arching me back and giving him full access to my neck, while his other hand found my center and pushed me over the edge.

I came against him barely able to move, but his strong hands held onto my body as he thrust up into me and found his own release.

Neither one of us said a word, and we stayed like that for a long time. Our bodies pressed together, our hearts racing against one another, and me wondering what the hell just happened.

CHAPTER 19

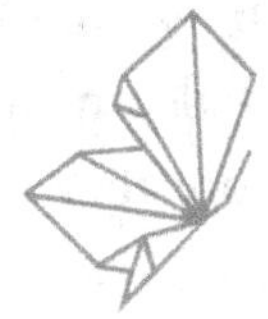

I didn't know how to feel or how to act. When I opened my eyes, my body was wrapped in Tucker's arm and in his scent. The spiciness of his cologne mixed with a smell that was pure Tucker. I was surrounded by him, drowning in everything he was, and I wasn't sure if I would ever be able to climb back out.

He stirred behind me and his arm around my waist tightened, pulling me closer into him. I tried not to breathe too hard because I wasn't ready for him to know I was awake. I wasn't ready for the spell we had been under last night to be broken.

I had never felt more alive than I did when I was with Tucker. It made me excited and scared at the same time. Scared wasn't the right word. I was terrified. I had been hurt before. There was no doubt about that, but I had never cared about a man like I had Tucker. No one had ever had the power to hurt me like he did. He had the power to change everything.

The feeling of his nose running along the back of my

neck caused me to take in a deep breath as he did the same, as if he was breathing me in.

"Good morning." His voice was rough with sleep, and my thighs tightened at the sound.

"Morning."

He placed a soft kiss on my shoulder before he pulled me onto my back and looked down at me. I was sure that I looked a mess. My hair more than likely resembled a bird's nest. I was completely naked except for my pair of panties that I managed to throw back on before Tucker threw me back on the bed and refused to let me put any other clothes on.

We were still covered in rainwater, dirt, and each other, but I felt beautiful.

When his eyes were on me, taking me in as if he was devouring me, it was hard to feel anything but beautiful. It wasn't a feeling I was used to.

He pushed my hair out of my face before he pressed his lips to mine. With that one kiss, most of my anxiety left me. I didn't know what this morning would hold for us. Would he pretend that it didn't happen? Would he treat me like a one-night stand? I didn't think I could handle either of those options.

But instead of letting that fear take over, Tucker caressed my body with his mouth and put my insecurities to rest. My body hummed as he worked his way down my body.

"Firecracker," he murmured against my belly button.

"Hmm?" My head was pressing back into my pillow and my fingers ran through his hair.

"It's noon." His words could barely be made out as he didn't remove his lips from my skin.

"Okay." I didn't give a damn what time it was.

"We're supposed to be at my parents' by one." His tongue traced the edge of my panties and I shot up in bed.

Tucker's grip tightened on my hips, and he held me in bed.

"What are you doing?" I pushed against his shoulders. "We have to get ready. I am not showing up at JoJo's house looking like this."

He smiled, one of those brilliant smiles of his that showed his dimples and made me melt. "You're not getting up until you kiss me."

"Tuck." Even though his words softened me, I was still ready to panic. We were going to his parents' for crying out loud.

"Kennedy, kiss me."

I looked into his eyes, and I couldn't resist him. I pressed my hand against his strong jaw and felt the stubble of his day-old beard against my hand. We were only a breath away from each other, but I could already taste him. I could taste his desire for me and mine for him. It was consuming me.

When our lips finally touched, I knew that I was completely screwed. There was no way that I would make it out of this unscathed, and there was no way we were making it to his parents' on time.

When we finally scurried down the stairs, we had five minutes until we had to be at Tucker's parents. Brooke, Liam, Jase, and Ryan were all sitting on the couch, and they looked like they had been sitting there waiting for us for a while.

"It's about damn time." Liam stood up from the couch as the others followed him.

"Shut up, Liam." Tucker wrapped his arm around my waist and pulled me against him.

"Well, you can be the ones to explain to JoJo that we are late because the two of you have been locked up in your room all night and morning." A smirk formed on Liam's handsome face.

"Don't be a jerk because you didn't get laid, Liam." That statement might have pissed me off if it hadn't just come out of my own mouth.

All the guys started laughing, and Brooke patted Liam on the stomach with a private smirk. It almost made me wonder if Liam did get laid. Obviously, Brooke and I needed some girl time to dish.

Tucker kissed the top of my head then led me out the door. "Let's go, Firecracker."

...

JoJo pulled me into a hug as soon as we walked in the door. It wasn't just one of those polite hugs you give to someone when you see them. She pulled me into her and her arms wrapped around me and squeezed me tight. It was the kind of hug I would assume a good mother would give. I hugged her back in the same way and held onto the moment with her.

"Really, JoJo. You just met her. Don't you miss me at all?" I could hear Liam's teasing behind me, and I turned my head to stick my tongue out at him like a child.

"Yes, dear." She coddled him as she let me out of her hug but held onto my hands. "But I just love her to pieces."

I smiled even bigger and made sure to look over at Liam's pouting face, but my gaze stopped on Tucker and the way he was taking us in. I didn't even know how to describe the look on his face. It wasn't something that I had ever seen before.

"My boy," a deep, loud voice boomed into the living room.

Tucker smiled and walked around his friends to get to a man who looked just like him, just older.

"Hey, Dad." The two men pulled each other into a hug and clapped each other's backs.

Tucker's dad had the same warm brown eyes of his son, or I guess Tucker had his, and they were filled with love and happiness. It was easy to see that this man was far different from the dad I grew up with, and he was genuinely happy to see his son.

"Well, how the hell are you?"

Tucker chuckled and looked over at me. "I'm doing good, Dad. Really good."

He held his hand out to me, and I moved away from his mother and toward him.

"Dad, I would like you to meet Kennedy Hayes."

"Hi, darlin'." His accent was stronger than his son's, but I loved it just the same.

"Hi. It's nice to meet you, Mr. Moore." I stuck my hand out to shake his, but he used my hand to pull me into him instead and wrapped me in a hug.

"Sorry, darlin'. We're a bit of a hugging family."

I smiled up at him, way up, since he was a good foot taller than me, just like his son.

"JoJo has told me a lot about you. I believe she has a girl crush on you."

I giggled and Tucker groaned.

"Really, Dad?"

"What? Is that not what you all call it?" He scratched at his clean-shaven face.

"No, Dad. Don't ever say girl crush again."

I smiled at Tucker's embarrassment and reassured his father. "No worries, Mr. Moore. I knew what you meant."

"Thanks, girl, and call me Dad or Arnie. Mr. Moore just sounds weird."

"Okay, Arnie."

We all moved into the dining room after Arnie and JoJo greeted and loved on everyone. Their house was beautiful and rustic. It reminded me of something you would see on the cover of a Martha Stewart magazine. Everything had its place, but the space was filled with love and family.

Almost every free surface was covered with pictures of Tucker and his sister. She had brown hair that matched her brother's, but her eyes were a soft blue instead of the chocolate brown that the rest of her family seemed to have. Most of the photos were from when they were younger, but it was easy to see how gorgeous she was and how much she adored her older brother.

We sat at a large round family table where everyone could see each other and talk easily. The conversation was relaxed and everyone was smiling and laughing. JoJo talked to me about a book that I had recommended to her that she had already managed to finish. She was fangirling hard over it, and it made me entirely giddy.

Tucker and the boys talked sports and fishing. Tucker kept his hand on my leg, his thumb rubbing circles on my skin, his touch driving me insane.

Even when he wasn't talking to me, he would turn to me every few minutes to make sure that I was okay or to see what I was talking about with his mom. His attentiveness was getting to me more than his touch was. I didn't know where we stood. Were we exclusive? Was this just sex?

I didn't want to be that girl either. The girl who

demanded a title for what we were. Who needed more than what he was willing to give.

My worries and fears bubbled up to the surface as I sat there looking around me. JoJo was laughing at something Brooke was talking about. The guys all seemed captivated by a fishing story Arnie was telling, and I was just sitting there, worrying my lip between my teeth.

Tucker looked over at me momentarily, and I smiled at him. He smiled back and turned back to his dad, but quickly looked back at me.

"You okay?" he whispered close to my ear.

"Yeah. Of course." I nodded my head.

He pulled back slightly and looked me over. I smiled at him again, but I wasn't sure if I was convincing either one of us.

He slid his hand along my face gripping my jaw then leaned his head into mine. He devoured my lips and stole my breath.

When he pulled away from me, I felt light-headed and swoony, and I wished there was no one else in the room. But Tucker had managed to push my insecurities down once again.

He placed his forehead against mine as he ran his fingers through my straight hair.

"You get me?" His words were barely a whisper, but I heard them loud and clear.

"I get you." And I did. There was no mistaking the statement he had just made by kissing me like that in front of his family and friends, and when he settled back into his seat, I couldn't stop smiling. Everyone was looking at us while also trying to pretend they were still having a conversation, and I blushed as Tucker took my hand into his.

By the time it was time for us to leave, my stomach was full and my worries were gone. I felt grounded, yet carefree, and deliriously happy. I promised JoJo that I would text her when we made it home, and I also promised her that I would read the book she recommended so we could talk about it.

She pulled me into another long hug before I made my way out the door. "Take care of my boy, Kennedy. Don't hurt him. He deserves good."

"Trust me. If anyone hurts anyone, it will probably be the other way around."

She smiled down at me like she understood exactly what I meant, and I was sure that she did. Tucker acted just like his father, and she was clearly as in love with him as she had ever been. She knew the power these men could have on a woman.

"One word of advice, honey." She leaned in closer even though no one else was near us. "Those men in our books will never hold a candle to the Moore men. Remember that."

I giggled, but I knew exactly what she meant. Tucker was surpassing them all.

CHAPTER 20

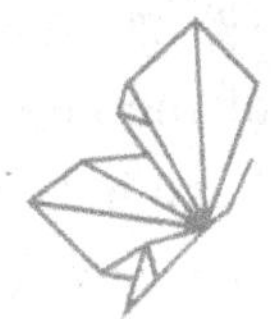

"We're going out tonight." Liam rubbed his hands together.

"But we have to leave early in the morning." Brooke looked around our room that the two of us were currently lying in.

"So, get everything packed up tonight, but we're going out to the bar. Get ready." He closed the door behind him, and Brooke and I looked at each other.

"I'm doing your hair and makeup."

I groaned. Loud.

"You have to look nice for your boyfriend," she teased.

"He is not my boyfriend."

"Then what is he exactly?"

"Umm," I hesitated. "I'm not really sure, to be honest."

"Well then let's make you so hot that there will be absolutely no confusion."

I buried my head under my pillow, but the more I thought about it the more her idea sounded good.

"Deal." I peeked out from behind my pillow.

She squealed then started running around the room like a maniac.

"You do know we have to get all of this packed tonight." I waved my hand around at all her clothes and hair and makeup products that were thrown all over the place.

"That is not top priority right now."

I was hauled up out of the bed, and she pushed on my shoulders to get me to sit down in front of the mirror.

"Now let the master do her work."

I laughed at her, but the look on her face made me shut up.

For good reason too. When I finally stood in the mirror, fully dressed and ready to go, I was almost as excited as she was.

I looked like myself, just a much sexier version.

My long, black hair fell in soft curls down my back, and Brooke had managed to give it volume that normally wasn't there. The makeup around my eyes was dark and smoky, and it made my green eyes pop in a way that I had never been able to manage on my own. They looked alluring and almost seductive. Words that had never been used to describe me. Ever.

I was wearing one of Brooke's dresses, and because she was much smaller than me, the black material clung to my skin and showed off every single one of my curves. Normally, I would have hated it, but I loved the way it looked on me. I felt beautiful. I felt sexy even.

"Please just put them on."

I looked down at my bare feet then back at Brooke who was swinging a pair of black heels from her hand.

"I. Will. Fall." I sounded out every word to make sure she heard me clearly that time.

"I promise that I will not let you fall. Just try them on. If you hate them, you can take them off."

I grumbled but slipped my feet into the shoes. I grew about four inches instantly. And my legs. Did heels always do this to other girl's legs? Because my legs looked awesome. I spun around in a circle. Honestly, just checking myself out.

Brooke looked like a giddy schoolgirl behind me. "You have to wear them. I lied you are not allowed to take them off."

"I'm not taking them off, but if I fall, I will kill you."

"Deal."

We made our way down the stairs, and I could hear the guys talking and laughing in the living room. Brooke was in front of me, dressed similarly to me, but she was used to it. I wasn't. I felt nervous. My heart was racing and my hands were sweaty.

When we finally made it to the bottom, I tried to pretend like I wasn't dressed any differently than normal. I imagined that I was walking around in a pair of my Chuck Taylors and jeans. Comfortable. Not at all exposed.

But then I heard it, the sharp intake of his breath.

I finally looked up at him. He was wearing a black long sleeve button-up shirt that was rolled up to his forearms with a pair of dark blue jeans. He looked hot. He looked...

"Holy shit."

Tucker was staring at my legs. His hungry gaze traveling over my body. His eyes tracked over every detail, taking his time, taking it all in. When he reached my eyes, he stalked toward me and buried his hands in my hair. He tugged me toward him, hard, and a shot of lust went through me. His lips crashed against mine, and I couldn't stop my moan as his body pressed against me.

"You're going to mess up her makeup." I distantly heard Brooke say from my side, but I didn't give a crap about my makeup. I didn't care that they were standing there watching the two of us while went at each other like a couple of teenagers. All I cared about was that I was in Tucker's arms and his lips were pressed against mine.

I felt drunk, and I hadn't even had one drop of alcohol. My body was tingling. My knees weak. My heart racing. His tongue traced my lips and I followed its path before sucking it into my mouth. His hands on my back tightened, and I felt my dress rise a little on my hip as the fabric bunched under his fist.

I wanted him. I needed him. Every single part of me was desperate for his touch.

"Well now that I'm hard."

I pulled my mouth away from Tucker when Ryan's words made it into my foggy mind.

"Really, Ryan?" Brooke's hands were on her hips.

"What? That was hot as fuck."

Tucker's hands turned my head back in his direction and placed a soft, quick kiss to my lips.

"You look so damn beautiful." He breathed against my lips.

"Thanks, Tuck." I tucked a strand of hair behind my ear.

He continued to stare down at me without saying anything else, and everyone else was clearly waiting on us to leave.

"What are you doing?" I whispered to him.

"I'm trying to convince myself that I actually want to see my old friends tonight instead of marching you upstairs and fucking the shit out of you."

My thighs clenched and I whimpered causing his eyes to darken even further.

"Firecracker." His voice was a warning.

"I don't need to meet your friends."

His hand moved to my hip. His grip almost painful.

"Oh no, you don't." Liam pulled Tucker's arm causing his hand to slip off my body. "A lot of people are meeting up with us, and we need to leave now before we never get you two out of the house."

"You're right." Tucker didn't look like he thought he was right. He looked like he wanted to throw me over his shoulder and carry me up the stairs. Which wasn't a bad plan at all.

...

We walked into a small bar, and Tucker kept me tucked into his side. The place was crowded, and I saw Brooke's eyes light up when she saw all the men that were greeting the guys as we walked in.

The only time Tucker let go of me was when someone would stop to hug him or slap his shoulder. He introduced me to almost everyone. You know, his good friend Kennedy.

I wasn't expecting him to confess his undying love, but I thought maybe, I don't know, that he would introduce me as more than just his friend. But instead of acting like I cared, I planted a big smile on my face and pretended like I wasn't affected at all.

I knew it was unfair of me to be upset. We had spent one night together for crying out loud and we hadn't talked about being anything more, but it was impossible for me not to be hurt. By the way he had treated me all day, I had thought that we were more than just friends. Maybe he just wanted to be friends with benefits?

I wasn't sure how I felt about that.

We walked up to a table that had several guys sitting around it and a few women who were hanging on to them. The women were beautiful too. The type of girls I was used to seeing Tucker around.

He pulled a chair out for me to sit down, and I tugged on the hem of my dress to cover more of my thighs. Who decided this dress was a good idea again?

Tucker sat down beside me and introduced me and Brooke to everyone. I was too stuck in my own head to remember any of their names, but I nodded my head and said my hellos. Tucker put his hand on my knee and my anxiety settled a small bit.

I looked up at his profile. He was talking to one of the men who was sitting across the table, and he looked so carefree and happy. His jaw was still covered in scruff, and I decided that it was my absolute favorite look on him. His skin was tanner than normal from our days in the sun, and he looked unreal. Too good to be true. Too good for me. Too good to exist in my world.

I saw a flash of red hair, but I didn't pay much attention until I saw her saddle up next to Tucker.

My Tucker.

She ran her blood red fingers down his arm and acted like seeing him tonight was the best thing that had happened to her all year. Not that I could blame her. He was the best thing that had ever happened to me as well.

"Tucker, you should have called me. I didn't know you were back in town."

"Sorry, Julie. We just came in to see the family and my boys."

He slowly moved her hand off him, but I was still staring daggers at her. I never wanted to rip another girl's hair out so badly in all my life. I was the girl who complimented other girls in the bathroom. I was not the jealous girl. At least not until now.

I felt a hand touch my shoulder, and I pulled my glare away from Tucker. There was another woman standing on the opposite side of me, except this woman was my favorite person in the world.

She leaned close to me and whispered in my ear, "Let's go to the bar."

I nodded my head then scooted my chair back to follow her. I saw Tucker's gaze flash to me, but I didn't stop to tell him where I was going. I just got up and followed my best friend.

"Jealousy isn't a good look on you," Brooke said as she handed me a shot.

"I'm not jealous." I pouted. I actually pouted.

"Okaaayy," she exaggeratedly drug the word out.

"I'm just frustrated." I threw the shot back.

"Hey! We were supposed to take those shots together."

"Then I'll get another one." I waved down the bartender.

"If it makes any difference at all, Tucker hasn't taken his eyes off you since you got up." She wiggled her eyebrows up and down.

"It doesn't." I raised my second shot, and she hit hers against mine before we downed the contents.

"Hey, ladies. Can I buy you all a drink?" I looked at the guy who was standing behind us. Brooke's smile became bigger when she looked at him, and I knew why. He was hot.

Like really hot. His head was covered in a baseball cap, his smile was sexy, and his body was built. It was easy to see even through his clothes.

"Hi. I'm Brooke." Brooke placed her hand in his, and his sexy smile became even hotter.

"And what's your name, sweetheart?" He turned to me.

"I'm Kennedy."

I didn't stick my hand out to him because I'm awkward and I forget how to act in normal situations when hot guys are around. He brushed my awkwardness off though, and he slipped my hand into his much larger one.

"It's nice to meet you ladies. I'm James."

He flicked his hand out and the bartender stepped in front of us. I was already feeling the effects of the two tequila shots that we had just taken, but I needed alcohol to get through the night so I threw caution to the wind and ordered a margarita.

Why the hell not?

I felt heat against my back. Pressed completely against the back of me, and I looked over my shoulder. Tucker was there staring daggers right at James.

"Tucker, what's up, man?" James slapped Tucker on the shoulder, but Tucker didn't look like he was happy to see him at all.

"Hey, James. I'm just coming up here to get my girl." He wrapped his arm around my middle. "It seems she ran off without telling me."

Excuse me?

I jabbed my elbow into his stomach to give him a warning to quit being a jerk, but he barely even budged. I wasn't even sure if he felt it.

"This is your girl?" James looked down at me, but before

I could answer with a big fat negative, the bartender set our drinks down in front of us.

James pulled his wallet out of his jeans, but Tucker beat him to it. He held out a twenty-dollar bill and James grumbled.

"Now, Tucker. I offered to buy these ladies a drink."

"Well, James. I'm sorry, bud, but no other man is buying my girl a drink."

I. WAS. FUMING.

"I wasn't your girl a few minutes ago when you were introducing me to your friends."

I heard Brooke snort, and when I looked over, she was hiding her smile by taking a sip of her drink.

"We didn't talk about how you wanted me to introduce you," he growled into my ear.

I turned to face him. "Yet, you didn't care what we talked about when you came over here to piss all over me."

"Kennedy." His voice was a warning, but I didn't care.

"Tucker," I said back in the exact same tone.

He was staring down at me, but he didn't have near as much height on me as usual with the heels I was wearing. When he didn't say anything else after a moment, I started walking away from him and back toward the table.

Screw him and that damn margarita.

I didn't make it but a few steps when I was tugged back against him.

"Don't do that shit." He growled, low enough that only I could hear him.

"Do what? Practically ignore you all evening then let you sit beside me while another man has his hands all over me?"

His grip tightened around me.

"I didn't ignore you."

"Whatever, Tuck. I don't even care."

"Yes. You do." He pressed a barely there kiss behind my ear.

"Not anymore." I attempted to stomp off, but he didn't allow it. Instead, he threw me over his shoulder and stormed toward the door.

"Tucker!!! My dress." I frantically tugged against the fabric to make sure it was covering my butt.

He slapped my ass, hard, and I yelped. He used the same hand to hold on to the fabric on my dress keeping me covered. The people around us cheered. They were all drunk and excited that Tucker Moore was carrying his girl out of the bar, but not me. I was furious.

"I am so damn mad at you, Tucker."

"I got that, Firecracker." He continued to walk, and I felt the temperature change when we stepped outside.

"Put me down." My words were pretty jumbled since my body was bouncing against his shoulder.

"Not happening." And he didn't. He carried me the whole way to the truck, and only set me on my feet then.

"Get in the truck." He pulled the door open.

"What is with you? You can't just throw me over your shoulder when you're not getting your way."

"It's worked so far." He shrugged his shoulders. "Get in the truck."

"What about everyone else?" I asked with my arms crossed. There was no way that I wanted to get into that truck alone with him.

"They can catch a cab."

"I'm not leaving Brooke."

"Liam has her. She'll be fine."

"Tucker," I groaned.

"Kennedy, you are about a minute away from getting fucked in the back seat of this truck. If you want the rest of them here to see it, then fine. I'll go get them." He waved his arm back toward the bar.

I wanted to be mad at the words he just said. I really did, but my body betrayed me and my thighs clenched together.

"That's not happening." My words weren't convincing, even to me.

He crowded my space and pressed me up against the truck. "Is that why your breath just became faster and your nipples hardened? Because it's not happening?"

I pulled my arms tighter over my chest and attempted to cover my breasts, but I only succeeded in putting them further on display.

"You're an asshole."

"We've known this, but you still like me." He smirked. That damn smirk that I love so much with his stupid perfect dimples.

"So you think."

His smirk dropped and he leaned in closer. "You're telling me that you don't want me to bend you over, hike up this fucking dress, and bury myself inside of you?"

I shivered and let out the tiniest moan. *My traitorous damn body!*

"That's what I thought. Get in the truck."

I stomped around him on shaky legs and climbed into the truck. My whole damn body was buzzing with anticipation, and although I was still pissed at him, I wanted him. Bad.

We drove in silence for the first few minutes, him watching the road and me looking out the window at basically nothing since it was pitch black outside.

"You can't stay mad at me forever."

"Watch me." I crossed my arms.

My body jolted forward when he slammed on the brakes.

"What the hell are you doing?" He was pulling over onto the side of the abandoned road, and I momentarily looked down to make sure the doors were locked before he managed to get us mugged.

"I wasn't trying to ignore you." He scrubbed his hand down his face as if he was irritated.

"I don't even care, Tucker." I was trying so hard not to care. "Just take me home so I can go to bed."

"Stop saying that you don't care," he growled before he unclicked my seat belt and dragged me across the cab of the truck. My resolve to stay mad was really difficult when my legs were straddling him.

The steering wheel dug into my back when I tried to put some much-needed space between us.

"Stop acting like you don't."

He groaned, his frustration with me clear. He stared into my eyes. It was so dark inside the cab of the truck that he was the only thing I could really make out.

"Tuck," I breathed out his name. Ready to just go home. Ready to forget this night even happened.

But instead of letting me do that, he wrapped his hand in my hair and closed the space between us. When his lips touched mine, I was no longer mad at him, no longer ready to go home. I just wanted him. Nothing else mattered.

Our kiss was messy, rushed, and frantic. It wasn't a kiss of want. It was need. Need to erase what had happened tonight. Need to be closer to each other.

He tugged on my hair, almost to the point of pain, and I

arched back giving him full access to my neck. He kissed, licked, and bit, and I was a writhing mess on top of him.

My dress was riding high on my thighs, and I rubbed myself against him, aching for more.

"Fuck," he whispered against my neck. His breath hot against my already overheated skin.

He gripped my dress in his hands and pulled it over my head leaving me in a pair of lace black panties and a matching strapless bra. My bra was jerked down, making quick work of the fabric that was hiding me from him.

His tongue ran over my skin then his mouth latched onto my nipple. The steering wheel was digging into the skin of my back, but I didn't care. He could mark me, leave scars, and I would still want more. Need more.

I frantically worked the buttons of his shirt, my fingers slipping and struggling to get them undone. He pulled himself away from my breasts long enough to assist me, jerking both his button-up and his T-shirt over his head.

The moon light was shining through the window and shining straight on him. Every ridge of his abs visible. The sharp rise and fall of his chest mesmerizing.

The sound of his belt buckle being worked open caught my attention, and I sat up on my knees to give him room to free himself. He fumbled around in his pants for a condom, and I had to stop myself from laughing at the frustration on his face. All laughter was gone when he finally pulled it from his wallet and tore it open with his teeth. There was just something so damn hot about it. The determination in his eyes. His eagerness to get to me.

He slid the condom on, and I pulled my panties to the side and followed its path. His moan filled the truck as I settled fully onto him. I contracted around him, and his hands gripped my hips.

"You are so fucking wet," he sounded breathless, and I loved it.

I began to move on him. The constricted space forcing us closer to each other. Skin dragging against skin as I lifted and dropped back down. The smell of his spicy cologne filled the space and drove my lust even further. I began working my hips in small circles, and he devoured my mouth, his tongue matching the speed of our bodies.

Sweat pebbled against my skin and made my body slick against his. Our breathing was hard, and I breathed in everything Tucker would give me. I swallowed his moans. I drank in his pleasure. I made it my own.

I could feel myself falling over the edge, just needing something, anything, and Tucker knew it too. He thrust up into me, taking away my control, and his thumbed grazed against my clit. His teeth clamped down around my nipple, and I was lost. I screamed out as my orgasm crashed into me. I thrashed against him, and he rode it out, coming with me. My name on his lips.

My body went slack against him. My face buried in his neck. His hand traced a path down my back, slick with sweat, causing goose bumps to break out on my skin. My body clenched around him, and he groaned low in my ear.

"Remind me to make you mad at me more often." He chuckled, causing my body to softly bounce against his.

I couldn't bring myself to lift my arms so instead, I bit down on his shoulder. His hand on my back coming to a sudden stop.

"Don't be an ass." I drug my nose against his neck breathing in his scent further.

He laughed softly again, but then seemed to sober up. "I'm sorry, you know. I didn't mean for you to think I was ignoring you. I just didn't want to scare you away. I didn't want to introduce you as my girlfriend if you aren't ready for that."

I nodded my head against him because I knew I was overreacting.

"Are you ready for that?" His voice was vulnerable and they matched his words.

But instead of answering him, I screamed and clung closer to him.

"What the fuck?" He struggled to jerk up his pants as the flashlight shined in the window.

There was a series of loud, sharp raps on the window, and Tucker's body stiffened below me.

I scurried back to my side of the truck and threw my dress over my head as Tucker managed to pull his pants up without buttoning or zipping them. He rolled down the window a few inches after he made sure I was covered, and I could barely make out the police officer that was standing outside the window with his flashlight shining in my eyes.

"Excuse me, folks." His deep southern twang came through the window.

"Yes, sir." Tucker rolled the window down fully.

"Tucker Moore?"

"Bobby Smith?"

"Hey, man. How the hell are you?" The cop clicked the flashlight off, and I was thanking God.

"I'm good, man. Was better just a few minutes ago, though."

I smacked Tucker in his still naked chest and Officer Smith laughed.

"Man, what are you now? Twenty-eight years old? Haven't you figured out how to take it to the house yet?"

"I know, but did you see her?" He hiked his thumb in my direction, and I shrunk into myself. "I couldn't help it. She's a little vixen."

"Oh my God, Tucker." I buried my face in my hands.

"Well, this is your warning, Moore," he said with laughter. "Get her home."

"Yes, sir." Tucker saluted him and pulled his T-shirt over his head.

"Bye, Tucker."

"Bye, Bobby."

Tucker turned to me when the window was finally rolled back up.

"I can't believe you got us in trouble." He buttoned his pants and started the truck.

"Me?" I pointed to myself incredulously. "You are the one who pulled the damn truck over and pulled me on top of you."

"Yeah, but you're the one who wore that damn dress," he waved his hand in the direction of the fabric that was barely covering any of my skin, "and then you went and flirted with some asshole I went to high school with."

He pulled out onto the road and into the direction of the cabin.

"First of all, I didn't flirt with him. Secondly, that doesn't make me responsible for us getting in trouble with the cops."

"Yes. It does," he grumbled. "You made me fucking jealous, and I needed you."

I smiled a small smile and looked out the window. I shouldn't have been happy about his jealousy, but I was. I loved knowing that he needed me because the only thing I was sure about was the fact that I desperately needed him.

CHAPTER 21

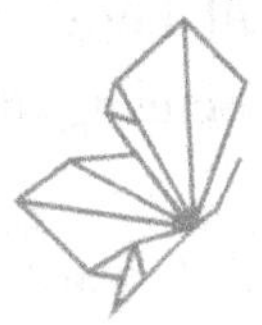

The next morning, I woke up with a headache but still managed to have a smile on my face. Once we finally made it home, Tucker and I took advantage of having the cabin alone, and we tainted every surface we could. By the time I fell into bed, I was sore, exhausted, and deliriously happy.

We were packing everything up to leave which meant I didn't get to lie in bed and get lost in Tucker like I wanted to. Instead, I was helping Brooke cram all her stuff back into her bags.

"How did you manage to get all of this in here to start with?" I laid on top of the bag while she attempted to zip it.

"Very carefully," she huffed out.

"Do you all need help?"

I turned to the sound of Tucker's voice in the doorway and smiled up at him.

"I think we may be able to handle the zipping, but we could use some help carrying them down."

He looked me over from top to bottom; taking in my

short shorts and my tank top. His gaze was slow, calculated, heated.

"I don't know how you expect me to get anything done when you're lying there dressed like that."

I smirked. "I could think of a few things you could do."

"Really, guys? I'm still here," Brooke said, looking up from the zipper she was focusing on. I had almost forgotten she was there.

Tucker chuckled, and I watched the way his dimple popped out.

"I actually thought you guys would be cute once you got together, but you're actually pretty nauseating."

"Whatever." I shoved her arm causing her to fall on her ass.

I got up from her bag and grabbed mine. I wasn't looking forward to heading home. Not in the least. A series of thoughts kept running through my head. Spiking my anxiety.

Would things change once we got home? Would it go back to the way it was?

To top it off, I knew that I had dinner with my family the next day then I would be shooting the staff of Rock Bottom the day after.

A nervous wreck was an understatement.

I was losing my damn mind.

We said our goodbyes to Jase and Ryan, and I could tell that the guys would really miss them. They joked and harassed each other, but they were lifelong friends, and they knew what they meant to each other without having to get sappy.

"It's such a shame," Jase said as he wrapped me in a hug.

"What is?"

"You and Tucker. We really would have been great together." He winked at me, and I giggled.

"Okay, asshole. Hands off." Tucker was smiling though. He knew his friend was only joking, but there was a hint of threat in his tone.

By the time we finally hit the road, I felt like I was coming out of my skin. It was as if that perfect bubble that I had been living in the last few days had finally burst, and I was left scattered trying to figure out which way was up and which way was down.

I plugged my headphones into my ears and rested my head against my seat. I needed to get out of my own head. I was my own worst enemy.

Nothing had changed. Tucker was still being amazing, and he had given me no reason to believe that he wouldn't stay that way.

The music ran through me and helped calm me somewhat. I opened my eyes when I felt someone watching me and looked in front of me. Tucker was driving, and I could see him glancing at me through the rearview mirror.

I smiled at him, but it obviously wasn't believable. He tilted his head to the side and studied me momentarily before turning his attention back to the road. When we stopped for gas, he pulled me into him and kissed the top of my head.

"You okay?"

I looked up at him and saw the concern in his eyes.

"Yeah. I'm just tired."

"You sure?" He didn't look like he believed me, and it unnerved me that he could already read me so well.

"Positive."

He didn't push me any further, and when we got back

into the car, I managed to fall asleep. I didn't wake up until I felt Tucker lift me out of the car. It was dark outside, and although I had probably just slept four hours, I was exhausted.

"Hey there, sleepy head." He kissed my forehead and my heart fluttered.

"Hey." I scrubbed my eyes as he sat me down on my feet.

"I ordered us some pizza for dinner. It should be here soon."

"Okay." I walked up the stairs like a zombie with Tucker trailing behind me carrying our bags.

When I got to my door, he stopped with me and didn't even glance toward his. He just waited patiently for me to unlock my door then dropped his bag inside the door before carrying mine to the room.

"I think I'm going to take a shower before the food gets here," I said as I kicked my shoes off.

"Okay." He laid down on my bed, and I knew he was tired from the long drive.

I stepped into the spray of the hot shower, and instantly my muscles began to relax. Letting my head fall back, I let the water fall over my face and wash away my tension. I focused on letting my anxiety wash down the drain, but it shot up again when the shower curtain moved open.

Covering myself with my hands, I said, "What are you doing?"

"Taking a shower." Tucker was completely bare as he stepped into the shower with me as if it was the most normal thing in the world.

I started to step out of the spray so he could get in, but he boxed me in instead, holding me close to his body and putting us both in the water.

His strong hands ran over my hair, each strand getting soaked by the water. He worked his way down my body, rubbing my arms, softly caressing my belly.

"Thank you for taking me to Tennessee." My voice was quiet, his hands almost putting me in a coma.

"You're welcome. I wouldn't have wanted it any other way."

I sighed, and he gripped my chin in his hand tilting it up to face him. His lips touched mine. Soft. Tender. Loving.

"I need you, babe." His words played across my lips and all I could do was nod in agreement.

He turned me away from him, my back pressed to his front, and he ran his hands down my body. His skin scorched mine in their barely there touch.

"Tucker," I moaned.

His lips pressed to my neck as his hands moved to my breast. I could feel his hardness digging into my back and my arousal pooling between my thighs.

He didn't waste time either. One hand remained on my breast, touching, teasing, and torturing my nipple, while the other hand moved down my stomach to my center. His fingers moved in slow, lazy circles over my clit, and I felt breathless by the time he bent me over and moved my hands to the shower wall.

His fingers ran down my back tracing the rivets of water that ran down my skin. Using his foot, he pushed my legs apart until they couldn't go any further, and his hands on my hips arched me back leaving me completely exposed to him. Ready for anything he was willing to give me.

When he pressed into me, I momentarily realized that he didn't have a condom on, but the feel of him was too intense, too good, to make him stop. He stopped for a moment when he was fully seated inside me, and I squirmed, my body begging him to move. With the next thrust, I got my wish.

He pulled out of me slowly then rammed back into me with so much power that I was barely able to hold myself up on the slippery tile wall.

"Oh, fuck." The words slipped out of my mouth.

He growled as he did it again, but this time I was better prepared for it and braced myself for the impact. My body contracted around him with every thrust. Our moans and the slap of our skin were the only sounds that could be heard.

"You feel so fucking good."

I looked over my shoulder at the sound of his voice to see him staring down at where we were connected.

I pushed back into him with his next thrust, and he clamped his eyes shut. When they opened again, they were almost black. Dark. Hungry. Lethal.

He wrapped his hand in my hair, pulling my head back, forcing my back to arch almost to the point of pain. His other hand dug into my hip. His fingers pressed into my skin, branding me.

My legs shook as he pounded into me. My breath ragged. My heart raced.

Tucker slammed into me forcing my body forward. My hands slipped and I barely managed to catch myself as my orgasm ripped through me, but Tucker held my body close to him as he milked his own pleasure from my body.

After our breathing returned to normal, Tucker helped me stand, still holding me close, providing me strength through my weakness. He peppered gentle kisses over my face before pouring shampoo into his hand.

We didn't talk as he lathered up my hair and rinsed it out. We just watched each other as he soaped up my body being gentle as he ran his hand over my center. He quickly washed himself off before turning off the shower and wrapping me in a towel. He hung a towel low on his hips showing off the deep muscles that disappeared underneath, and my mouth watered.

"Stop looking at me like that, Firecracker, or I'm going to put your ass on that counter and fuck you again."

I blinked up at him but then a drop of water ran off his neck and made its way down his body, and I couldn't stop myself from watching its path.

The next thing I knew, I was lifted in the air and my ass hit the counter as my towel was ripped from my body.

Turned out that Tucker made good on his threats, and the pizza was ice cold by the time we made it out of my room.

CHAPTER 22

I stared in the mirror and saw someone that I used to pretend to be. My hair was pulled back in a severe bun, my body covered in a chiffon blouse that I found buried in the very back of my closet, and a pair of black trousers. I felt like an imposter, but I knew that it was what my mother would want to see me in, and as much as it made me feel like I was smothering, I didn't want to cause a riff.

Tucker had told me again that I didn't have to go and even offered to go with me, but I couldn't expose him to my family. Not yet at least. I couldn't stand to sit around a dinner table and watch them judge him, and I knew they would. They judged everyone. Even their so-called friends.

When I stepped up to the doorway of my childhood home, my hands shook and I could feel my anxiety pumping through me as if it was a real, living thing. Being here should have brought a feeling of home, of family, but all I could think about when I took in the familiar floral scent was memories of never being good enough for them. The urge to run was overwhelming, but I knew I would never hear the end of it if I did.

I raised my hand and knocked softly against the heavy wood door. It was one of my mother's pet peeves. She couldn't stand it when someone "banged on a door like a maniac" as she liked to say. My other hand was clutched on my bag, the bag that was heavy with the weight of the business school paperwork inside. Paperwork that I was going to talk to my parents about tonight.

I hadn't even talked to Brooke about it because I knew she would try to talk me out of it, but she didn't understand.

The door opened moments later, and I smiled a tight smile at my mother.

"Hello, Kennedy. I'm glad you finally made it."

I looked down at my phone and saw that I was ten minutes early.

"Hi, Mother." I stepped into the house and looked around. It looked practically the same as it always had except for new furnishings that my mom bought to keep up with the ever-changing style. The house was large with only the nicest things on display, and I knew that nothing in that front room was ever touched. It was all for show. Trust me, I had experienced the wrath of Mrs. Hayes when I had accidentally broken a vase throwing a ball in the house. You would have thought I burned the place down.

"Your brother and Jessica are in the foyer with your father," she said as she began walking in that direction.

"Jessica's here?" I asked, confused why she would be present for our family announcement.

"Yes."

I trailed behind her and took deep breaths to help me get through the evening. I was already being defensive in my own mind and nothing had happened yet. Everything was fine. I just needed to keep reminding myself of that.

I stepped into the room behind my mother, and my father looked up from his conversation with my brother.

"Kennedy." He gave me a curt nod, which I returned.

My brother, Justin, turned his head in my direction before standing. Always the gentleman.

"Hello, Kennedy."

"Hi, Justin." I stood awkwardly feeling like I didn't belong in this situation at all. Not knowing what to do with myself.

"Hi, Jessica." I barely glanced in her direction.

"Kennedy." Her smile was saccharine sweet and just as fake as she was.

I took a seat on the couch with my father and looked around the room. No one was talking, but they all seemed so content to be in each other's presence.

"Well, since everyone is here," my brother reached out and grabbed Jessica's hand. She looked absolutely perfect, as she always did.

I looked to my brother and a moment of panic overtook me.

"I think it's finally time to make our announcement."

He smiled at both of my parents. Before looking back to me. It was obvious that I was the only one who hadn't already been privy to the announcement.

"Jessica and I are engaged."

Something deep inside of me sunk at his words. Something caved in on itself.

I had been compared to Jessica all my life. Always compared and always lacking.

I gripped my bag tighter against me and thought about

the school paperwork that lay inside. The paperwork that wouldn't even matter. It wouldn't make a difference against her.

My mother was grinning from ear to ear, and I didn't think I had ever seen her so happy. So unconditionally proud.

I took a deep, audible breath.

"Kennedy, aren't you happy for your brother?" My mother's voice echoed through my head.

Was I happy for him?

Was I happy for our family?

"I'm..." my voice broke. I didn't know what I was feeling.

There was a tightness in my chest that hadn't been there moments before. I felt like I was suffocating.

"Yes. I'm so happy for you both." I planted a fake smile on my face.

Jessica smiled at me, and the memories of the way she had treated me over the years came flooding back to me. The laughs of her and her friends, the way she would snicker when my mother talked about my weight.

I didn't return her smile and I saw her jolt back slightly, almost unnoticeably, and it fed my anger.

My hands balled into fists, and I counted to ten in my head. I wasn't the same girl I used to be. I wouldn't let any of them have this much effect on me.

"Kennedy." My mother's voice was soft and for a second I thought she might actually see that this was somehow hurting me. That she might see that her daughter needed her, but it was stupid of me. Every time I thought my mother would step up and actually be a mom, she let me down monumentally. "Jessica would like for you to be a bridesmaid, but you'll need to lose some more weight to fit in the dress we have selected."

I stared at my mother like I had never seen her before. Every bad thing she had ever said to me bubbled to the surface. Every time she judged me, criticized me, hurt me. Every ounce of hope that I had ever held onto about her changing, about her finally loving me for me, evaporated in that instant.

The woman standing in front of me was a stranger to me. Someone that I had truly never known, and someone that I wished I never had.

"I hate you."

She jerked back at my words, and it fueled me. I burned with my hate for her.

"Kennedy," my dad's voice boomed through the room, but the fear that used to run through me at the sound of his anger was gone.

"What?" I turned my angry gaze to him. "What can you possibly have to say to me? Are you going to tell me to not talk to my mother like that? Well, guess what, she has never been a mother to me."

"I'm sorr..." Jessica's words cut off when I looked up at her. She was standing there in a perfect light pink dress that hit right below her knee. Her nails were covered in a French manicure, and she reminded me of my mother. Her perfect little mini-me. I hated her even more.

"Kennedy, stop this right now." I turned my gaze to my brother. "You are ruining everything. Mother, I told you she didn't need to be in the wedding."

I watched my brother as I took in his words. As I took in how much he had become just like our parents.

"I hope you and Jessica are happy together," I said to my brother.

His eyes turned to me, completely unforgiving in his expectations.

I pulled the business school paperwork out of my bag and laid it on the table in front of me. "Thank you all for making this decision easy for me."

My mother's eyes were glued to the paperwork before she looked up at me with shock on her face.

I walked out of the house and none of them spoke another word to me. I made it to my car, and only then, did the tears begin to fall. And they poured.

...

I pulled over on the side of the road when I could no longer see clearly. My sobs were racking through my body, and I wiped at my face with the back of my hand. I was far enough away from my parents' house that the feeling of immediate threat had left me, but I wasn't far enough away to feel the protection of my friends. Of my home.

My phone tumbled to the floor when I tried to pull it out of my bag causing me to cry harder. I finally managed to wrangle it out from under my seat and hit my speed dial for Brooke. My finger hesitated over Tucker's name, but there was no way that I wanted him to see me like this. He couldn't. I needed Brooke.

"Hey, babe. That was quick." The sound of her voice pushed my anxiety down further. She was still at work, and I could hear the chaos of the salon in the background.

"Brooke." I sounded as horrible as I felt.

"Kennedy? Are you okay? Where are you?" Her words were rushed. Panicked.

"I'm on the side of Hatcher Lane. Can you come get me?"

"I'm on my way."

I took a deep breath and a sob is all that managed to come out.

"Breathe for me, Kennedy. It will be okay. I promise. All we need is each other." She sounded as wounded as I felt, and I knew that she was feeling every bit of my pain. It was just who she was. She didn't have any idea what hurt me, but all she knew was that I was hurt. There would never be a moment in my life where that girl wasn't there for me.

I stayed on the phone with her. Not even talking. Her listening to me cry. Me listening to her breathe and tell me that everything would be okay.

When a car that I didn't recognize pulled up next to me, my body immediately stiffened, but my best friend jumped out of the passenger seat and waved goodbye to the car. My driver side door was jerked open and she immediately pulled me into her arms.

"Who was that?" I managed to say through my tears.

"A girl from the salon. What happened?" She brushed the hair out of my face and wiped my tears off my cheeks.

"Jessica."

"What about her?" Her face hardened.

"It's her. That's who my brother is engaged to."

She took a deep breath and closed her eyes. When they opened, her blue eyes were filled with sympathy. She knew how bad Jessica had treated me growing up. She knew how deep my wounds were from my family, and it hurt her too.

"Kennedy," she whispered my name. The hurt clear in voice.

"The worst part is that he knows. You know? He knows how she treated me. He was there for me once upon a time."

"He's an asshole." She put my hand in hers.

"I know."

"They don't deserve you."

"Then why does it hurt so badly?" I looked up at her and searched for answers. Answers I desperately needed.

"Because they should be better. You deserve to have an amazing birth family, but instead, you ended up with me."

A small smile curved on my lips for the first time since I stepped into my parents' house.

"I know it hurts, and it's going to, babe. But we have each other, and I love you like you are my sister. You are my sister. We don't need them." They were words that she had said to me many times before, but the truth of them had never rang as clear as they did in that moment.

She was right. I had her. I had Tucker. I didn't need anyone else.

CHAPTER 23

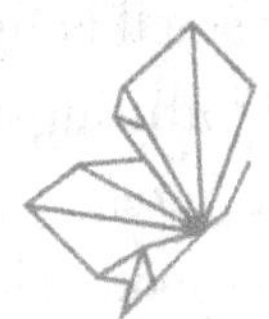

Brooke drove us home, and I was thankful. Even though she had made me feel significantly better, I couldn't stop the tears from falling down my face. I was too overwhelmed. Too sensitive. Too raw.

When we pulled up outside our apartment building, I was ready to jump out of the car to get to Tucker. I didn't realize how badly I needed him until that moment. The feeling consumed me.

I opened the door to the car and was climbing out, when Brooke grabbed my wrist to stop me.

"Kennedy, hold on just a second."

I wasn't listening though. I had no interest in sitting there a second longer. My only thought was getting to Tucker. His touch would take everything away. I craved it.

I should have listened to her though.

When I turned back toward our apartment, my heart came to a complete halt.

Tucker was standing in the doorway to our building talking to a woman. He was facing me, and I could only see the back of her head. He ran his hand over her forehead and tucked her hair behind her ear. Something he constantly did to me. Something that I loved.

I couldn't catch my breath.

His body shook with laughter as she said something to him. When he tugged her small body into his and kissed her on the forehead, I stopped torturing myself and looked away.

He knew I wouldn't be here.

I knew that this was too good to be true.

There was a valuable lesson to be learned from my parents, and it was that no one could be trusted. No one except for Brooke.

She was still in the car, and she was looking up at me with pity in her eyes. It was a look that I hated. I despised it.

"Get in, love. Let's go for a drive."

I didn't have to think long on what she said. I wasn't walking into our building, I was running, and I didn't care where we ended up.

...

It was one o'clock in the morning by the time the taxi pulled up in front of our building. I was drunk as a skunk and so was the guy who was sitting beside me. Brooke was giving me dirty looks from my other side, but I was avoiding looking in her direction.

We had drive around for about an hour before we ended up at a hole in the wall bar. The tequila shots were flowing and although Brooke begged me to slow down, I didn't listen to her. I just wanted to completely erase the day, and alcohol was my only option to do so.

The only time I did listen to Brooke was when she

reminded me that my final shoot with Rock Bottom was the next day at noon. Her words penetrated my drunken brain enough for me to realize that I needed to go home, but not enough for me to realize I needed to go home alone.

"What about you and Liam?" I asked, curiously.

"What about me and Liam?" She looked away from me as she took a sip of her drink.

"You never told me what happened between you two. Do you like him?"

She stared down at her drink for a moment before looking back at me. "It doesn't matter what happened between us. It's in the past. Liam doesn't want anything with me and that is all that matters."

"Guys fucking suck."

She nodded her head in agreement before raising her glass to mine.

"Cheers," we both said in unison before downing the rest of our drinks.

Tucker had blown my phone up around eleven, and I tortured myself by listening to one of his voicemails. He sounded sincere as he talked about him being worried that I hadn't made it home from my parents' yet. It made me want to march into his apartment and demand to know if he was worried about me when he was with another woman. Instead, I turned off my phone and didn't look at it again. I wasn't his business to worry about anymore.

I wasn't his concern.

The guy sitting next to me was only concerned with one thing and that was exactly what I needed. He could help me forget this day. To forget Tucker.

I giggled as I missed a step but my newfound friend,

whose name I couldn't remember, caught me and smiled down at me. Brooke wasn't smiling though. She was pissed.

She had no right to be though. She was always the one telling me that I needed to get out more. That I needed to get laid.

We followed Brooke to our floor, his arms wrapped around my waist. They felt foreign on my skin, wrong almost, but I wouldn't let it get to me. I needed this. I didn't care who he was.

Brooke stopped suddenly when she walked into our door, and I ran into her back.

"Whoa there." The guy whose name I forgot pulled me back against him. I turned my head to smile at him but I stopped short when I heard his voice.

A voice that had no business talking to me.

"Who in the fuck are you?"

I looked over at Tucker and drew in a sharp breath. He looked like shit. I had never seen him look anything other than perfect, but there he stood completely disheveled. He looked worried, he looked upset, and I wanted to run to him to take it all away. Then thoughts of him with that other woman flashed into my mind, and I straightened my spine and hardened my heart.

"Ummm, Kennedy." The guy's hands on my hips tightened as he looked at the rage in Tucker's face.

"Don't fucking talk to her." Tucker stormed toward us. "If you plan on living through the night, I suggest you get your fucking hands off my girl and leave immediately."

"Fuck you, Tucker," I yelled. "You do not have to leave." I looked behind me.

"I think I'm going to go." His hands let go of my hips and he backed toward the door while keeping his eyes on Tucker.

When the door closed behind him, I walked past Tucker to my bedroom.

"Where in the hell do you think you are going?" He grabbed my wrist before I could completely get away, and I saw Brooke sneak into her bedroom out of the corner of my eye.

"I'm going to bed, Tucker. I've had a horrible day, and I'm tired." I jerked my arm but his grip held strong.

"What happened? Why were you with that guy?" His voice was still angry but I could see the vulnerability in his eyes. It almost broke me. Almost.

"Why not, Tucker? We're nothing more than a couple fuck buddies, right? We should be able to fuck whoever we want."

He jerked back from me like I had physically hit him and my arm dropped to my side like it weighed a hundred pounds.

"So, this past weekend meant nothing?" His brown eyes were boring into mine waiting for me to answer.

"Apparently not."

He stared down at me for several seconds. It wasn't a look that I liked. It was as if he had never truly seen me before, but I guess it was fitting considering I had never expected to see this side of him either.

He didn't say another word. He just turned his back to me and walked out. The sound of the slamming door echoing throughout the empty room.

...

The sound of my alarm going off sliced through my head as if it was actually assaulting me. I could barely open my eyes even though my room had very little light shining into it. I managed to hit my phone enough to make the noise stop before I ran to my bathroom to empty the contents of my stomach.

Memories of the day before ran through my head, and I prayed that it was all a nightmare. Every last bit of it. But I knew it wasn't. The pain was too real. Too raw. I felt it everywhere.

Brooke walked into my bathroom as I wiped my mouth with a piece of toilet paper.

"How are you feeling?"

"Please don't yell at me." I laid my head against the toilet.

"How are you feeling?" she whispered while leaning against the bathroom wall.

"Like shit."

"You should after last night."

I flopped onto the bathroom floor and let the coolness of the tile seep into my skin.

"I barely remember last night."

"Do you remember destroying Tucker?" She crossed her arms over her chest.

"You're taking his side?" I peeked up at her.

"I'm not taking anyone's side. What I am saying is that he looked fucking destroyed last night. He didn't look like someone who was cheating on you just a few hours before."

I thought about what she just said, but it didn't make any sense. I knew what I saw. I wasn't crazy.

"But you saw him." I sat back up and grabbed my stomach when I felt like I was going to lose its contents again.

"I know, but maybe there is an explanation. Maybe we didn't see what we thought we saw."

"My life isn't a romance movie, Brooke. I'm the girl who gets cheated on and ends up alone surrounded by her books and cats. I'm not the one who ends up with happily ever after."

"I don't believe that." She shook her head.

"Well, you should start believing it. The sooner we figure it out the less likely we are to get hurt."

"Maybe you should just talk to him," she said softly, knowing I wouldn't like her idea.

"I have to get ready for work."

She turned her back and walked out of my bathroom with a shake of her head. I could feel her disappointment radiating off her, but it didn't change anything. I didn't want to see Tucker. I had trusted him, completely, and the only thing that got me was heartbreak.

CHAPTER 24

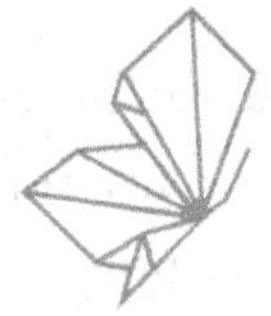

I got myself together the best that I could and prayed that no one noticed that I had been puking and crying all morning. I filled my lungs with fresh air before I walked into Rock Bottom and some of my nervousness left me because I knew I would have my camera in my hand soon.

Chloe was standing just inside the restaurant when I walked inside, and she smiled at me before walking over.

"What's up, buttercup?"

She was far too peppy. At least for a hungover Kennedy to deal with.

"Hey, Chloe." I looked around the room at the group of fifteen to twenty people all dressed similarly in black uniforms. "Where do you want me to start?"

"Are you okay?" She tilted her head to the side and studied me.

"I'm fine. Why?" I could fake it. I knew I could.

"You don't look like yourself. You kind of look like someone stole your puppy. A puppy that you've been wanting for a really long time."

I took a deep breath and tried my hardest to hold myself together.

"I'm okay. I didn't have the best night last night."

"Well, we're going to have a great day. I promise."

I hoped she was right because I didn't think that I could handle anymore today.

Chloe introduced me to the staff, which consisted of chefs, kitchen staff, servers, bartenders, and hostesses. I said my hellos then I began shooting.

We moved around the restaurant taking photos in the dining area and in the kitchen. I took photos of the staff grouped together. Photos of them pretending to work. By the time an hour rolled around, I felt lighter.

When it was time for me to shoot Chloe, I was in a much better mood, and she had me laughing when I looked through the lens at her cross-eyed face.

"I will take these photos and use them. You won't get any good ones." I laughed.

"You are no fun." She put her hands on her slender hips then posed like she had a former career in modeling.

"Oh. The owners are here." She waved behind me, and I pulled my face away from my camera and straightened out my shirt.

I turned toward them with my professional face on, and it lasted all of two seconds. My whole world came to a screeching halt.

I looked around the room searching for something. I had no idea what I was looking for. Maybe someone to jump out and tell me that I was on a hidden camera show. That this was all a joke.

Tucker was staring at me, but he wasn't seeing me. His stare was blank. He didn't care anymore.

"You own this place?" I asked incredulously.

None of this made sense.

"With Liam," he said nonchalantly as Liam poked his head around Tucker's shoulder.

"Hey, Kennedy."

I looked to Liam, but I wasn't interested in talking to him. There was only one man I wanted answers from.

"How could you lie to me about this? You said you only worked here." I stepped toward him, and Chloe looked back and forth between us.

"That's rich. Coming from you." He flicked his hand out in my direction. "What was it you told me? We're nothing but a couple of fuck buddies."

Chloe gasped, and I knew how unprofessional this was. It didn't matter anyway. I didn't get this job due to my talent.

"Oh, please act like I mean something more to you. I saw you with that woman yesterday." He looked a little shocked and it only fueled me further. "What? You didn't think I knew? So, I'm the bad guy because I got caught? It doesn't matter what you do behind my back?"

"What are you talking about?" He was searching my face.

"Stop lying to me!" I was becoming hysterical. "I saw you with her outside our building. I needed you, Tucker. I fucking needed you. My family crushed me, and there you stood holding another woman in your arms. Do you know how bad you hurt me?" My voice cracked, and I hated it. I hated showing him how weak he had made me.

He took a step toward me, and I held out my hand to stop him.

"Don't."

"I'll kill them."

"Don't worry about me. Go worry about whoever else you've been sleeping with."

"You mean her?" He pointed to the corner of the room, and my eyes clashed with the woman's who I had seen him with just the day before. I physically jolted back at seeing her here, and my breath caught in my throat.

"That's my sister, Kennedy."

I looked from the girl to him and back. "What?"

"She's my sister. I wasn't cheating on you."

I took a deep breath, and I felt like my world was collapsing around me. I didn't know what to do. I didn't know what to say.

"You should have let me go to that dinner with you. Why didn't you call me?"

"I wasn't thinking, Tucker. I was just trying to get to you."

"I tried calling you. Why did you bring that asshole home with you? What were you thinking?" He ran his hand down his face, his frustration clear.

"I was trying to forget you. To hurt you back." My voice sounded as fragile as I felt.

He looked at me, and I could see the fury and the pain written all over his face. I wanted nothing more than to take it all away.

"Why don't you take a minute to compose yourself then we'll finish the shoot."

I searched his face looking for more. This couldn't be the end of us. He couldn't just dismiss me so easily. But he didn't give me the opportunity to look for long because he turned on his heel and stormed away from me and back into hiding behind the door to the back of the restaurant.

Everyone was looking at me. Wide eyes and even wider

open jaws. Nobody knew what to say or what to do, and I didn't blame them.

"Kennedy."

I looked up at Liam except he looked blurry. Clouded by my tears.

"Yeah?"

"Why don't you let Chloe take you to the bathroom? Give yourself a few minutes." His voice was soft. Much softer than Tucker's was a few minutes ago.

I nodded my head, but didn't move. I had no clue what I was doing. The only thing I could think about was the look on Tucker's face, and it kept flashing over and over in my mind.

I felt a hand on my arm, and I looked to my left expecting Chloe. But I was dead wrong. The girl standing next to me was the last person I expected. The girl I hated only moments ago.

"Come on, sweets." She put her hand in mine. "Let's go to the bathroom."

I let her pull me behind her. When we stepped into the bathroom, I stared at her. Really took her in for the first time, and I felt like a complete idiot. I had seen pictures of her in her parents' house. I had no idea how I didn't realize it before.

She ran a paper towel under the sink before pressing the cold towel under my eyes. Wiping away the tears that I hadn't even noticed falling down my cheeks.

"I'm Sophie, by the way." She continued to run the cold cloth over my face. Washing away the traces of my pain.

I nodded my head, but I couldn't form words yet. I was too scared that I would break down crying.

She tucked a piece of hair behind my ear and looked over my face. "So, you're in love with my brother, huh?"

Laughter bubbled out of me suddenly, and I couldn't help it. I had just met this girl, accused her of sleeping with her brother, and now we were talking about me being in love with him. Apparently, she could read me much better than her brother. She smiled at my laughter and cocked her head to the side.

She was so damn nice, and I had been looking forward to meeting her. And now I'd ruined it. Her brother hated me. The man I loved wanted nothing to do with me.

My laughter caught in my throat and quickly changed over to a sob. The change was so sudden, and I could see the worry all over her face. She didn't even know me, and here I was, completely losing my shit in front of her.

She pulled me into her arms and buried my face in her chest as I fell apart. I don't know how much time passed. All I know is that she continued to hold me until I could finally breathe again.

When I pulled my head away from her, she wiped her fingers under my eyes and looked at me with so much sympathy that it caused my chest to hurt even more.

"If you don't want to finish this shoot today, I can tell my brother to fuck off."

I laughed a strangled, deep laugh and shook my head.

"No. I need to finish it. This is my career."

"Okay. Well in that case," she pulled a small makeup bag out of her purse, "let's get you cleaned up."

CHAPTER 25

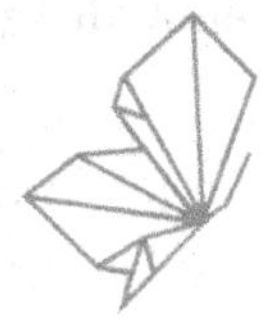

Most of the staff was gone when we walked back out into the dining room, and for that, I was thankful. Tucker narrowed his eyes on his sister's arm that was wrapped in mine as we made our way to where he, Liam, and Chloe were standing, but I looked away from him.

I had to get through this and looking at him was the quickest way for me to fail.

"Okay. So where do you want to start?" I asked, my voice much more gravelly than normal.

Nobody said anything at first so I looked over at Tucker to see him watching me. His expression blank.

Liam cleared his throat, and I turned my attention to him.

"I think we'd like some pictures by the bar then we'll do whatever you suggest."

I nodded my head and got all my camera equipment ready.

When I pressed my camera to my face, I stared at Tucker

and Liam through the lens. It was safer this way. Less vulnerable. My camera was my safety net.

I took their pictures. Liam smiling while Tucker looked like he could kill someone at any moment. I could barely even see Liam though. I was taking advantage of my excuse to take in Tucker. I didn't know if I would have this opportunity again.

"Chloe, do you want to get in the picture," I called out from behind my lens. I needed a distraction if I wanted these pictures to turn out at least decent. "You should sit on the bar between them."

Chloe did as I suggested and I continued to shoot. We made our way around the restaurant. Tucker seemed to relax some after a while, and I finally managed to get some images where he didn't look like an asshole. Because he wasn't. He didn't need to be portrayed that way. Even if I was hurt by him. Even if we managed to hurt each other.

When we finally wrapped up, I immediately began packing up my equipment. I looked up when Chloe walked up beside me, and when I saw her smiling face, it filled me with disappointment that it wasn't Tucker.

"Hey." I zipped up my camera bag.

"Do you want to stay and have a celebratory drink with us?" she asked hesitantly.

"No. I don't think so." I looked over at Tucker who was staring directly at me. "It's been a long day. I'm going to head home and work on these images."

"You sure?" She cocked her head to the side.

"Yeah. Hopefully, I'll have all these images to you in a couple days."

"Okay. That sounds good."

"I'll talk to you later?" I lifted my bag onto my shoulder.

"Of course."

I walked all the way home. The weather was starting to turn cooler, and I wrapped my arms around myself to keep the chill away.

So many things ran through my mind as I mindlessly took each step toward my apartment. My apartment that was right next door to Tucker's. Would he bring women home with him again? I couldn't bear the thought of hearing him in his room with another woman. The thought was like a sucker punch to my stomach.

How did we get here? Why did I jump to conclusions? Why did I bring that guy home with me? Why did he lie to me?

That last question had been lying dormant in my mind, but now that I thought about it, the more pissed off I became. What was his plan all along? Was I just a damn game to him? Was nothing between us real?

By the time I made it back to my apartment, I was filled with sadness, anxiety, and fury. As soon as one emotion would take the lead, another thought would pop into my head, and the game would change again.

Exhaustion was the strongest at that moment, and I wanted nothing more than to dive face first into my bed and not come out for a week.

I opened my front door and sighed in relief when I didn't see Brooke. I knew she would question about how today went, and I wasn't ready to talk about it. Not yet. Not after everything that happened.

I sat down at my desk and entered my memory card into my computer. The images downloaded one after another. Picture after picture of Tucker's face flashed across my screen, and once again, misery took the lead.

I felt pathetic as I clung onto every image of him. I took in his beautiful brown eyes that were burning holes into my camera. His lips that were usually upturned and playful were the complete opposite. He looked dark and desolate. He looked damn handsome, but it wasn't him. And I was the one to do this to him. I was the one to hurt him.

Fuck. I really hurt him.

I had no idea how to fix it. I wasn't even sure if I could, but I knew for certain that I couldn't fix it today. We both needed time to cool off. We both needed time to think. And if I was lucky, Tucker would realize how badly I needed him, and hopefully, he would need me too.

CHAPTER 26

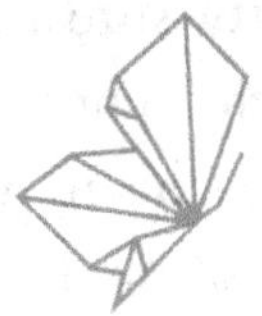

It had been exactly one week since I laid eyes on Tucker. Seven long, torturous days. Seven days where I felt the loneliest I had ever felt. I'd thought about going to his apartment every day, but each time I managed to talk myself out of it.

I was still mad at him for lying to me about Rock Bottom, I was so ashamed of myself for the way I had treated him, and I was scared to death that he wasn't going to want me anymore. That was my biggest fear of all.

My need to see him was consuming me, but I was even more consumed by my fear of his rejection. It terrified me. I couldn't handle it.

Brooke had encouraged me to go to him. She was mad about his lie to me as well, but she was more disappointed in me. Understandably so. Hell, I was disappointed in myself. How could she not be?

I hadn't heard him either. I lay in bed at night, perfectly still, praying that I heard him. Just something to give me the tiniest piece of him. Something to let me know he was okay.

But I also laid in fear; fear that I would hear another woman. Fear that I would hear him moving on.

Three loud raps at the door pulled my attention away from my Kindle. I looked down at myself and cringed. I was wearing my Gryffindor pajama bottoms with a white tank top, and I was pretty sure that I had been wearing them for three days straight. There was a stain on the front of my shirt, and I wasn't even sure where it came from. My hair was in a knot on top of my head, and I was a little bit scared to look in the mirror. I knew that I looked like a hot mess.

I cautiously pulled the door open and peeked into the hallway. My breath rushed out of me when I saw Tucker standing there. He looked handsome as ever in a black suit with a white dress shirt. He wore no tie and the top couple buttons were undone making him look impossibly sexy.

"Hey." I ran my hand over my hair and wished that I had at least taken a moment to make sure I looked okay. Here he stood looking like the bachelor that he was, and I reeked of heartbreak. It seeped from my pores.

"I need you to sign this." He shoved a few sheets of paper into my hands, and I stared at his vacant eyes.

"Okay." I looked down at the paper and saw that it was a disclosure agreement. "What is this for?"

"I need your permission to use your photographs. We have some interest in publishing them, and it will be good for advertisement."

"Oh. Okay. Sure." Normally, I would have asked where they were publishing them, but it was obvious by Tucker's curt words that he had no interest in talking to me more than he had to. I would sign it regardless. I would give him anything he needed.

"Do you want to come in?" My voice was as small as I felt. "I need to grab a pen."

I started heading inside, but he stopped me with the click of a pen.

"I have one."

He didn't look at me as he handed the pen over to me careful not to allow our skin to touch, and it crushed me.

I pressed the paper against the front door and quickly signed my name where it was flagged to do so before handing it back to him. He still didn't look up at me, his eyes directly on the paper, so I held them when he tried to pull them away from me. Forcing him to look up.

"I'm sorry, Tuck."

His pupils dilated, but otherwise, there was no change, he was completely stoic.

"Thanks for signing these." He pulled on the papers again and this time I let them slip from my fingers. As easily as I had allowed him to.

Without another word, he walked away without a backward glance, and for the second time in seven long, torturous, lonely days my heart shattered into a million pieces.

...

On day ten post-Tucker, Brooke finally dragged me out of the apartment. I hadn't had a photo shoot in those ten days, and I was thankful that I had blocked that time off in case I was still needed for Rock Bottom. I needed my camera in my hand, but I needed the time to wallow more. The images I sent to Chloe were amazing. I know that it was my own work, but I was blown away by how good they turned out. I had never been so proud of my work.

Chloe sent me an email raving about the photographs, but I didn't hear anything about them from Tucker. He didn't even mention them when he came to have me sign the disclosure agreement. I was worried and stressed that he didn't like them, and the thought of Tucker's disapproval of my work hurt me far more than my parents' ever could.

I had spent the last ten days doing nothing but editing images, reading books, and drowning myself in rocky road ice cream. Today was the first day that I put clothes on that weren't pajamas even though my yoga pants and long-sleeved T-shirt practically felt like pajamas.

I put on my oversized sunglasses as we left our apartment building, and with every step I took, I searched for Tucker. When we finally stepped outside, I sighed and breathed in the fresh air. It tasted strange on my tongue.

I could see Brooke watching me out of the corner of her eye. Probably waiting for me to break down, and after the way I have acted the last ten days, I didn't blame her. But I didn't have any tears left. I was completely dried out.

I tugged the hem of my shirt as we began walking down the sidewalk. We had decided that we were going to walk to go get lunch, and it felt good to be out of the apartment. I felt slightly like a vampire after not being in direct sunlight for so many days, but the sun warmed my skin against the chill in the air and I was thankful.

We were almost to the small café that we both loved when I completely regretted my decision to leave the four walls of my home that had been keeping me safe from the world. Safe from reality.

My brother was stepping out of a restaurant with Jessica by his side except he didn't really look like my brother. One of his eyes was bruised with purple, green, and yellow colors swirling around and showing that the bruise was probably days old. The left side of his bottom lip was swollen and a small cut tore through his normally pursed lips.

He glanced at me before turning his gaze to his fiancée, and I thought that I made it out without him noticing me until his gaze snapped back to mine.

Pure fury rested there, and I return his stare hoping mine read the same.

I hope he could see how badly he's hurt me.

"Kennedy." He nodded his head at me politely, always the diplomat.

"What the hell happened to you?" I wasn't going to talk to him, but I couldn't help it. I had to know.

"Don't act like you don't know," he practically growled at me.

I jolted back slightly at the venom in his voice, but I prayed he didn't see it. I would not falter in front of him. I looked at Brooke but she just shrugged her shoulders.

"I don't know what you're talking about." I think I would remember if I knew what happened to him. It would probably be the highlight of my damn year.

"So you're telling me that you didn't sic your little boyfriend on me?"

I shook my head no, but then Tucker's words came back to me. *I'll kill them.*

"What?" It couldn't be true. Tucker didn't even care about me anymore.

"Your thug of a boyfriend paid me a little visit the other day. Like he has the right to tell me what to do or don't do. Like he has the right to tell me what to do with my sister." He was practically in my face now, but I didn't back down. I wouldn't show him any fear. "He told me to stay away from you, but maybe I should have told him the same. You're nothing but trash."

The next thing that happened was like an outer body experience. A hand flew through the air and slapped my brother's face with a power I didn't know I possessed. Except, I didn't possess it. My best friend did.

Her perfectly pink manicured hand made a loud sound when it connected with his cheek, and I couldn't stop from smiling when I saw that she had managed to reopen the cut on his lip and a trickle of blood trailed down his chin. He looked momentarily stunned and so did Jessica who was hanging off his arm.

"If you ever talk to my best friend that way again, I will do far worse than Tucker Moore managed to do to you." She was pointing her finger into his face, and I had to physically work at not busting out in laughter.

My brother opened his mouth to say something, but when Brooke stepped closer to him, he very smartly shut his mouth. He stared at me for several moments. His anger rolling off him in waves, and for the first time in ten days, a genuine smile formed on my face.

...

"I cannot believe that just happened." I slid into the booth and looked at my best friend who was bouncing on her toes like a boxer.

"I can." She swung her arms around in what I think she thought was a boxing move but didn't resemble anything I'd ever seen on television. "I am so pumped right now."

"Sit down before our server thinks we're crazy and kicks us out."

She plopped down in the booth across from me, but she didn't drop the shit-eating grin from her face.

"I should join MMA," she said seriously, and I rolled my eyes.

"Let's not get ahead of ourselves here. You slapped one person."

"I know." Her voice was giddy. "But did you see that slap? It was amazing."

"It was amazing." I nodded in agreement. "I would pay good money to see it again."

"I would have paid to see Tucker kick his ass." She was still smiling, but her words practically plunged into my chest. Why did he do it?

Hope exploded in my chest like wildfire. I couldn't allow myself to believe it. I couldn't get my hopes up just to be dashed again. I couldn't handle his rejection a second time.

"Yeah. It would have been awesome." I picked up my menu and fiddled with the tethered edge.

"What's going through that head of yours, Kennedy?"

"Tucker," I replied honestly.

"What about him?" She rested her chin on her palms.

"Everything. How much I miss him. How big of an idiot I have been. How badly I want to see him." I ran my fingers through my hair. "I'm just a mess really."

"Why don't you talk to him? Put yourself out there."

"Because I'm scared." It was the truest statement I had said in a long time.

CHAPTER 27

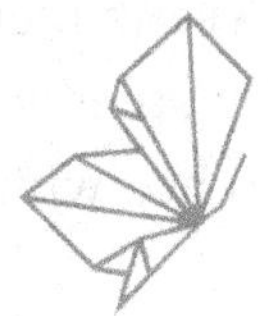

Twenty days post-Tucker, I woke up in a panic when I heard screaming in the living room. I jumped out of bed and grabbed the closest thing I could find that resembled a weapon. My bedroom light flipped on and I stared with wide eyes at my best friend as she stared wide-eyed at me.

"What are you doing?" She laughed.

"Me?" I yelled. "What are you doing? Getting murdered?"

"No. That was my excited scream. Why? What were you going to do cast a spell on my murderer?" She pointed to my replica wand, and I set it down on my bed while I tried to get my heart rate under control.

"I could have at least stabbed someone with it."

"That's what he said." She bent over laughing, and I breathed through my nose so I wouldn't kill my best friend. "Please be serious." She rolled her eyes. "You would die if something happened to your wand."

"Enough about my wand." I waved my hands around like a lunatic. "Why were you screaming?"

"Oh yeah. Because of this."

She pulled a magazine out from behind her back and held it out to me. It was a magazine I had seen a million times. A magazine that I owned hundreds of copies of, but this one was different.

The word Architect was written across the top in bold white letters just like every other copy that rested in a crate by my desk, but the difference with this one was that Rock Bottom graced the cover.

Tucker's Rock Bottom.

The large agate chandelier sparkled in the lighting and created light and shadows throughout the amazing space. The photographer had managed to capture the room in a way that made it look enchanting. Magical. It was my photo. It was my work.

The magazine dropped from my hands and landed with a thud on the floor. My hands were trembling and I stared down at them. Brooke slipped my shaking hands into hers and leveled her eyes to look at me.

"Kennedy?" she asked cautiously. Like she was working with a caged animal.

"Is that really an Architect Magazine?"

She nodded her head slowly.

"Is that really my photo?"

Her lips picked up at the corners and she nodded her head again.

"Is this a joke?" I looked up at her and tears fell down my cheeks.

"No, babe. It's not." She squeezed my hands in hers.

Then I screamed. Brooke buckled under my weight when I jumped into her arms. But we didn't care, we were a fit of giggles and cheers, and I could barely breathe. I could barely think.

My hair was covering her face, and I'm pretty sure I accidentally kneed her in the crotch in my excitement. Brooke pushed me off her and I fell onto my butt. She pushed her hair out of her face and her face was in as big of a grin as mine was.

That was the thing about Brooke. My joy would always mean as much to her as it did me and my pain would always wound her.

"Well, are we going to look at the article?"

The article. Shit. I didn't even think about that.

I grabbed the magazine from the floor and started flipping through the pages until I spotted a picture of Tucker and Liam looking handsome against the backdrop of Rock Bottom. It made my chest ache. It made me want to see him, to touch him. I traced the edge of his face with my finger and took in every detail of him. I was there that day. I took the picture, but he was still mesmerizing.

Brooke cleared her throat, and I looked up.

She motioned her hand as if to say "get on with it."

So, I did. I devoured every word of the article.

Every time the interviewer asked Tucker a question, I held my breath as I read his answer. He talked about how hard he and Liam had worked to build Rock Bottom from the ground up. He talked about their friendship. He talked about Chloe. He talked about his family, but what really caught my attention was that he talked about me.

Interviewer: The design of your restaurant is extraordinary. The space started off as a rundown building. You even have a photograph

of the original building hanging in your restaurant. Where did you get your inspiration?

Tucker Moore: That original photograph actually came from the photographer who shot the images that will be featured with this article, Kennedy Hayes. When I first saw her photography, I knew I had to have her. Her vision is so strong and so creative. I wouldn't have settled for a different photographer. She once told me that she falls in love with old buildings. She falls in love with their character, their fading and chipping paint, the story that they have to tell. She falls in love with the idea of all the lives that have happened inside those four walls. Love, laughter, and loss. How could you not be inspired by that?

My heart was pounding.

Interviewer: I agree. She sounds like an incredible photographer.

Tucker Moore: She is. She's actually the inspiration behind our next endeavor. We have purchased an abandoned building downtown that used to be a mill many, many years ago that we are going to be turning into a bar.

Interview: Wow. Do you have a name yet?

Tucker Moore: Firecracker.

The magazine fell to my lap and I stared at the floor. I could hear my heartbeat in my ears, and it was taunting me. I swear it was repeating over and over. Go to him. Go to him. Go to him.

I picked the magazine back up in my trembling hands

and held it against my chest. What now? What do I do? Does this mean that he doesn't completely hate me?

How could I be so stupid? I should have gone to him and confronted him when I saw him with his sister. Instead, I was reckless. I hit my rock bottom, and I was trying to climb my way out of the hellhole of pain my family had put me in. I needed to feel something else. Anything. In return, I screwed everything up.

"Well."

I startled when Brooke talked, completely forgetting that she was in the room.

"I... I..." I took a deep breath to help calm my nerves. "I don't know what to say."

"Do you love him?" Her words were soft, hesitant.

"Of course, I do." I had no doubt about that. That was the one thing I was one hundred percent certain about.

"Then it is time for you to fight for your man."

Fuck. She was right.

CHAPTER 28

"What exactly is the plan again?" I walked through the aisle of slutty Halloween costumes trailing behind Brooke and Sophie. I wasn't even sure how I got into this situation.

"We're going to show up at the Rock Bottom Halloween party, and you are going to knock my brother off his feet." Sophie held up a Wonder Woman costume that looked like the skirt was exactly three inches long, and I shook my head no.

"But what if he doesn't want me there? I don't want to upset him at his restaurant." My fingers skimmed over a mummy costume, and I prayed that they let me pick something like it. Something that covered all my goodies.

"Did you read the article?" She put her hands on her hips. "He wants you there."

Running my hands through my hair, I let out a sigh. I heard what she was saying and I understood why she thought that, but I was still scared to death. What if I was too late?

"What about this?" Brooke held up a costume in her hand, and if it wasn't for the hat, I would have no idea what it was.

"Is that supposed to be a witch?" I pulled the skirt toward me to get a better look.

"Yeah. It's a sexy witch." Brooke shook her hips and I shook my head.

"That is more like slutty witch, and quite frankly, it's a disgrace."

Brooke rolled her eyes and placed the costume back on the shelf.

"I didn't know you were so passionate about witches." Sophie looked at me like I was an alien.

"Oh, she's passionate about anything she doesn't want to do." Brooke smiled at me with a wink.

I walked away from them and picked up a Mary Poppins costume. It was adorable.

"Umm, no." Brooke looked over my shoulder.

"Why not?" I held the costume up to my body and looked at myself in the mirror.

"We want him on his knees begging to have you back. Not running away because you look like a grandma."

My elbow connected with her stomach and she laughed. "It's the truth."

"I've got an idea." We both turned to look at Sophie. "You can try that on if you agree to try on one costume that each of us chooses then we'll pick our favorite one."

I hesitated but then thought "what the hell?" If I don't like it, I won't buy it so I could at least appease them. They didn't need to know that I had no plans on actually wearing their choices.

I put on my Mary Poppins costume first and when I

looked in the mirror, I frowned. Brooke was right. I looked frumpy. Not sexy at all.

When I walked out to show the girls, Brooke held her tongue but looked smug as hell.

"Next," Sophie called out before I completely made it out of the dressing room.

Brooke's choice was next. When she handed it to me, I almost handed it right back.

"Where's the rest of the costume?" I called through the curtain.

"Just put it on."

I squeezed into the cheap fabric skirt and then pulled the top over my head. I think it was supposed to be Poison Ivy, but I looked like I was trying to get laid. By anyone who was willing. By someone who would probably leave me with an itch afterward.

"Not happening." I turned in the mirror and could almost see the curve of my ass cheek.

The curtain was pulled back, and I thanked God that I had some clothes on even if they only covered a few inches of skin.

"You look hot," Brooke crooned, but Sophie shook her head.

"It's my turn now." She handed me a long black costume before pulling the curtain closed again.

I gawked at the costume when I realized it was made of leather, skintight leather, but I shimmied into it anyways. I knew I wouldn't hear the end of it until I did.

The black body suit went all the way down to my ankles and ended just above my breasts. The top was strapless and the sweetheart neckline curved perfectly over each breast making my rack look amazing.

Sophie peeked her head into the curtain. "Need help zipping it up?"

"Yeah." I held the fabric against my chest as she tugged the zipper up my back.

I looked at myself in the mirror, and I blinked. Hard. Who was this girl? Where had she been?

The leather suit ran along every curve of my body. It accentuated the flare of my hips, the curve of my ass, and every inch of my legs. They were areas that I had always hated about myself. They were areas that I now couldn't stop staring at.

My body looked amazing. I had never said those words before. It stopped me dead in my tracks. I looked good. Damn good.

The weeks of running with Tucker had transformed my body in ways I hadn't even taken the time to notice.

I took a deep breath and put my hand on my stomach to try to stop the flutter of butterflies.

"What am I supposed to be?" I looked up at Sophie to see her looking at me with a devilish smile on her face.

"Cat Woman." She dangled a mask from her hand, and I grinned.

...

It was the night before Halloween, and I wasn't even sure how we got here. I was at Tucker's cabin less than a month ago, but it seemed like that was a lifetime away. It had been too long since I saw him. Too long since I touched him.

My need to see him was consuming me, but my fear was greater. Every time I let myself think about the possibilities of tonight, my fear would rear its ugly head and remind me of all the times I failed. My fear lived inside me and it taunted me with ugly words that had been repeated to me so many times throughout my life.

You're not good enough. You're not good enough. You're not good enough.

It didn't matter what my parents, my brother, or my ex-boyfriends criticized me about. It always came back to one thing.

You're not good enough.

But I wasn't going to let it beat me. Tucker was the most amazing man I had ever met, and I would let him decide if I was good enough or not. I wouldn't let my own fear ruin the one thing in life that I truly wanted.

"Holy shit, Kennedy."

I turned from the mirror I was currently standing in to look at my best friend. She was dressed as a cheetah, full makeup, covered in spots, and it completely fit her personality.

"What?" I adjusted my Cat Woman mask on my face, being careful not to mess up my hair and makeup she had just spent an hour doing.

Sophie walked into my room looking cute as can be dressed as a mermaid. Baby blue mermaid hair and all.

"My brother won't know what the hell to do when he sees you. That's what."

I looked in the mirror again and smiled. My body was covered in the leather body suit. My feet in a pair of heeled booties that I borrowed from Brooke that make my legs look a million times better than they did on their own. My black hair was stick straight falling over my shoulders and tucked under my mask. But then there were my eyes.

Brooke applied enough smoky makeup around my eyes

to satisfy the pickiest of drag queens, but the effect was amazing when I put on my mask. My eyes popped in a way that they never had before. I looked catlike. I looked feral. My lips shined in the light as a bright cherry red coated my lips, and I couldn't stop looking at myself.

I felt like a vamped up version of myself. I was still me, but now I was sexy, sultry, and confident. I had never felt that way in my life.

The place was completely packed when we walked into Rock Bottom. It made pride bloom in my chest for both Tucker and Liam. It looked amazing too. They had elegant Halloween decorations throughout the space.

Black and diamond encrusted pumpkins. Black and white candles scattered throughout the space creating an even more sultry effect than normal. Black spider webs hung from the ceiling and little diamond spiders twinkled in the lights.

People were packed into the space dressed in costumes that ranged from slutty nurses to zombies. Their hands were holding colorful drinks that looked like they were Halloween themed, and everyone looked like they were having an amazing time. I searched the faces around me, but I didn't recognize anyone. No Chloe. No Liam. No Tucker.

Sophie waved us forward and Brooke and I followed behind her, pushing our way to the bar. The very crowded bar.

We finally squeezed through the bodies and Sophie raised her hand trying to get the attention of the slammed bartender. When she saw that it was going to be a while before the bartender made it to us, she leaned her back against the bar and scanned our surroundings.

"Does anyone see him?" I chewed on my lip as I tried to peek behind each mask to see if they hid Tucker.

"Not yet. He's here though." Sophie held up her phone. "He just texted me a little bit ago."

"You didn't tell him I was coming though, right?" I didn't know why it mattered so much to me, but I worried that if he knew I was here he wouldn't show his face.

"And miss his reaction when he sees you? Hell no."

Fingertips trailed across my back and I held my breath. Shit, shit, shit. I wasn't ready for this. I was going to hyperventilate.

"Well, well, well. What do we have here?"

I turned my attention over my shoulder and stared into the bright blue eyes of Jase. Fuck, he was hot.

His chest was completely bare, and I worked my gaze down his impressive ridges of muscle to see he was wearing nothing but a pair of black Calvin Klein underwear and a pair of Chuck Taylor's.

"What the hell are you supposed to be?" Sophie's voice worked its way through my brain and reminded me that I was standing there staring at a half-naked Jase with my mouth hanging open.

"I'm an underwear model. Isn't it obvious?" He put his hands on his hips and it made his abs constrict under the movement.

Sophie snorted a very unladylike sound, and he turned his sharp eyes on her.

"Very original there, Jase."

He put his hand over his heart. "Wow. A compliment from Sophie Moore. I thought I'd never see the day."

Sophie rolled her eyes but didn't reply.

"Well, Cat Woman," he brought his attention back to

me, "are you here to get my boy back or do I get my chance to sweep you off your feet tonight?"

"Sorry, Jase. I'm here on a mission." I winked at him. I felt so much more powerful in the costume.

"I would tell you knock him dead, but he's going to die when he sees you. You look smokin'." With that, he kissed me on my cheek and was gone again, disappearing in the sea of bodies.

"I seriously can't stand that asshole." Sophie was staring daggers in the direction that Jase just disappeared.

"What's the story there?" Brooke nodded her head in the same direction.

"Not one I want to get into tonight."

Sophie's face looked flushed, and I knew that there was something going on between them. I just wasn't sure what.

After thirty minutes of not seeing Tucker, I was getting frustrated. My heart raced any time a guy would walk by me that had a similar build to Tucker, but as soon as I saw that their eyes weren't chocolate brown ones with a small fleck of gold, I got even more irritable.

I excused myself from the girls to run to the restroom to give myself a moment to breathe. The body suit seemed to be getting tighter and tighter as the night went on, but I knew it was due to my own anxiety and the crushing feeling that tonight wouldn't work out.

I stared at myself in the mirror and really looked into my own eyes. I could see my fear staring back at me. It was taunting me, letting me know that it was in charge. It was always in charge. I quickly looked away.

The urge to run out of there was overwhelming. The thought of being in my apartment surrounded by my things was comforting, but it hadn't felt right in quite some time. It hadn't felt right to be alone in my space without Tucker since I met him. Damn him for destroying my comfort zone. He obliterated it.

Not tonight. I wouldn't run tonight. Tucker deserved more than a girl who was willing to run. He deserved a girl that would fight for him. He deserved more than I could ever give him. He deserved a girl who was braver than me, but tonight I was Cat Woman. I stared at myself in the mirror again. Tonight, I wasn't the scared girl who ran from her fears. Tonight, I was a fucking super hero.

CHAPTER 29

There was a different woman stepping out of the restroom than the one who walked in it only moments before. I stood up straighter, my steps were surer, and I was on a mission.

Tucker would either forgive me or he wouldn't, but I wasn't giving up until I tried.

I spotted Sophie and Brooke still at the bar as soon as I stepped out, but they weren't alone. Two men were standing in front of them talking, and I knew, I just knew it was him.

He was standing there in a black suit and black cape. His normally unruly hair was combed back perfectly, and although I knew in the moment I saw his mask that Sophie had set me up, he looked amazing.

"Batman."

His brown eyes flew to me as soon as I spoke the words, and I knew he wasn't expecting me to be here. That was clearly evident by the shock on his face.

He didn't say a word for a moment or two. He just slowly ran his eyes over me from the top of my cat mask to the tip of my booted toes. Chill bumps broke out across my skin and anxiety bloomed in my belly. He made me nervous. He made me feel alive.

"Holy shit." His voice was a whisper, barely there, only meant for me, and my eyes flew up to meet his.

"Hi," I squeaked out, having no idea what to say.

He didn't reply though. Instead, he ran his hands roughly through his hair, completely messing it up, and tugged on the ends while staring at me with a mixture of lust and anger. I could see the two emotions dueling in his eyes.

I looked to my friends for a clue as to what to do or say, but Sophie was pretending to talk to Liam while they both watched us out of the corner of their eyes while Brooke just stared at the ceiling as soon as I looked at her. Great help.

"Look, Tuck." I didn't know where I was going, but I had to say something. I couldn't just stand here while he stared at me.

My voice broke something inside of him. As soon as I said his name, the name I called him, he wrapped my right hand in his and charged his way through the crowd to the back of the restaurant. I tried to keep up in my boots as he took long, powerful strides, but there were a few times that I was sure that I would fall on my face.

The door slammed shut behind us as we made it into the back, and although the volume dropped significantly, there were a whole new plethora of sounds. Pans banging, cooks talking, dishes clanging against each other. It reminded me of how much Tucker was responsible for. Of how much he had accomplished.

He continued to pull me toward the back of the building until we came to a space I had never been to before. He pulled a key from his pocket, opened the door, and then pulled me in after him.

A large desk filled most of the space with a sleek black chair situated behind it. Shelves ran along one wall and were filled with books, binders, and documents. I imagined him working alone in this room. I could see him running his hands through his hair when he was frustrated and him biting his lip when he was concentrating hard.

The click of the lock drew my attention away from taking in the office and back to the man who I had fallen desperately in love with.

His normally brown eyes were almost black and a thrill ran through me. He had the power to completely destroy me, ruin me, but I didn't want a perfect fairy tale with anyone else. I didn't need a happily ever after. All I needed was whatever he was willing to give. I needed it like my last breath.

He stepped closer to me, and I took a step back against his desk to help hold myself up. I felt like my knees would buckle at any moment.

I didn't speak because I didn't want to break the spell he seemed to be under. The one that was clouding my head as fiercely as it was clouding his. I didn't want him to remember that I was the girl who ruined us. That I was the girl he didn't want.

He stopped when he was barely an inch away from me. I could feel his breath against my face as he drug ragged breaths in and out. I looked up at him begging him to do something, to say something.

His hand touched the side of my neck and I jumped slightly at the feel of his skin on mine. That one touch had me falling apart. He pushed me over the edge and I was like an avalanche falling from the top. There was no stopping it. No graceful downfall. I was plummeting down at full speed and I wasn't sure what would be left of me when I stopped. If I ever stopped.

A whimper left my mouth as his hand crawled up my neck and caressed my cheek. He lifted the mask gently, pulling it away from my face, removing my façade, stripping me of my false bravado.

"You are so damn beautiful." His words a whisper on my lips.

Taunting me.

"Please, Tucker."

I couldn't take anymore. My need for him was a desperation. My heart thundered in my chest.

He threaded his fingers in my hair. Both hands cradling my head, angling my face up to his, putting him in complete control.

He tugged my hair back sharply, but not painfully, and I gasped at the sudden change of pace. He took full advantage too. He traced my lips with his tongue, pulling back when I desperately tried to press my lips against his. His mouth evaded mine and pressed a light kiss against my neck. I was sure he could feel my heavy pulse against his lips. He could feel the quick rhythm pounding against his tongue.

His hands trailed down my body. My skin burned in the path of his hands, the thin layer of leather not protecting me in the least. His fingers bit into the skin of my hips, and I winced slightly at the pain before he spun me around like a rag doll and pressed his front to my back.

His face tucked into the crook of my neck breathing me in. My chest rose and fell in rapid succession. Arousal and fear of what was happening between us were battling inside me. One barely taking the lead before the other would fight its way back to the top.

His hands roamed over my leather costume. One hand running over my belly through the center of my breasts until it reached my chest. The other crept down my thigh barely missing where I needed him the most. Causing me to groan in frustration.

"What's wrong, Kennedy?" he whispered against my skin, his mouth resting just below my ear. "Do you need my cock or my mouth? Tell me what you need from your fuck buddy."

His words cut me like a knife.

Deep.

Scarring.

"Tuck." I didn't know what to say. I didn't know how to correct what I had done.

"Yeah?" His teeth grazed against my sensitive skin. "Did your last fuck buddy not give you what you need? Did he not know how to work your body the way I do?"

I straightened my spine against him, but I didn't answer. He knew that guy left my apartment. He forced him to.

He pushed on the center of my back and I let him. He pushed me until my chest pressed against his desk, my ass on full display still pressed against him. He ran his hands down my back and over my ass.

"Did you wear this for me, Firecracker?"

A tear ran down my temple and landed on his desk, but I wouldn't dare wipe it away. He needed this. This was his revenge. I would let him have it. I wasn't sure how I would survive it, but I would give it to him just the same.

The zipper of my body suit slowly moved down my body. The sound of its teeth unlocking from one another echoing throughout the room. My body didn't care about his cruel words. It just needed him. My heart be damned.

His rough fingertips ran down my naked back then he reached his hand inside the fabric, his palm against my stomach. His tender touch betraying his words. He lifted my body back against him before gently turning me around and sitting me on the edge of his desk.

His gaze ran over my lace covered breasts before moving to my face. As soon as his eyes met mine, his entire demeanor changed. I could see the shift in his eyes. I could feel it throughout my entire body. It pierced my soul.

"Kennedy." His pain was clear.

I blinked my eyes closed and willed my tears to quit falling.

The feeling of his lips against my cheek caused a sob to pour out of me as he caught my tears. His lips now wet as they moved across my skin.

"God, babe. I am so sorry." His words were broken and so was I.

Tears streamed down my face, but I looked through them to see him. To see the sincerity on his face.

"Tucker, I don't know what to do. I'm so sorry."

He wrapped me in his arms, my half naked chest pressed against him.

"You don't have to do anything. We both fucked up. We've both been so selfish."

He was right, but his sins weren't equal with mine.

He deserved more than I was giving him.

His hands wrapped in my hair once more, this time gentler, and he arched my neck until my lips were reaching up to meet his. I could taste my tears on his lips when he pressed them against mine. His movements were hungry but reserved. I could practically feel his tension radiating under my fingertips. He was so controlled and so restrained.

I hated it.

I didn't want him to water down what he was feeling for me. If he was angry, I wanted him to bruise my lips with his anger. If he was hurt, I wanted him to take it out on me. I would take anything he would give me, but I couldn't stand to watch him hold himself back while I fell completely apart.

"Please, Tuck," I whispered against his parted lips.

"What do you want from me, Kennedy?" His chest heaved against mine.

"Show me that I am not alone in this."

I pushed his costume from his shoulders. My fingers fumbled along the buttons, and I had to slow my trembling hands down to accomplish the task. He stepped back away from me before helping me to my feet. His hands worked their way around my body pulling the tight leather fabric from my skin, and I kicked off my shoes instantly dropping me down about four inches.

He laughed a deep throaty laugh when I went from reaching his chin to barely making it over his shoulder. I shrugged my shoulders, and he smiled. That damn smile of his with his deep dimples that I absolutely adored.

With a flick of his fingers, my bra fell to the floor and his perfect smile slipped from his lips and his laughing eyes became feral.

He lifted me, his hands gripping my ass, and laid me back against the desk. I looked up at him and watched his eyes as they raked over my body hungrily. I squirmed under his stare, but he placed a hand on my stomach that stopped my movements and my anxiety.

He pressed his lips to mine, soft, gentle, loving, and my

gasp of breath got lost in his mouth as he bit down on my lip. He worked his way down my body, taking his time, and devouring every inch of my flesh. He dragged my nipple into his mouth. His tongue flicking rapidly, his teeth drawing out a delicious ache.

I gripped his hair tightly in my fingers begging him to give me more. I would take more of anything he was willing to give me. Every touch set me on fire, and I craved the next second that his skin would connect with mine.

He took his time, driving me crazy with his mouth, as he worked his way down my body. He gripped my hands in his as he nipped my hip bones causing my thighs to clench. Then he looked up at me, his eyes staring into mine, as he laid a gentle kiss over my panties.

I fought the urge to look away from him, to hide from his gaze, but I knew I couldn't. Not with Tucker. Not anymore.

He hooked his fingers in my panties and slowly slid them down my legs, watching me the whole time.

He pressed his lips against my sex, gently, teasing, and he stared up at me with fire in his eyes.

"Don't take your eyes off me, Firecracker."

He didn't wait for my response, and I suppose he really didn't need to considering I had been able to take my eyes off him since the moment we met. He ran his tongue through my flesh, and I arched off the table begging for more. But he was there knowing exactly what I needed.

He sucked my clit into his mouth causing me to scream in pleasure, and it didn't even cross my mind that there were hundreds of other people under that same roof. I didn't care who heard me. All that mattered in the moment was him.

All that had ever mattered was him. I watched him as he completely consumed me, and I knew that no matter how much I tried to protect myself, I never stood a chance against him.

He had weaseled his way into my heart on day one, and when I looked down into his dark brown eyes, I knew that I was completely in love with him.

He lifted me from our position on the desk and moved us into his desk chair. He easily maneuvered me off his lap and spun me around so I was facing away from him. The uncomfortableness of my weight being lifted by his hands alone didn't hit me until after I was already situated back on his lap. Normally, it was the biggest thing on my mind, but with him, I rarely thought about it.

Tucker slid into me and my back slid against his chest. He moved my hair off my shoulder and tasted the sensitive skin of my neck. I worked myself up and down on him, I rolled my hips, and I set the speed. Tucker felt so incredibly close to me even though I couldn't see him. But God, I could feel him.

"Look how beautiful you are." He gripped my hair in his hand and turned my face to look at the computer screen before pressing his lips softly against my neck.

I stared at my reflection. My body in control of both mine and Tucker's pleasure. I watched my body as I moved against him. I watched his hands as they caressed parts of my body that I had always hated, and suddenly with his hands against my skin, I didn't hate it so much.

I looked at myself in the reflection, and for a moment, I imagined what Tucker saw when he looked at me. I thought about what I must look like if I wasn't constantly critiquing every small thing about me. If I wasn't filled with insecurities. For the first time in my entire life, I felt unmistakably beautiful.

Tucker had my insecurities in his hands, and he didn't force me to see myself differently. Instead, he held me tightly as they began to fall away and I let myself fall completely apart with them. Tucker whispered how beautiful I was in my ear as we both cliff dived over the edge. We clung to each other as we tried to catch our breath, and I knew in that moment that I would never let go.

CHAPTER 30

Walking back out into the restaurant, I felt like I was in a different universe. I was back in my skintight leather body suit, but it now felt completely different against my skin. My body was still on fire from Tucker's touch. My hand was in Tucker's as he led the way back to where our friends stood, and as we walked back to where we stood just moments before, I let my fear creep back in.

I considered myself a pretty strong girl. I knew what I wanted out of life, and I had a plan of how I was going to get it. It was a plan that I had stuck to for a very long time. But my plan was fucked. I didn't know where I fit in to my plan or where my plan fit into my life anymore. I couldn't see a plan that didn't have Tucker in it.

Brooke and Sophie were grinning like a couple of goons when we stepped up beside them, and I had to look away to stop from laughing at the expression on Brooke's face.

"So did you two fuck and make up?"

Tucker smacked Liam so hard on the back of the head that I was sure he would have a headache for days to come.

"Seriously?" Tucker ran his thumb over my knuckles.

"What?" Liam rubbed the back of his head. "I want to know if I won the bet or not."

"You all bet on us?" I looked around at our friends.

"Technically, I was the one betting on you." Chloe made her way through Liam and Tucker, and I smiled when I saw her dark fairy costume. The exact way I imagined her the first time we met. "These other clowns were betting against you."

"That was before I saw the cat suit," Liam waved his hand in my direction. "I didn't know she was going to dress like that."

"So naive," Chloe purred before pulling me into a hug. "You look hot," she lifted on to her tiptoes to whisper in my ear.

"Thanks, Chloe."

"No worries. I got my girls back. I already told Tucker how big of an idiot he was to let you slip through his fingers."

Tucker was staring daggers at Chloe, and I couldn't stop my smile.

"So how much money did you win anyway?"

"Oh, I didn't win any money." Chloe grinned wickedly. "But Liam and Jase now have to clean my apartment this weekend in their underwear."

Everyone laughed except for Liam. I had no clue where Jase had went, but I doubted he minded the underwear part of the bet considering he was parading around in it in public.

"You girls can come over and eat popcorn with me while it happens if you want."

"I'm in," Brooke raised her hand, and Sophie nodded her head in agreement.

"Kennedy?"

"Not happening," Tucker spoke before I could.

"Aww." Chloe patted his chest. "Jealousy looks so damn cute on you."

Jealousy really didn't look that cute on Tucker. Especially when it was happening every five minutes. Tucker, Chloe, and Liam had to get back to work so the rest of us ladies decided to enjoy ourselves and gossip. Naturally.

We had finally managed to score a booth, courtesy of the owners, and the girls were leaning across the table hanging on to my every word about how things had gone down in his office when I felt someone settle into my booth beside me.

"Hey, ladies."

"Hi," I said hesitantly.

There was something about a guy who would sit down uninvited and interrupt our conversation that really turned me off, but before I could tell him to get lost, Tucker was there.

He didn't even give the poor guy a chance to defend himself. He just pulled the guy up by his arm, whispered something in his ear, and pushed him in a direction that was opposite from where we were sitting.

"Really, Tucker. He was cute," Brooke whined as Tucker sat down beside me.

"Then he should have sat next to you and not her." He nuzzled his face into my neck and placed a soft, subtle kiss there.

I couldn't remember for the life of me why I was getting frustrated with him. I couldn't think at all when his lips were on me.

"Are you ready to get out of here?" His lips moved against the skin of my ear.

I nodded my head but no words came out.

Tucker scooted out of the booth and pulled me out behind him.

"Bye, girls. We're leaving," I waved to Brooke and Sophie.

"Really? Just like that?" Brooke called out.

"What happened to chicks before dicks?" Sophie laughed beside her.

"Shut up." I shook my head at them.

"Keep the boots on," Chloe's voice called out, and I had to look around for her because I didn't even know she was around.

But Tucker didn't give me time to reply to her. He pulled me out of Rock Bottom like a man on a mission, and I prayed that his mission was me.

We walked home hand in hand. No words were spoken. It was a blissful silence knowing that we were here together. There was no need for words.

When we made it to our floor, Tucker pulled me right past my apartment door and pulled his keys out of his pocket. I didn't argue. I wanted to be wherever he was and I didn't care where we ended up. As we made our way into his apartment, I realized that I had never been in his bedroom before. We had spent so much time together, but never in there.

His large bed was covered in a black comforter that was left unmade. His furniture was nice. All black stained wood that screamed masculinity and fit him perfectly. I didn't get much time to take in the rest of the room because I was quickly thrown onto the bed as soon as we made it through the doorway.

My back bounced against the mattress then Tucker's strong hands flipped me onto my stomach. He didn't waste any time. My outfit was gone in a flash. I was laid completely bare in front of him.

He removed his clothes. His fingers stealthily moving over buttons and zippers. I lay in front of him and watched in fascination as his body came into view. I had seen it only hours before, but I would never get used to it.

My breath caught in my throat as he dropped to his knee and crawled over me. He tenderly pushed my hair out of my face and stared down at me. His dark brown eyes were captivating, and I could feel myself getting lost in everything they were saying without saying a word.

He drug his bottom lip against mine. Not a kiss. A barely there touch. But I still felt my body arching off the bed, begging for more.

"I'm sorry."

I shook my head. "No. I'm the one who's sorry."

"I should have never lied to you about the restaurant." His voice was so sincere, and I knew that he meant it. But I still didn't understand.

"Why did you lie?"

Gripping my hands in his, he lifted them near my head and pressed them into the bed. His movements slow and calculated.

"I knew those photos were yours the first day I asked you."

He nodded his head when I narrowed my eyes.

"And I saw how protective you were of them. I saw the way your eyes lit up just looking at them. You basically hated me at that point, but I knew I had to have you. I needed you to take the photos of Rock Bottom, but I knew you wouldn't think I was asking because I really wanted you."

He was right. I probably wouldn't have.

"You are so fucking talented, Kennedy."

My gaze avoided his as I ran it down his chest, but he gripped my chin in his hand and forced me to look at him.

"I don't care what anyone else has ever told you. I don't care if anyone else believes it." He shook his head. "You have to know how talented you are. You need to believe in yourself."

I let his words fill me up. I let them drown out the doubt that always creeped there.

"I believe in you."

I let out a small moan and his eyes lit with fire.

He pressed a kiss to the center of my chest before moving his mouth along my collarbone. His lips spilled words of beauty against my skin, and I drank them in like I was ravenous.

"You are so damn beautiful."

"I crave the taste of your skin."

"I crave all of you."

His lips finally made their way back to mine. He created a storm inside me. Part of me felt like a whirlwind of madness while the other part of me felt like I was finally letting go of the breath I had been holding. Knowing that I was exactly where I was meant to be.

As his tongue danced with mine, I felt off balanced, but he was always there to catch my fall. He caught my whimpers in his mouth and made my pulse spike with his teeth. Our bodies were pressed together and although our mouths were the only things engaged, I felt him more than I had ever felt him before.

I felt him in a way that I knew would leave a scar.

He worked his way down my body worshiping every inch of skin he touched, and when he finally slid inside me, my body was on fire. He moved slowly in and out of me, taking his time, savoring the moment.

Our skin was slick with sweat and his hands glided over my thighs as he pulled them around him. Standing with me in his arms, he moved us to a wide armchair that I hadn't even noticed was in the corner of his room. He settled me on top of him, and I immediately began to move. I used his shoulders as leverage as I rocked my body against his.

It didn't take long before I felt myself falling apart around him, and he knew it too. He wrapped his arms around me, his face buried in my neck, and his whispered words into my ear caused me to completely shatter.

"I love you."

It was frightening to know that despite myself, in the amount of time that it took to take one breath, I could so easily lose myself in him. I was drowning in his reckless love, and I never wanted to come up for a breath. It was incurable and I would never be able to escape it, but at the end of the day, I needed him far more than I needed my next breath.

And as my body shook around his and I watched pure ecstasy fill his eyes, there was only one thought in my head.

"I love you too."

CHAPTER 31

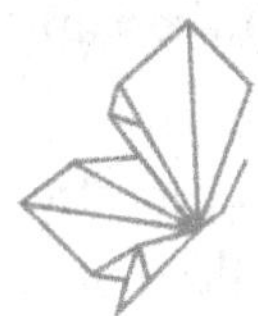

We had been inseparable. Both of us had been busy with work, but I hadn't had one night where I slept alone. On nights where Tucker was at the restaurant late, he would crawl into my bed when he finally made it home and silently curl around my body. When we both had the evening off, we would order food, veg out in front of the television, and get lost in our own little bubble. In the mornings, we got up and went jogging just like we had before.

We talked about what we had both done. I apologized for not trusting him. He apologized for lying to me.

He told me the reason he kept it a secret that he owned Rock Bottom. He said he knew I wouldn't take the job if I knew he owned it. He said that I would think I didn't earn it, and the more I thought about his words, the more I knew he was right. I wouldn't have. I would have felt like I was being handed it. Regardless of whether I deserved it or not.

The makeup sex after that conversation was out of the world.

It was on day eight after our makeup that my family hit me with another blow.

I had just finished shooting the wedding of the amazing couple I had just shot engagement photos for the month before, and I was blissfully happy. It's hard not to feed off that kind of love when you're capturing the perfect images for them to remember it by.

I was completely worn out after eight hours of shooting, but I couldn't drop the smile that was on my face. That was until I checked my mail.

Pulling my mail from my slot, I made my way up the stairs and started flipping through the bills and junk mail until I came to a letter that was addressed to me in perfect calligraphy handwriting.

My hands shook as I ripped the perfect cream envelope open.

Mr. and Mrs. Charles Hayes
request the pleasure of your company
at the marriage of their son
Dr. Justin Charles Hayes
to
Ms. Jessica Nicole Russell
on Saturday, the thirtieth of November

at six o'clock in the evening: at Greenbrier Country Club

Reception to follow

. . .

Every word hammered into me as my heart hammered in my chest. I knew it was coming. I freaking knew it, but I hoped. A single thread of hope. It was so powerful yet so dangerous.

It was that hope that caused my chest to feel like it was caving in.

It was less than twenty days away. I hoped that my brother would realize how badly he hurt me. I hoped that he would make a decision that wouldn't completely destroy the last piece of a relationship that I was still holding onto. A relationship that was so easily destroyed by an expensive invitation. An invitation that I was sure my mother had met with several designers before she made the final decision. And Jessica I'm sure she was there, but she would have no say. She had no clue what she was walking into with my mother.

I walked into my apartment in a daze, and Tucker was sitting on my couch with his feet on the table and a beer in his hand.

My first reaction was to ask him to leave. To go into my room and bury myself in my sadness, but I wouldn't. He deserved far better than that from me.

"Hey, Firecracker." He smiled his perfect dimpled smile and the pressure on my chest lessened.

"Hey."

"What's wrong?"

"I..." I didn't really know how to put into words what I was feeling so I just handed him the invitation before I plopped down on the couch beside him.

He was silent as he read the words on the pearlescent

card in his hand then he set it along with his beer on the coffee table and pulled me into his lap.

I tucked myself into him and rested my head on his chest.

"Talk to me, Kennedy," he whispered against the top of my head.

"I don't know what to say. I'm just hurt. It's stupid really." I shrugged my shoulders.

"It's not stupid. They don't deserve your pain, but it's okay that you feel it." He rubbed his hand up and down my spine.

"I just hate that I let them hurt me. I knew this was coming, but I hoped it wouldn't. I hoped they would change."

Tucker nodded his head and kissed my forehead. "What can I do?"

I thought about his question for a moment and realized that he was already doing it. He was making things better by just being there.

"Just make me forget for a while." I looked up into his eyes, which turned darker at my words.

"Now that I can do." He lifted me in his arms, carried me to my room, and made me forget everything including my name.

...

"Not happening." I shook my head in protest.

"Come on. Don't be a party pooper." Chloe bounced in her seat with excitement.

"I'm not a party pooper. I just don't sing."

"Don't let her lie," Tucker said from beside me. "She sings in the shower all the time, and it is amazing."

I elbowed him in his stomach, which only caused him to laugh. He had just told me the other day that my voice was amazingly horrible. I didn't take it as a dis either. I knew how bad my voice was, but I typically rocked it anyway. What I didn't do was showcase it in a bar full of people with a karaoke mic in my hand.

"See." Chloe waved her arms around, the alcohol she was drinking clearly loosening her up. "Come on. It will be just us girls. It will be amazeballs."

She and Brooke both stood up and I hesitated before Tucker gave me a gentle push.

I straightened my shirt, threw a dirty look over my shoulder at Tucker, and then followed the girls on stage. The guy running the sound equipment put a microphone in each of our hands, and I stared down at the thing and prayed that it burst into flames.

Instead, the music started and Brooke hooked her arm in mine with a giant smile on her face. I was about to embarrass myself in front of this entire bar, but for that smile on my bestie's face, I would do just about anything.

The music began to pump through the speakers and I laughed when the words "Like a Virgin" by Madonna lit up across the karaoke screen.

Then we rocked the shit out of it.

A full on girl band happened on stage, and although we probably sounded hideous, the crowd of people loved us and sang along to the words.

By the time we made it back to the table, I was sweaty, laughing, and feeling drunk on life. I leaned into Tucker and planted a kiss onto his smiling lips.

He pushed a piece of hair off my sweaty forehead. "I've been thinking."

"About?"

"About how we haven't been on a proper date."

I had to wrack my brain, but he was right, we really hadn't.

I put my hand on my chest, shocked. "What kind of girl am I? You haven't even taken me on a date, and I've already given it up to you?"

He grinned a wicked grin. Only one dimple popping out. "I'm pretty damn persuasive. You couldn't resist my charm."

"Oh shit. It's getting deep in here."

He pulled me into his chest and chuckled against my head.

"I'm being serious though. I know you're busy all week with shoots, but what about next weekend. Let's get away for a few days."

"A getaway?" I pulled away and looked back up at him. "How is that a date?"

"Well, we can go on dates during our getaway. We need some time to ourselves." He nuzzled into my neck and I softened around him.

"How long of a getaway are we talking?"

"Maybe a week," he said nonchalantly.

"A week?" I shrieked. "I can't be gone a week."

"Yes, you can. I already looked in your planner and the only thing you have scheduled that week and it's at my restaurant. We can reschedule."

That damn smirk. It made me want to smack him and rip off my clothes at the same time.

"Where do you plan on going?" I crossed my arms over my chest.

"That's a surprise."

"No. I don't like surprises."

"Too bad."

"I'm not going unless you tell me." I did a smirk of my own.

"Yeah, you are. I already spent a lot of money to book it, and you'll feel too guilty to let me do that."

"Seriously, Tucker?" I asked, exasperated.

"Seriously."

"You're an asshole."

"I know."

"But I love you anyway."

"I know that too."

I pushed him in his chest, which didn't even cause him to budge.

"But I love you more." He pressed his lips against mine in a gentle kiss and I shook my head. There was no way that he could love me more than I loved him.

CHAPTER 32

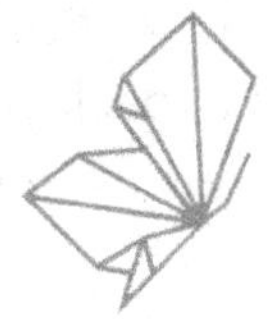

Nothing in this world made me want to kill my best friend more than when I found out she was conspiring against me. I came home from an engagement shoot that I did right outside Tucker's newly purchased bar, Firecracker, to find my suitcases packed and waiting by the door.

Tucker and I were set to head to the airport at nine in the evening, and I was refusing to pack until he told me where we were going.

"What is this?" I pointed down at the offensive pieces of luggage.

"Your bags." Brooke poked her head out of the kitchen and smiled at me.

"And who may I ask packed my bags? Did you let Tucker in there when I specifically told you to guard my shit from him?"

"Nope." She popped the p.

"Then how?" I thought about it for a second before realization finally hit me.

"You broke friend code," I screeched and pointed my finger at her.

"I did not break friend code. I helped my stubborn friend in her time of need."

"This is not my time of need." My hands were now on my hips.

"Yes. It is. You needed to pack your bags but you have no idea where you are going and what to take. I do, so I helped you out."

I narrowed my eyes at her. "You know where we're going?"

"Oh did I say that. Oops." She didn't look like she was one bit sorry.

"You have to tell me." I grabbed her arm and pulled her toward me.

"Not happening."

"I will let you do my makeup any time you want for the next month."

"Really?"

I had her. I knew I had her, but I needed to sweeten the deal.

"Yeah. I'll even let you put slut dust on me if you want to." I wagged my eyebrows.

"Seriously?" She was getting excited.

"Of course. We're best friends."

"Oh, wow. Okay. Tucker is taking you..." She looked around the room like she was making sure he was nowhere in sight.

"Yeah?"

"On a secret trip." She wiped her brow dramatically. "Wow. I'm glad I finally got that out."

"I hate you." I stomped toward my bedroom to see what

all she had packed.

"No, you don't."

She was right. I didn't. I never would.

...

I looked up at the sign in front of me.

There was no fucking way.

It wasn't happening.

It couldn't be true.

Departure: Fiumicino- Rome, Italy

I stopped dead in my tracks and stared at the words in front of me.

Rome.

Italy.

One of the most architecturally rich places in the world.

A place I had always dreamed of going.

He was taking me to Rome.

"Firecracker, are you coming?" Tucker called from in front of me, both of our carry-ons hanging off his arms.

"What?" I squeaked the word out. I wasn't even sure if he could hear me.

"Are you coming?" He adjusted one of the straps on his shoulder.

"Tucker?" I was still staring at the sign.

"Yeah?"

"Are we going to Rome?" My voice cracked and I knew I was close to losing it.

"Yeah."

I finally dropped my gaze to him, and he looked so damn

adorable standing there holding our bags with a hopeful look on his face. His normal confidence was gone, and in its place was his vulnerability.

I finally broke out of my stupor and I ran to where he stood. He wasn't expecting it when I launched myself into his arms, but he managed to recover before we both hit the ground.

I kissed him deeply. Our tongues tangling in a dance that was far too inappropriate for the middle of the airport. Dozens of people were walking around us in a rush trying to get to their destination. They didn't care that we were having a moment. They only cared that we were in their way.

"What was that for?" Tucker asked when we finally came up for air.

"For this." I held my arms out in the air, and he gripped his arms behind me before I fell. "For you being you."

"So you are happy with your surprise?"

"Happy doesn't cut it."

...

My hands shook around my camera as I continued to take shot after shot of the Colosseum. We had been in the Colosseum for what felt like hours now and I was sure Tucker was ready to leave, but he stood next to me without saying a word while I tried to capture the best angles and lighting.

"This is amazing." I finally pulled the camera away from my face.

"It really is." He nodded his head.

"Where to next?" I was already tired after waiting in the

hour-long line to get in, but I wouldn't waste my time in Rome.

We passed out once we finally made it our hotel. Our bodies tired from being cramped in tiny seats on the plane for such a long flight. Tucker was probably much sorer than I was since he allowed me to use him as a pillow during our flight, but we both needed the sleep.

When we woke up this morning, we walked the streets of Rome dipping into small shops and tasting amazing food. Then we came to the Colosseum because I couldn't take not seeing it any longer.

"I figured we'd go get lunch then some gelato then head home to get ready for our date." He pulled me in close to him, our hips touching.

"Our date?"

"Yes. I told you I would take you on a proper date once we got here."

"We're in Rome. I think that's the ultimate date."

"I still want to take you out for a nice dinner." He placed a kiss on my jaw and butterflies took off in my stomach. "Okay?"

"Okay."

...

By the time I was ready for our date, I felt like a ball of nerves. I had on a simple lace black dress that was packed in my bag that I had never seen before with a pair of black heels. I shook out my hands as I stared at myself in the mirror.

Tucker was waiting for me right outside that door. Probably sitting on the bed wondering why I was taking so long.

Hell, I didn't know why I was taking so long, but there I stood, staring at my large eyes that were filled with anxiety.

Taking a deep breath, I finally pulled the door handle open and stepped out of the bathroom I had been holed up in for the last hour or so.

Tucker was sitting in a chair by the window and stood up as I walked into the room. He was dressed in a black suit with a black dress shirt. He wore no tie and the top couple buttons were undone, and he looked devilishly handsome.

"Wow, Kennedy. You look gorgeous."

"Thank you. So do you. Well, I mean..." What the hell was I saying? "You do look gorgeous, but men don't like being called gorgeous. So you look very handsome."

He smiled his deep dimpled smile. "Are you nervous, Firecracker?"

"No. Why would I be nervous?" I fidgeted with the hem of my dress.

"You seem nervous." He edged toward me and twirled a piece of my hair between his fingers.

"Nope. I'm good."

"You sure?" He pressed his lips gently to mine. "Because you have no reason to be. It's just you and me."

"I know." I let out a deep breath and some of my anxiety went out with it.

"Okay. So let's do this."

We walked hand in hand out of the swank boutique hotel we were staying in and onto the streets of Rome. There was a black car waiting for us along the street, and Tucker opened the door for me before sliding in himself.

"Where are we going on this date?"

"Surprise." He shrugged his shoulders.

"Another surprise? When are these surprises going to

end?" I wasn't really against his surprises. Yes. I had a need to be in control, but if I was willing to give my control up to anyone, it would be him.

"Hopefully never," he whispered against my ear before he pressed his lips to my jaw.

My arms broke out in chill bumps, and I swear I practically swooned in the backseat of the car.

After driving for about ten minutes, Tucker pulled a thin black blindfold from his suit pocket and dangled it in front of my face.

"What the heck is that?" I pointed to it like he was holding a snake.

"It's a blindfold." He smirked.

"Well I know that, but what is it for?"

"It's for you. I can't have you peeking at my surprise."

"Fine." I pouted.

His smirk got bigger.

He gently placed the blindfold over my eyes and secured it at the back of my head. Then he held my hand in his and peppered kisses along my jaw and neck. My stomach tightened when his tongue ran along my collarbone.

"What are you doing?" I whispered, hyper aware of the driver who could clearly see us.

"Distracting you." He trailed his hand along my knee as he whispered in my ear. "Is it working?" He nipped my earlobe, and it took everything inside me not to cry out.

"Yes," I said in a breathy moan.

"Good, because we're here." He pressed one last kiss to my lips then pulled away from me as the car pulled to a stop.

I groaned in frustration and Tucker's deep chuckle echoed through the car.

I heard a door open then Tucker helped me out of the

car. The night was cool, and a slight breeze whipped my hair around. We began walking forward. One of Tucker's hands was in mine and the other was guiding my back.

"There are several steps ahead of us. Just let me guide you."

I nodded my head. I trusted him completely.

As we climbed the steps one by one, I wracked my brain for where he could be taking me. I tried to think about what I knew of Rome and what places had stairs, but the options were endless and I had no idea where we were.

There was a loud creak of a door opening. A heavy door. An old door. Then Tucker's hand on my back pushed me forward and I could feel the air change around me.

I could smell candles. That I was certain of, but there was something else. One of my favorite smells in the world. The smell of an old building.

I took a deep breath and let it fill my lungs. I could taste the history on my tongue without ever laying my eyes on the building.

A chair scraped against the floor and Tucker helped me take a seat. Finally, he removed my blindfold.

I couldn't breathe.

I looked around me at the architecture, the art, and the history that surrounded me, and I couldn't breathe.

I was sitting at a table that was set for two, candles littering the surface, plates filled with beautiful food, and I didn't know what to do.

"Are you okay?" Tucker was sitting across from me, and I didn't see another person around.

"How did you do this?" I squeaked out. "This isn't possible."

"Everything is possible." He shrugged.

"We are on our first date," I did air quotes with my fingers as I said the word date, "and you bring me to the Sistine Chapel?" I was starting to sound hysterical.

I looked up at the ceiling, at the amazing detail of the art that surrounded us. I took in the curves of the wall. The details in the wood. I had never been in a more beautiful place. I had never been so in love with a single moment of my life.

"You don't like it?" He looked really concerned now.

"Like it? Are you kidding me? I can't believe it. No other guy will ever be able to compare to this, Tucker. You've ruined me."

"That was the plan." His dimples popped out and I fell so deeply in love with him in that moment.

"I love you," I breathed out.

"I love you too, Firecracker." And I knew he meant every word.

"So what now?" My hands shook in my lap.

I, Kennedy Hayes, the girl who had never been good enough, the girl who had lived her life riddled with fear of failing, sat in a room filled with greatness. I was surrounded by grandeur and magic, and I had never felt more enchanted.

It was my own fairy tale. One made specifically for me.

"Now we enjoy our dinner in the Sistine Chapel."

"And then?" My heart hammered in my chest.

"Then I'm going to love you for the rest of your life."

Just like that, all my fears disappeared. I forgot about the girl I used to be. I forgot about all the times I wasn't enough. I forgot about all the people who didn't give me the love I deserved. I stared into the eyes of a man who loved me for who I was, and I realized that he was the one who made me forget it all. Including the date, November thirtieth, the day of my brother's wedding.

And I realized in that moment that this trip was more than an amazing getaway. It was Tucker's way of protecting me from the demons that had haunted me for years. He would always protect me.

Falling in love with Tucker was the most dangerous kind of love. He had more power over me than anyone ever had. He had the power to destroy me.

But his love was also uninhibited, passionate, and fearless.

He didn't love me because I was perfect. He loved me despite everything. He knew all my flaws and he loved me despite them. It was such a rare love. It was pure even though it had once been tainted. Even though I had tested it with my own insecurities and fears. He taught me to love. A love that was so strong I never dreamed it was possible. I was deeply in love with him and irrevocably in love with myself. He flipped my world upside down, but the greatest adventures happened when I finally let my controlled world slip through my fingers and went bottoms up.

EPILOGUE
1 YEAR LATER

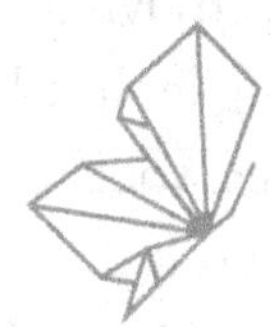

God. She was so beautiful.

She didn't know it either.

She constantly hid behind her glasses and her photography, her deep-seated insecurities that her parents engraved in her making her forget how incredible she is.

But when she let go and forgot her fears, dear God. I never stood a chance.

Not a chance in hell.

She was standing in front of me dressed in a pair of ripped up blue jeans, her white Chuck Taylors, and a simple white T-shirt, and fuck, she was gorgeous. Her jet-black hair was straight down her back and her dark rimmed glasses framed her bright green eyes. She was laughing at something that Chloe was saying, something that was probably insane knowing her, and she looked happy. I wanted nothing more than to make her happy.

Firecrackers was packed to the brim, the grand opening a huge success, and I was sitting at the bar with my three best friends watching my girl fit into my life flawlessly.

"When are you going to do it?" Jase asked from beside me.

"Do what?"

"Wife that girl up." He pointed his beer toward Kennedy. "If I was you, I would have done it months ago."

"You need to back off my girl before I kick your ass, Jase." I took a sip of my whiskey, enjoying the burn of the liquor.

"I'd definitely put a ring on it if I was getting that jealous over her. I mean you named your new bar after the girl." He laughed, and I smiled to myself.

"You know what. You're right." I stood up from the stool I was sitting on.

"What do you mean I'm right?" He coughed around his beer.

"I mean that you are right. I'm a damn fool if I don't go wife that girl up."

I walked away from my friends with Jase's jaw practically sitting on the bar and Liam smiling.

Of course he knew all about my plan. We didn't keep a thing from each other.

I stepped up to my girl who was surrounded by her best friends. It made me ecstatic that my sister and she had become so close. It made my life so much easier. Unless they talked about our sex life. I wasn't comfortable with that.

I wrapped Kennedy in my arms and pressed a kiss to her neck. She didn't turn around to see me. She knew it was me from my touch alone. I could tell by the way her body instantly relaxed against me.

"You better watch out," she whispered for only me to hear. "My boyfriend is around here somewhere, and he gets really jealous." There was laughter in her voice, and I smiled as I ran my nose against her skin.

"He's an idiot if he lets you run around this place by yourself looking like this."

She scuffed. "I'm in a T-shirt and jeans."

"Yet your still the most beautiful woman in here."

"Keep talking." She pushed back further into my body. "Maybe we'll have to hide out. My boyfriend never talks to me like this."

I dug my fingers into her side causing her to laugh because she knew damn well that I told her how beautiful she was every day.

"He really is an idiot then. If you were mine, I would have put a ring on it by now."

"Is that so?" She giggled.

"Yeah. It is," I whispered into her ear. Completely serious now.

I slowly peeled her body away from mine before I dropped to one knee. The room around me fell silent and I could see her body trembling in front of me.

"Firecracker."

"Yeah?" She still hadn't turned around and her hands were now covering her face.

"Look at me, Firecracker."

She slowly turned toward me and I could see her glasses were fogging up with her tears.

She looked down at me, and fuck, it was the most beautiful I had ever seen her. She was completely vulnerable, a look that she reserved for only the few people she completely trusted, and I felt so damn lucky that I was one of those people.

I gripped her small shaking hands in mine.

"Firecracker, I love you so much."

She sniffled, hard.

"I never imagined that the sassy, bossy girl next door would be the one to knock me on my ass, but here I am."

The crowd around us laughed softly.

"All of my doubts about life, all the fears I've ever had, they all disappear when I look at you. I think I may have loved you from that first time you ran over me in the stairwell. You literally crashed into my life and didn't give me a chance. Everything I've done from that moment on, every decision I've made, has been for you. When I open my eyes in the morning, I search for you. When I fall asleep at night, I miss you. My dreams don't do you justice. You surpass anything I could ever have imagined. I want to be the one who makes you smile every day and the one who holds you when this world becomes too much. But most of all, I want to love you for the rest of my life. So do me a favor, Firecracker, and say yes to marrying me because, babe, my heart is useless without you. It's seen the rarest kind of beauty in you, and it won't settle for anything else."

Her hiccup rang loud through the completely silent space, and I could hear my heartbeat racing in my chest.

She wiped her hands underneath her glasses as she began shaking her head up and down.

"Is that a yes?" I let out a nervous chuckle.

"Yes. Yes. Of course it's a yes." Her words were jumbled and anxious and perfect.

She launched herself at me and I didn't react in time to stop us from landing on the floor. My back hit the hardwood floor with a thud, but when her lips connected with mine, nothing else registered. She was all I could feel. She was all that I could see.

And, fuck, she was enough.

She would always be more than enough.
She was everything.

TROUBLE WITH THE HOTSHOT BOSS

Keep reading for a sneak peek of Trouble with the Hotshot Boss.

PROLOGUE
SOPHIE

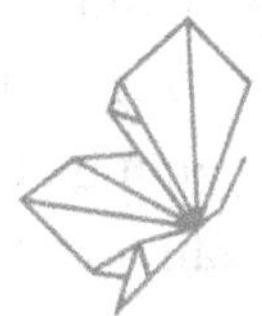

FIVE YEARS EARLIER

I was a little bit tipsy, but I knew with one hundred percent certainty that Jase Hale was the hottest boy I had ever seen.

I had known that fact since I first laid eyes on him at ten years old. Not that I understood what hot was at that age, but I knew there was a reason I couldn't stop smiling when I was around him.

It had nothing to do with the fact that he and my brother loved spending time with me. It was the opposite actually.

But I didn't care.

It was my eighteenth birthday, and he was here.

They all were. My brother, Tucker, and all of his best friends.

They were a bit shocked by all the alcohol I had managed to commandeer without their help, but I wasn't the same little girl they had all left behind once they graduated high school.

Jase knew it too. He didn't check my ass out in my skin-tight jeans like I was his best friend's little sister.

And he had been watching me all night.

"You want another drink?" I leaned against the wall beside him and turned my head to take him in fully.

"I'm good." He shook the cup in his hand, but he turned his head to look at me. We were so close to each other. I could practically feel the tingle of the mint gum in his mouth. "I think you've had enough too."

I rolled my eyes dramatically. "I've barely drunk anything."

"Happy birthday, Soph." Elliott, a boy from my grade, walked by, and I smiled before turning back to Jase.

He was scowling at Elliott's back.

"Tucker's having fun."

Jase's gaze moved to follow mine where Tucker was sitting around the kitchen table playing some sort of drinking game. His head was thrown back in laughter, and I was genuinely happy that he was here. I missed him.

"He needs to relax. He works too hard."

"What about you?" I licked my dry lips. "Have you been working too hard too?" I watched him as his eyes stayed glued to my lips. "When are you going to have some fun?"

His gaze bounced back to mine. "I have plenty of fun."

I didn't let him see how badly those simple words affected me.

"Well, let's have some fun tonight."

His pupils flared, just slightly, but I noticed. When he didn't answer, I knew I would have to push him harder.

"Don't be a chicken." I threaded my fingers with his and tugged him away from the wall.

"Where are we going?" He set his cup down on the counter nearest him, but he didn't try to stop me.

"You'll see." I tightened my fingers and pulled him through the crowd of people that had all come out to celebrate my birthday. It didn't matter that they were all there though. The only thing that mattered was him.

He didn't hesitate as he followed me.

We walked out the back door, and as soon as the door closed behind us, the sound of the party cut off. It was only the two of us.

"You know there are bears and shit out here, right?" Jase asked as I led him to a trail that led through the trees at the edge of the backyard.

"Why, Jase Hale, are you scared?" I turned back to look at him, but I didn't dare let go of his hand. It was the first time he had ever let me touch him like this. It was the first time I had even dared.

"I'm smart." He smirked.

"My family has been coming to this cabin for as long as I can remember, and I have never seen a bear. Unless you think a squirrel might get us?" I bugged my eyes out as if I was truly scared.

"Very funny." He kicked a stick off the trail, and I laughed.

My parents' cabin sat practically on the top of a mountain, and they would die if they knew I was using it to throw a party. They thought that I went out with my girlfriends tonight and then planned to stay at one of their houses.

I felt guilty, but I wouldn't have this opportunity again.

I came to a stop when the trees thinned and all you could see were the stars in the sky. I dropped Jase's hand as I sat down on the ground, and I prayed that he would sit down beside me instead of taking off back toward the party.

I knew that he would rather be there.

But he didn't even seem to consider it.

He watched me as I leaned back on the ground and stared up at the sky then he joined me.

Our shoulders touched just barely, and neither of us spoke for several minutes as we listened to the quiet sounds of the world around us.

"So..." I hesitated, and I hated that I did. "Do you have any girlfriends at school?"

"Girlfriends?" He turned his head toward me, but I didn't meet his gaze. "As in plural?"

"Girlfriends. Girlfriend. Whichever." For some reason, the thought of him having one single girlfriend versus an entire volleyball team after him really bothered me.

"No." He chuckled and tucked his arm behind his head. "I'm still holding out for a set of twins to make my girlfriends dream come true."

I jabbed him in the side with my elbow and he rubbed the spot as his deep chuckle echoed through the air.

"What about you? Did the vultures come out as soon as your brother left?"

I laughed at the thought. Sure, I was pretty enough, but the thought that some guy was vying for the opportunity to get to me was laughable. My brother wasn't that scary.

"Oh yeah." I rolled my eyes. "They all came out of the woodwork as soon as Tucker crossed the county line."

"Figures." He said the word under his breath. "Why aren't you in there with one of them?" He hiked his thumb over his shoulder toward the direction of the cabin.

I rolled toward him and stared at the small scar that ran

just along the base of his chin. I wanted to touch it. I had wanted to touch it since the day I saw him crash his skateboard.

"Because I'm here with you."

He didn't move away from me as he had done so many times before. My forearm was pressed against his side, and I could smell him so clearly. He didn't smell like any other boy I knew. There was a slight hint of spicy cologne, but it was something below that pulled me in.

"We should get back." He said the words, but he didn't move.

I shook my head. "No one is missing us."

"Sophie." He said my name as if he was pained.

"Don't." I laid my hand on his chest. "Not tonight."

He stared at me then, really looked at me, and for the first time in my life, I loved what I saw in his eyes.

"What are you doing?" His voice was gruff and made my stomach tighten.

"Nothing I haven't done before." It was a lie. I had no damn clue what I was doing.

I just knew that I wanted to do it with him.

I had always wanted it to be with him.

Jase ran his hand down his face in frustration, and it was easy to see that he was warring with himself.

"Your brother." He looked back over his shoulder toward the cabin and my heart started hammering in my chest.

"Isn't here." I moved an inch closer to him before I reached up and hesitantly ran my finger over that small scar.

His eyes jerked back to mine.

He looked so serious, feuding with himself, and I felt a surge of excitement at the thought of challenging him. I wasn't the same little girl that he, my brother, and their friends used to pick on.

I let my fingers trail down his chin to the base of his neck and my breath caught as he swallowed down his nerves beneath them.

"Sophie." My name was a whisper on his lips, and I let them fuel me.

I pushed up on my knees and quickly draped one leg over his before he could stop me. I was straddling him, closer than I had ever been to him before, but he caught my hips in his hands before I could press them against his.

"What are you doing?" His voice was slightly panicked as he started to sit up, but that only moved his body closer to mine.

I let my arms fall to the top of his shoulders, and I couldn't miss the way his eyes stalked the rise and fall of my chest.

"I don't know," I answered honestly. "But please don't make me stop."

His eyes slammed shut, and I forced myself down against him despite the weak push of his hands against my hips. His hands tightened against me—the pressure of his fingertips against my skin unlike anything I had ever felt before.

His gaze met mine for only a moment before something inside of him snapped. I had been waiting for that shatter of his control for as long as I could remember.

He forced his hands into my hair as he jerked me forward—closing the tiny gap that remained between us, and he swallowed the sound of my shock with his lips against mine.

Everything around us fell away.

The first taste of his lips made me feel like I was starving.

That simple touch and I felt completely off-balance. I couldn't bring him close enough to me.

It wasn't at all what I had dreamed my first kiss with Jase would be like.

He was always in control. He was the flirt, the lady's man, but this Jase—he was as desperate as I was.

His hands fumbled over my body and his mouth crashed with mine. He bit my bottom lip and my hips pressed against his frantically.

I wasn't sure what I wanted from him, but I knew that I needed more.

His fingers tangled in my hair and I was surprised by how much my stomached tightened when he pulled my head back roughly. His mouth moved over my chin and down my neck, and I could feel his ravenousness in his kiss.

It only fueled my own need.

I moaned as I pressed my chest against his, and I prayed his tongue couldn't feel the rapid beat of my heart against my neck. I had no clue what I was doing, but it didn't matter.

Nothing mattered in that moment.

Jase's hand pushed the bottom of my t-shirt up my stomach, but he hesitated. I could feel the uncertainty in the falter of his touch and the shudder of his body beneath mine.

I didn't want him to be uncertain about me.

I couldn't stand it.

I brought my own hands to meet his at the bunched fabric of my shirt, and I pulled it over my head without a second thought.

He looked like he was in a daze as he took in my breasts, and I thanked God that I borrowed the tiny lace bra that was almost a full size too small for me from one of my friends. He wouldn't be looking at one of my white cotton bras with that same desire.

His finger dipped just inside the lace before he ran it along the edge. The rapid rise and fall of my chest came to a quivering halt as he leaned down, his gaze on mine, and ran his tongue against the thin fabric.

I could feel the hint of his tongue against my nipple, but it wasn't enough. I moved to drop the strap of my bra, but Jase quickly pushed my hand away. His teeth scraped against my nipple through the fabric, and I knew—I just knew that this was how I was going to die.

It was too much and not enough at the exact same time.

It was everything but just a taste.

He moved his mouth to the other breast, and my skin became covered in goose bumps as he blew the gentlest breath against the fabric he had just wet with his tongue.

My fingers wrapped in his hair, and I was almost embarrassed by the way I couldn't stop rolling my hips against his.

I had never felt like this before.

Not even close.

Not when I ran my own fingers against myself to try to figure out what this whole sex thing was all about and definitely not when I had been kissed by anyone else.

I tugged on the fabric of Jase's t-shirt, and he moved away from me only slightly to allow me to pull it over his head.

I didn't hesitate, I pressed my own mouth against his chest and tasted the skin that had probably been featured in too many teenage girls' dreams to count.

He groaned, low and deep, as my tongue ran over the base of his neck, and air hit my breasts as he slowly lowered my bra off my body. I pressed my naked chest against his, the feeling more than I knew it could be, and I cried out as he quickly flipped us. His body now hovering over mine.

He didn't unbutton my jeans as his finger slipped under the fabric and ran from one hip to the other. My stomach trembled under his touch, but I held my breath as he lowered his mouth and pressed a gentle kiss right below my belly button. I was so captivated by watching his mouth that I barely noticed his hand that slid beneath my jeans.

It wasn't until I felt the lightest touch against my center that my hips surged forward, and I had to bite my lip to stop myself from crying out.

Jase was working his way up my body with his mouth and his hand seemed to move with the same laziness as he pushed a finger through me and growled at the amount of wetness that he found.

I wanted to cover my face, but my arm was pinned under Jase's body. Instead, I let my fingers press against the front of his jeans.

He groaned, and his teeth scraped against the skin covering my collarbone.

When I felt how hard he was under my touch, I was no longer embarrassed by my own arousal.

He didn't give me time to worry about it anyway.

He began moving the heel of his hand against me in the tiniest circles, and I could barely remember my own name let alone any reason to be embarrassed.

Jase's mouth met mine and I gave him everything in my kiss as he took everything from my body. Our teeth clashed as we nipped at each other's lips. His tongue fought mine as I pushed my hips harder against his hand.

I was so close, so damn close, and I felt like I was going to break.

I was falling apart, I could feel it, but I didn't care.

Jase was holding onto me, and that was all that mattered.

I was surrounded by the smell of him, the taste of him was on my tongue, and I didn't care what happened next.

Until my brother's voice echoed through the trees around us. "Sophie!"

Jase's body tensed on top of mine, and I felt and saw his regret before he even uttered a word.

"Shit." He jerked his hand out of my pants and scrambled for his t-shirt just as he tossed my bra in my direction.

I held it against my chest, but I didn't make any move to put it on. I was too busy watching Jase. Watching him freak out. Watching him be a fucking coward.

There was no going back to what we just had.

"Sophie." My name was once again a whisper on his lips, but this time it was in panic. "Put your fucking clothes on."

I didn't do as he said.

I just sat there in complete shock at what had just happened. Not that I was about to hook up with Jase Hale, one of my brother's best friends and the guy I had been in love with for as long as I could remember.

I would never have regretted that.

Jase stood and dusted the dirt and leaves from his clothes as his gaze searched the tree line for my brother. He picked up my shirt and shook it out quickly before tossing it to me.

"Get dressed," he growled at me.

I slid my arms into my bra and slowly clasped it behind my back. Tucker's voice called out my name again, but I wasn't worried about my brother. This wasn't about him.

"Sophie." Jase started to pace. "I swear to God."

"Leave." I looked up at him. I didn't know what he saw when he looked down at me, but I knew my hair was still a mess from his hands and my skin was still burning from his touch. "Just go, Jase."

He stared down at me. There was conflict in his gaze. He didn't want to leave me, but he also didn't care about me enough to stay.

I could hear Tucker's footsteps as he made his way toward us, and I knew that Jase could too.

I wasn't being fair.

But neither was he.

None of it mattered though.

Because Jase took off in the opposite direction of Tucker, and I swore to myself that I would never let Jase Hale close enough to hurt me ever again.

Keep reading Trouble with the Hotshot Boss!

DIDN'T GET ENOUGH?

**You've fallen for the trouble.
Now it's time to meet the cowboys who'll ruin
you for anyone else.**

If you like your romance dirty-mouthed, slow-burn, high heat, and downright addictive, you'll want to head straight to the Calloway Ranch.

Keep Reading for a sneak peek of
Cowboy Casual!

CHAPTER 1
BLAIRE

The photos landed in my inbox at 5:37 p.m. Another email, this one with the subject line URGENT: For Review- Grant Chandler Jr.

I barely blinked. Just another Thursday at Senator Monroe's office, where my job as press assistant meant I spent half my time putting out fires before they spread all over the internet. A few clicks, some carefully crafted lies, and by dinner, the world would be slightly less on fire and my father's re-election chances marginally more secure.

I spent four years at Duke getting my marketing degree, and here I was, a glorified janitor for my father's indiscretions and political messes. My professors would be proud to see that their star pupil's primary skill set had become making scandals disappear before they hit the trending page.

But the name at the top of the email wasn't my father's. It was my fiancé's.

The Chandlers had been bankrolling my father's campaigns since before I came to live with him, their hedge

287

fund fortune buying the influence that kept both families comfortable. Four years ago, my father seated me next to Grant at a fundraiser. I was finishing my last year at Duke, and my father's eyes gleamed with approval every time Grant leaned in to whisper something that made me laugh.

Two hours and three glasses of merlot later, I'd mistaken his calculated attention for charm, and the next morning, roses crowded my tiny apartment doorway with a note that simply read, "Dinner? -Grant."

That one yes led to a diamond ring that had been on my finger for the last fourteen months, and now the wedding was a little over a hundred days away.

I opened the email, and the images loaded one by one. I noticed Grant first, then his assistant, who was splayed across his mahogany desk. Her blouse was unbuttoned, and his fingers tangled in her dark hair while the other hand gripped her skirt, wrinkling the expensive fabric I'd complemented her on last month. There was a hunger in his eyes I'd never seen in our bedroom.

More images followed as I scrolled, each one a blow. My stomach clenched. There they were in a D.C. hotel elevator, and the timestamp mocked me. Taken exactly fifteen days after the engagement party my father had thrown for us. Another showed them at some dimly lit bar. Grant wore a navy suit with a pale blue tie I'd tied for him the morning of his keynote speech. She draped her thigh across him, and his hand disappeared beneath the hem of her dress.

I scrolled through the evidence of his betrayal. In some, they were alone. In others, they exchanged secretive touches at campaign events where I stood just yards away, smiling for donors while his fingers found her waist.

The first photo was from thirteen months ago, and the most recent was from yesterday afternoon.

My vision blurred as I stared at the photos. A laugh from the bullpen made me flinch, and my gaze landed on the framed picture on my desk. Grant and I were at the Children's Hospital benefit. Grant's hand gripped my hip, his fingers digging in enough to remind me to stand straighter for the cameras. I'd wanted to wear the black dress I'd picked out myself, but he'd replaced it with the lavender gown that was hanging in our closet when I returned from work. "Trust me," he'd said, his voice firm.

I waited for the rage, for the tears, but found neither. Instead, my fingers shook against the keyboard as the room tilted and narrowed around me. In that moment, I felt the snap of that invisible thread that bound me to this life, to my father's ambitions and Grant's possessive hands.

In its absence came the rush, the flood, the name I'd locked away years ago.

Colt.

I physically recoiled from my own thoughts. *No. Not now. Not him.* I'd buried him beneath years of careful compartmentalization, sealed him away in the darkest corner of my heart where dangerous things belonged. He'd gutted me in ways Grant's betrayal couldn't touch, yet here he was, the first name my mind reached for.

The contradiction made me sick. Hating him and the physical ache of wanting him after all these years. I feared what that meant about who I really was beneath all these perfect, polished lies I'd wrapped around myself like expensive armor that suddenly felt paper thin.

I stood so fast my chair clipped the wall and made the edges of my vision pulse. There was a ringing in my ears as I willed myself not to look at the humiliating photos again. Everyone in this office would see them soon enough, and I should have been doing damage control. That was my job, but I suddenly couldn't give a shit about this job.

Instead, I walked straight out into the hall, closing my office door behind me with a soft click. My heels echoed on the tile as I moved, mechanical and purposeful, each step meant to keep the panic from overtaking me.

The hallway outside my office was lined with campaign posters, and today the images of my father felt like sentries watching me, silent and expectant. I tried to draw a full breath, but the air stuck in my throat and went nowhere.

I picked up my pace, crossing the bullpen and weaving past the clutch of interns hunched over their laptops. Someone tried to get my attention, but I brushed past, offering only a brittle smile I hoped passed for apologetic. The elevator was slow as hell, so I ducked into the stairwell, grateful for the emptiness and the way the steps forced my body to move.

Three flights down, I stopped, leaning against the cool cement wall. My phone buzzed in my pocket, and I yanked it out, half expecting a message from Grant. But it was my father's assistant's name looking back at me.

Judy: Senator Monroe would like for you to meet him in his office immediately.

I stared down at the screen as if my entire future hadn't just imploded.

I should have been thinking about Grant. His betrayal. The years I'd spent smoothing his rough edges, convincing myself we were in love instead of two people playing assigned roles in someone else's strategy. I should have been furious or at least humiliated. But standing in that cold stairwell, an emptiness clawed through my chest, a ravenous, familiar void that didn't belong to Grant at all.

The realization ached inside me like a bruise pressed too hard, spreading from my sternum outward until even my fingertips felt tender with the truth I'd spent years denying. My body remembered what my brain had worked overtime to forget. His thumb tracing the freckles across my collarbone, the lake water dripping from his eyelashes as he surfaced beside me, the way my name sounded like a prayer when he whispered it against my neck at dawn. I hated how easily these memories returned, how they still burned beneath my skin while Grant's betrayal felt like nothing more than a paper cut.

I despised myself for it, for looking at evidence of my fiancé's infidelity and feeling only relief tangled with shame. The pain of losing Colt had carved hollows inside me I'd filled with pretty lies and my father's approval.

I started to turn back toward my father's office, because that's what the text demanded and that's what a dutiful daughter would do. But my body revolted. My hand hovered above the banister, knuckles white against the chipped paint, and I looked up the stairwell, concrete spiraling overhead.

Then my gaze dropped, my ears ringing, and saw an exit sign pulsing red at the base of the stairs like a dare. I pressed downward, footsteps echoing against the steps, and the farther I got from the office, the easier it was to breathe. My body was moving faster than my thoughts, and that felt like freedom.

By the time I hit the last step, my legs were numb. I didn't hesitate at the landing, didn't even process what I'd do next. Instead, I barreled toward the side exit, shoved open the steel door, and found myself in the narrow alley between the Monroe Senate offices and the looming black glass of Chandler & Chandler.

The sun hung low between the tall buildings, gilding the edges of everything it touched and forcing me to shield my eyes. When the door slammed behind me, I tried to breathe as my reflection fractured across the dark, mirrored windows of Grant's building. Three days ago, I'd walked through those same doors with his favorite sandwich and a smile, playing the role of the doting fiancée for an audience of receptionists.

I should've stopped to think and called my father. I should've done what I'd been trained to do. But all I could see was Grant's hand on another woman's thigh, and the way his smile had always held a flicker of calculation. For four years, I'd filed myself down, smoothed away any parts of me that might snag on propriety or expectation. Now something untamed and forgotten stirred beneath my ribs, screaming for me to be reckless, even as my father's voice in my head listed all the ways this would destroy everything I'd worked for.

I could feel myself being torn between the wild-hearted girl my mom had raised me to be and the dull woman my father had created.

Grant's building was emptying for the evening. Men and women in tailored suits filtered out the revolving doors, but I didn't slow down. I ignored the polite smiles offered by familiar faces. A few gazes caught on me, lingering a bit too long, and my skin prickled beneath their stares. The knowing glances made my stomach twist. Had they all seen the photos already? Or worse, had they watched Grant and his assistant slip in and out of his office for months while I'd been the oblivious fiancée?

I flattened my shaking hands against my skirt, smoothing wrinkles that had set in like permanent creases. My cheeks burned with each heartbeat, a flush I couldn't hide, but I lifted my chin and locked my shoulders back, marching into Grant's building before I could stop myself.

I passed the security desk, and the guard's eyes flicked up, then away. No need to check my ID when my father's face was on billboards and my fiancé's name was etched on the side of the building. I crossed to the elevator bank and jabbed my finger against the executive floor button, leaving a smudge on the polished brass.

The ride up was dizzying. Every surface in the elevator was a mirror, and three different women were reflected back at me. There was the Senator's daughter in her expensive suit and perfect posture purchased with years of correction. Then the jilted fiancé, with anger burning behind her trembling chin and firmly pressed lips where she'd learned to swallow her voice.

And then there was *her*. The one with wide eyes and color high in her cheeks, the one who looked like my mother. I wanted to scream at her, beg her to run, to fight, to do anything.

I'd let them kill her so slowly I hadn't even noticed she was dying.

The elevator groaned somewhere above me, the floor indicator ticking up, and I caught my mother's eyes in my reflection. Her dare and mischief flickered there, then disappeared beneath my father's careful mask. I touched my face, half-expecting to feel her sunlight warming my skin, but my fingers met only the sweat-damp foundation I'd applied that morning to cover my freckles.

My mother wouldn't recognize me if she saw me now, and I hated the way my mind still drifted to Colt, desperately wondering if he'd be the one person who could still see through to whatever remained of me.

What the hell was wrong with me? I should have been devastated about Grant, not feeling this treacherous relief.

The elevator jerked to a stop. I closed my eyes for a single, shaky breath, then wiped away a stray tear before it could mar my mascara. Just one tear was all I allowed myself to shed for the girl I used to be, the girl who'd been taught her worth came from men who never really loved her.

A soft chime announced my arrival as the doors parted to reveal a wall of windows framing the sunset-washed skyline. The remaining staff sat at their desks, sliding papers into briefcases and shutting down computers, their gazes carefully avoiding mine as I moved toward the frosted glass door that separated me from Grant's office.

Without knocking, I shoved open the door, and they sprang away from each other. His assistant met my gaze while her fingers straightened her shirt. Mascara tracks stained her cheeks.

Grant ran his fingers over his tie and offered his practiced smile. "Blaire, baby. What are you doing here?"

His assistant turned away, busying herself with paperwork on his desk, but I caught the way her hands shook.

I almost felt sorry for her.

"I thought we were meeting for dinner?" Grant's voice overlapped itself, the end of the sentence scraping against the beginning, like he was trying to race ahead of the silence

I'd brought into the room. He took a step around her, positioning himself directly in front of me.

"Don't act like you don't know that I've seen the photos." My voice was steady, but my hands trembled so hard I had to dig my nails into my palms to hold them still. "How long has this been going on?"

There was a twitch in his jaw, but he kept his mask perfectly in place. "Come on, don't do this here." He tried to close the space between us, palm open, but I jerked away so fast I nearly toppled a crystal award he'd won for service to his community off his bookshelf.

"Do not make a scene," he hissed, jaw clenched tight, and eyes darting to the open door behind me.

The command landed like a slap, and my heartbeat thundered in my ears as that wild-hearted Blaire clawed her way out.

"Should I whisper about you fucking your assistant, Grant?" I didn't recognize my own voice, how it carried across the room. "Would that be more convenient for you?"

His eyes darkened as his shoulders squared. "We should discuss this at home. Privately."

He reached for my elbow, but I stepped back. "No."

"Blaire." He said my name like he was speaking to a trained dog, and I recoiled.

"Don't touch me," I said, and I heard the tremor in my voice, which only made me angrier, but the look on Grant's face told me the words landed as I intended. "Nothing you say will change what you did."

"Blaire," he tried again, gentler now. "Let's take some time to think about how we want to handle this, okay? I'll call your father—"

"Of course you will," I cut in. "You're such a fucking coward, Grant."

He flinched. Not enough that anyone else would notice, but I'd spent four years learning the tells of Grant Chandler. The tic in his jaw, the flicker behind his eyes when his composure slipped. I recognized the look of a man cornered, and it thrilled and terrified me that I was the one who'd put him there.

"This is my office. People are watching," he hissed as he angled his body like he was going to shut the door. "Let's be smart about this."

"Smart," I repeated, and the laugh that escaped me was raw and humorless. "Where were your smarts when you were fucking her on your desk? Did you think no one would notice? Or did you think I wouldn't care?"

"I never meant for you to find out like this," he said calmly. "I was going to tell you. I— I needed the right time. You know how your father is. How important this is for all of us."

I could hardly breathe as I thought of my father's ambitions, my own perfectly curated life, and the unyielding gravity of "all of us." It made me want to scream.

"My father." The words clawed at my throat as my gaze fell to the ring on my finger, the weight of the diamond suddenly crushing every bone in my hand.

"Yes, your father, Blaire," he said, drawing out each word as if I were too stupid to keep up. He leaned in, dropping the mask of concern for something infinitely colder. "Don't act fucking daft. He'll get a handle on this, and we'll figure it out."

"There's nothing to figure out." I shook my head. "I can't do this."

"Where the fuck else would you go?" He laughed, and his words hit hard, harder than I'd braced for. "You live in my condo, Blaire. You work for your father, whose campaign is funded by mine. The life you live is because of me, so don't act like you're better than this."

I had grown used to Grant's cruel words, but somehow, they still sliced through me like a blade. He was right, wasn't he? My clothes hung in his closet, my career existed at my father's mercy, and even my engagement ring had been passed down through generations of Grant's family. But I had built this life too. I had sacrificed for it, shaped myself to fit in it.

The phone on his desk rang loudly, making me flinch. His assistant lunged for it, her voice a distant buzz until she thrust the receiver in my direction, her eyes wide with fear. "Ms. Monroe, it's your father."

My stomach dropped as I brushed past Grant, my fingers clumsy as they closed around the handset.

"Dad—"

"Come to my office. Now." His tone was so measured and so infuriatingly calm that rage flooded me, making my teeth clench so hard my jaw ached.

"No." The word ripped from my throat, and I shook my head even though he couldn't see me. "You don't get to ask me to swallow this. Not for you. Not for him."

"Don't be foolish, Blaire. Grant made a mistake. All men make mistakes." My father's voice slithered through the phone like poison. I locked eyes with Grant across the room, watching him watch me, and I felt like I was suffocating.

My fingers trembled against the ring, twisting it once, twice, before hesitating at the knuckle. The diamond caught the light, beautiful and cold. I yanked it off, wincing as it scraped my skin, then traced my finger over the pale indent left behind. I squeezed the metal in my palm until it bit into my flesh, drawing comfort from the pain.

"Go to hell, dad."

I hung up before I could hear my father's response, and the phone clattered into the cradle.

Grant's eyes darted between my face and the ring clenched in my fist. I thought he was about to plead, but instead, he said, "You're being childish."

I tried to move past him, but Grant moved faster. His hand shot out, catching my arm above the elbow. He held on like he thought he could will the moment backward, as if the world would reset if I stood still long enough.

The heat of his palm bled through my shirt, and I remembered every time he'd touched me gently for the camera, every time he'd squeezed my shoulder in public, always anchoring me to his side. I'd mistaken that pressure for security, but now it felt like a vise.

"You're not leaving until we talk about this." His voice dropped to a growl, low and ugly. He yanked me closer, pulling me off balance.

I twisted my arm, trying to pry him off, but his grip tightened, his thumb digging into the soft flesh inside my elbow.

"Grant," his assistant whispered his name from behind me, but he didn't acknowledge her.

"You're hurting me," I gasped, and this time, I wrenched free.

His face went slack with surprise, as if he couldn't believe I'd dare resist him.

"Never put your hands on me again," I said, my voice steadier than my heart, as the diamond's edge bit into my palm.

Ten years ago, on a night that still woke me up sweating, I'd stood in the gravel driveway of my grandmother's house and hurled Colt's necklace at his chest because I couldn't make him choose me.

But I couldn't bring myself to hurl this ring at Grant, couldn't bring myself to care enough. I opened my aching fist and let the ring fall to the ground, watching it bounce once before settling.

I thought he might grab for me again, but he just stared, mouth tight, as I stepped past him into the hall. I walked in a trance, the blood in my ears so loud I barely heard Grant call after me.

But his words chased me with a desperate, low chuckle. "You'll be back."

I forced myself to keep walking, and I didn't stop until I was jabbing my finger against the elevator button, then again, harder. I didn't want to think about what would happen if I didn't leave right now, if I let the old gravity pull me back toward the familiar controlling orbit of Grant, my father, and all the plans they'd fused around me like a glass cage.

The elevator doors finally slid open, and I stepped inside. Four years of my life stood behind me. Security, status, a future. I pressed my back against the wall and watched the doors close, avoiding looking at my reflection. My hands shook as I pulled out my phone and dialed my grandmother's number.

She answered on the third ring, her voice calm and steady as always. "Hello."

I opened my mouth, but nothing came out but a strangled sound somewhere between a gasp and a sob.

"Blaire?" Panic edged her voice, crackling through the connection. "What's wrong?"

"Can I come home?" The words tumbled out, raw and clumsy. I waited for the guilt, the flood of regret for throwing away everything I'd built, but all I felt was an overwhelming, dangerous relief that flooded through my chest like the first breath after nearly drowning.

"Always, baby." No questions, no hesitation.

I pressed the button for the ground floor. The elevator plunged downward, and with it came visions of Colt, the curve of his jaw, the calluses on his fingertips, the weight of judgment I'd find in his gaze. My lungs seized at the thought. I was going back to the place I'd fled a decade ago, back to where Colt Calloway's words had severed me from my roots, but now those same roots called me home.

The Calloway Ranch Series

Cowboy Casual
Available now!

Small Town Smokeshow
Coming May 12th, 2026
Preorder now!

JOIN US IN HOLLYWOOD!

Want first dibs on new releases, bonus scenes, exclusive giveaways, and behind-the-scenes updates?

Subscribe to my Newsletter!

Want to hang out where the real fun happens: early ARCs, spicy secrets, giveaways, and all the juicy gossip before anyone else?

Become a member of Hollywood!

ALSO BY HOLLY RENEE

The Calloway Ranch Series:

Cowboy Casual

Small Town Smokeshow

The Veiled Kingdom Series:

The Veiled Kingdom

The Hunted Heir

The Rivaled Crown

Stars and Shadows Series:

A Kingdom of Stars and Shadows

A Kingdom of Blood and Betrayal

A Kingdom of Venom and Vows

A Kingdom of Fire and Fate

The Good Girls Series:

Where Good Girls Go to Die

Where Bad Girls Go to Fall

Where Bad Boys are Ruined

The Boys of Clermont Bay Series:

The Touch of a Villain

The Fall of a God

The Taste of an Enemy

ACKNOWLEDGMENTS

Thank you to all the readers that have been such an amazing support!

As always, a huge thank you to my husband for supporting all my dreams. I think it's impossible for me to be any more in love with you than I am today. I love you.

Thank you to my mom, sisters, and best friends for always supporting me and pushing me to do more. I love you girls more than you can imagine!

Thank you to my entire team who I couldn't do this without!

ABOUT THE AUTHOR

Holly Renee is a USA Today bestselling author of romance that crackles with tension, swoons with heat, and leaves readers giddy with delicious banter. Whether she's whisking you off to a moon-drenched fantasy kingdom or a Tennessee ranch filled with heartbreak and horses, her stories are fast-paced, emotionally charged, and undeniably fun.

Born and raised in East Tennessee, Holly is a married mom of two, a lake enthusiast, a lifelong lover of pink, and hopelessly obsessed with the kind of love that makes you scream into your pillow.

Find her at www.authorhollyrenee.com.

www.ingramcontent.com/pod-product-compliance
Lightning Source LLC
Chambersburg PA
CBHW011806200726
48289CB00016B/2987